How to Fall for a Scoundrel

T0205081

BY KATE BATEMAN

HER MAJESTY'S REBELS

Second Duke's the Charm

RUTHLESS RIVALS

A Reckless Match
A Daring Pursuit
A Wicked Game

BOW STREET BACHELORS

This Earl of Mine
To Catch an Earl
The Princess and the Rogue

How to Fall for a Scoundrel

KATE BATEMAN

St. Martin's Paperbacks

This is a work of fiction. All of the characters, organizations, and events portrayed in this novel are either products of the author's imagination or are used fictitiously.

First published in the United States by St. Martin's Paperbacks, an imprint of St. Martin's Publishing Group.

HOW TO FALL FOR A SCOUNDREL

For information, address St. Martin's Publishing Group, 120 Broadway, New York, NY 10271.

www.stmartins.com

ISBN: 978-1-250-90737-0

Our books may be purchased in bulk for promotional, educational, or business use. Please contact your local bookseller or the Macmillan Corporate and Premium Sales Department at 1-800-221-7945, ext. 5442, or by email at MacmillanSpecialMarkets@macmillan.com.

Printed in the United States of America

St. Martin's Paperbacks edition / September 2024

10 9 8 7 6 5 4 3 2 1

For most of history,
Anonymous was a woman.

—VIRGINIA WOOLF

III

The Rules of a Gentleman Scoundrel

Rule #1: Never steal something from a man that he cannot afford to buy back.
Rule #2: Never rob an honest man.
Rule #3: Never go anywhere without a weapon.
Rule #4: Never mix theft with seduction.
Rule #5: Women, jobs, and duels—one at a time.
Rule #6: Always talk to the servants.
Rule #7: If it looks too good to be true, it probably is.
Rule #8: What you take, you sell. What you're given, you keep.

Chapter One

Eleanor Law had not expected to kiss anyone at Lady Chessington's annual Christmas ball, let alone a charming, anonymous scoundrel.

In retrospect, she could admit that she was partly to blame. For someone who prided herself on being observant, she'd been so busy watching her friend Daisy Hamilton dancing with a gentleman in an offensive yellow waistcoat that she'd failed to notice the yule bough hanging directly above her head. Nor had she paid much attention to the man who'd appeared silently at her side, until he spoke.

"Expecting a kiss?"

Ellie jumped and turned sharply. "I beg your pardon?"

The stranger was tall and brown haired, his skin a little bronzed, as if he'd recently returned from sunnier climes. His eyes were green? Or brown?—it was impossible to tell in the dim light—but it was his dimples that arrested her. The twin indents on either side of his mouth should have looked childish, ridiculous even, on a grown man, but instead they gave him a charming, piratical air that did something peculiar to her insides.

He sent a pointed glance upward, and Ellie followed the direction of his gaze, tilting her head back to see the ball of festive greenery attached to the alcove in which she stood. Blood rushed to her cheeks as she finally understood his inference.

"Oh, no—I—absolutely not! I hadn't even noticed it until just now."

His dark brows lifted in obvious amusement at her mortification, and the wicked sparkle in his eyes only added to her blush.

She cleared her throat. "For your information, sir, I am not some desperate spinster lingering under the mistletoe, praying for a kiss. My standing here is purely coincidental."

His smile widened at her quelling tone. "There's still one berry left."

Ellie cursed silently. Tradition held that one berry was removed every time a couple kissed beneath it; when no berries remained, no more kisses could be stolen.

She opened her mouth, just as he said, "Only a fool would waste such a golden opportunity."

He caught her hand and raised it to his lips with an elegant bow. Since neither of them was wearing gloves, his large fingers curled around hers, and her stomach somersaulted as his warm lips touched the back of her hand.

Flustered, she took a step back, deeper into the alcove, but instead of moving away, he stepped *closer*, angling his body so that his broad shoulders blocked her view of the room. Ellie's lips parted on a startled gasp at how effortlessly he'd maneuvered her, but before she could berate him, he touched his fingers to the underside of her chin, tilted her face up—and kissed her.

A jolt of something like faint lightning crackled through her at the unexpected contact. Blood pounded in her ears, but before she could do more than register the extraordinary sensation of his mouth on hers, it was over.

Her mystery man pulled back with a roguish smile, and she sucked in a breath, inhaling the delicious scent of his cologne while trying to decide if she should be flattered, insulted, or both.

He reached up and plucked the last mistletoe berry from the sprig. "There. All done."

Ellie blinked. Her lips still tingled.

Even though he'd only kissed her because she was conveniently beneath the mistletoe, she was still flustered. She was an unremarkable wallflower with neither a title nor a fortune to recommend her. *He* was clearly a shocking flirt who loved playing with fire.

Anyone could have seen them. There were over three hundred people here, all talking and dancing, some fewer than ten feet away. True, the kiss had been so brief, it could have been interpreted as him whispering in her ear, but even so, he'd been courting a scandal.

Ellie stared up into his face, certain she'd never seen him before in her life.

"Who *are* you?" she demanded hoarsely.

His eyes crinkled at the corners as he smiled down at her as if the two of them were complicit in some marvelous secret.

"Apart from the man who just kissed you? I have many names."

"You mean you possess a title?"

"Several. Although I rarely use most of them."

She almost stamped her foot at his deliberate evasiveness. "What should I call you, then?"

"Your latest conquest? Your most ardent admirer?" He swept her another extravagant bow.

Ellie rolled her eyes, but she couldn't help smiling too. There was something so playful about his outrageous flirtation that it was impossible to take him too seriously.

He turned to face the room again as if nothing had happened, and she took a steadying breath and tried to glean more clues about his identity.

The perfect cut of his dark jacket could only have come from one of the eye-wateringly expensive tailors on Bond Street, and a real diamond glittered on the gold bar brooch nestled in his white cravat. He clearly had money. And exquisite taste.

"I'm Eleanor. Eleanor Law."

His dimples reappeared. "I know who you are. You're the daughter of Sir Edward Law, the Lord Chief Justice."

"Then you have the advantage of me," she said pointedly.

He ignored the hint. "Do people call you Nellie?"

"Not if they expect me to answer."

"Noted. What do your friends call you? Elle? Nell?"

"Ellie."

"That's what I shall call you, then."

She raised her brows. "That's rather presumptuous. I don't think we can even be called acquaintances if I don't know your name."

"Ah, but mere acquaintances wouldn't have kissed, and we've already passed that awkward stage."

Oh, he was infuriating! Still, she couldn't deny that she was enjoying their sparring. She hadn't been so intrigued, nor so entertained, by a man for months.

She was about to demand his name again when Daisy bustled up, breathless and laughing from her waltz. She dismissed her partner with an elegant wave, shot Ellie's incriminatingly flushed cheeks a fascinated glance, then turned to their mystery companion with a wide, open smile.

"Good evening, sir. I see you've been keeping Ellie company. I don't believe I've had the pleasure."

He took her extended hand and bowed. "A regrettable omission, but easily remedied. You are Lady Dorothea Hamilton, are you not? Your father is the Duke of Dalkeith."

"He is. And you are . . . ?"

"Enchanted to meet you."

He shot Ellie a laughing, sidelong glance, as if he knew just how much his continued evasion was annoying her, then finally relented. "Henri Bonheur, Comte de Carabas. At your service."

Daisy smiled again, but Ellie narrowed her eyes. "A French name. Yet you have no trace of an accent."

"Why, thank you. My childhood tutor would be delighted to hear it. He always impressed upon me the need for perfection in all my endeavors."

He glanced across the crowded room and gave a little lift of his chin, as if acknowledging another acquaintance on the opposite side of the dance floor. "Alas, I must take my leave. Ellie, Lady Dorothea, it's been a *pleasure*."

He caught Ellie's eye on the word *pleasure*, and she cursed the heat that rose to her cheeks again. She ground her teeth, but sent him a sweet smile. "Good-bye, sir."

His dimples flashed. "Oh no. Let us say, *au revoir*. I'm quite certain we'll meet again very soon."

Chapter Two

Ellie shook her head as the scoundrel slipped into the crowd, stepping around the various groupings with ease. She tried to follow his movements, but without her spectacles, everything over six feet away became a frustrating blur, and she lost sight of him.

Daisy tapped her on the arm. "All right, tell me everything. Starting with why your cheeks are so pink. What on earth were you two discussing?"

Ellie absently touched her bottom lip with her fingertips. She could still feel the ghost of his kiss.

"Oh, umm, very little, really. I was just trying to discover his name."

"I'm not sure we're any the wiser now," Daisy said with a snort. "The *Comte de Carabas*? Wasn't that the name invented by the cat in the fairy tale 'Puss in Boots,' for his master?"

"It was!" Ellie gasped. "Although I think it was the *Marquis* of Carabas, in the tale. And 'bonheur' means 'good time' or 'lucky' in French. Henry Goodtime?" She gave an outraged huff. "That charlatan! He gave us a fake name!"

Daisy gave a delighted laugh. "How marvelous. I do love a handsome rogue. But *why*? Is he playing a game, to try to intrigue us? Or is he actually here under false pretenses? Maybe he's about to commit a crime!"

Professionally, Ellie and Daisy were two-thirds of the force behind King & Company, London's most discreet private investigation agency. Along with their friend Tess, Duchess of Wansford, they dealt with "sensitive problems" for clients, under the guise of assisting their fictional employer, Charles King.

"If he's a jewel thief, he'll have plenty of opportunities here tonight." Ellie tilted her head toward the glittering array of wealth clustered beneath the chandeliers: necklaces and tiaras on the women, pocket watches and tiepins on the men.

"He could be a card sharp," Daisy opined. "Maybe he's here to fleece the gentlemen at vingt-et-un or dice."

"I suppose we'll find out soon enough. If there's an outcry from the cardroom, or someone comes to King and Company tomorrow to report the loss of their favorite bracelet, at least we'll have a potential suspect."

Daisy gave a bawdy chuckle. "I volunteer to give him a thorough pat down to look for hidden loot."

"Very selfless," Ellie said drily. "It's a shame Tess isn't here. She might have recognized him."

"Speaking of potential new cases," Daisy said, "I was approached by a man named Bullock earlier. He said he'd heard that I knew Charles King, and asked for an introduction."

"Did you tell him to come to Lincoln's Inn Fields?"

"I did, but he insisted that he would only speak with Mr. King himself."

Ellie rolled her eyes. Some of the male clients requesting "Mr. King's" services had been extremely dismissive toward his "assistants," Ellie, Daisy, and Tess. A few had even refused to confide their business with an underling, especially if they were female.

"Then we'll have to tell him that Mr. King is too busy to accept any new clients," Ellie said firmly.

"Indeed. Life's too short to deal with 'gentlemen' who think we're inferior, overly excitable, and too feeble-minded to grasp the complexities of a criminal investigation."

Daisy's diatribe tailed off as a viscount approached, eager to accompany her in the next reel. She accepted with a smile, and Ellie glanced around to see if anyone was going to ask *her* to dance. Generally, she preferred to stay on the outskirts of the ballroom, happy to observe the dancing rather than take part, but "Henri Bonheur's" kiss had filled her with a strange, restless energy.

Her spirits lifted as a rather stocky, older man approached her, but they fell again when he introduced himself.

"Miss Law? I'm William Bullock, owner of the Egyptian Hall in Piccadilly. Perhaps you've heard of it?"

Ellie shook his offered hand. "Indeed, I have, Mr. Bullock. I went there to see Bonaparte's carriage when it first went on display, a few months ago."

"You and half of London." Bullock gave a contented chuckle. "That's been my most popular display to date. It's about to go on a tour of the country, so those in the provinces can see it too." His chest puffed out with pride, reminding her of a portly pigeon ruffling its feathers.

He pulled a large gold-cased pocket watch from his pocket, checked the time, then tucked it away again. "I hear you're acquainted with the investigator, Charles King?"

"That's true. I work as his legal researcher and aman-uensis. He's a friend of my father's," she added, with blithe disregard for the truth. Her father had never met her "employer," for the simple reason that the latter was entirely fictional. Still, she'd long ago learned that any mention of her father inferred a measure of gravitas to the situation, and impressed men like Bullock no end.

"Ah. Good. Quite so. In that case, I was wondering of you could make an introduction between Mr. King and myself. I'd like to engage his services for a sensitive matter."

"I'm afraid Mr. King prefers to keep himself *extremely* private." Ellie leaned a little closer, as if to impart a great secret. "I'm sure it will come as no surprise to you, Mr. Bullock, that Mr. King is, in fact, a *pseudonym* to conceal his real identity."

Bullock's eyes widened.

Ellie nodded solemnly. "That's how he's achieved such great success. His anonymity is one of his greatest assets. He's free to move through society, unremarked, without people clamming up around him."

Bullock nodded, his eyes scanning the crowd as if he hoped to decipher which earl, duke, or viscount might be the infamous investigator. "Of course! That makes perfect sense."

Ellie silently congratulated herself on her brilliance.

"I'd be willing to pay handsomely for his assistance, of course," Bullock murmured. "Money is no object. I'll give five hundred pounds."

Ellie bit back a groan of disappointment. All the income from King & Co. was split evenly between herself, Daisy, and Tess. But whereas Daisy and Tess both had additional funds of their own, thanks to being the daughter of a duke, and a duchess, respectively, every penny Ellie earned was going toward her own independence. With enough money, the choice of whether she married or not would be hers, to be made for love and not for financial necessity.

It pained her to turn down what sounded like a particularly lucrative job, but since there was no way Bullock could possibly meet Mr. King, it had to be done.

"I'm afraid there can be no exceptions," she said firmly. "I'm sorry. All communication must be done through either myself, Dorothea Hamilton, or Her Grace, the Duchess of Wansford."

Bullock let out an aggravated huff. "I already tried Miss Hamilton," he admitted. "She told me the same thing."

"And if Her Grace were here this evening, she'd agree."

Bullock gave an unhappy grunt. "That's a shame. I'm an honest man, Miss Law, and I've made my fortune through honest means. I like to look a man in the eye before I do business with him, and if Charles King can't trust me to keep his secret, then—"

"—he'll be unable to take your case," Ellie finished regretfully. "Mr. King is extremely—"

"Ah! Eleanor! There you are, my sweet! I've been looking for you all evening."

Ellie turned in surprise as "Henri Bonheur" appeared from behind a nearby pillar, dimples on full display.

"But you've only just—"

He didn't let her finish. He clasped her shoulders and pressed a firm kiss to both of her cheeks, in the French manner, as if they were old friends, then turned to Bullock with a disarming smile, hand outstretched.

"Henri Bonheur, Comte de Carabas."

Bullock was not immune to his magnetic charm. He shook hands automatically. "William Bullock."

"I see you've been making the acquaintance of my associate, Miss Law."

Bullock's brows lowered in confusion. "Associate?"

Bonheur leaned in, just as Ellie had done earlier, and, much to her annoyance, she couldn't prevent herself from bending forward, too, to hear what he was about to say.

"Indeed," he said with an air of mystery. "I can see you're a man of above common intelligence, Mr. Bullock—"

Bullock's chest expanded again.

"—and it has come to my attention that you've been asking to meet Mr. King."

"I have."

Bonheur lowered his voice to a whisper. "In that case, allow me to inform you that *I* am the man you seek."

"What?! No!" Ellie burst out. "What are you—?"

Bonheur sent her a glance that managed to be both laughing and chiding at once. He shook his head. "Now, now, Ellie. I appreciate your sterling efforts to keep my secret, but I've decided to take Mr. Bullock, here, into my confidence."

He slapped Bullock's shoulder, and the older man visibly preened.

"I trust we can be assured of your *utmost* discretion in this matter?"

"Of course," Bullock blustered immediately. "Absolutely. A hundred percent. Does this mean you'll take my case? It's just a straightforward theft, not the sort of thing you usually deal with, I know, but your reputation is second to none, and I want the best."

"For five hundred pounds? Of course I'll take it. But we can't discuss it here. You may call at my office, at number seven, Lincoln's Inn Fields, tomorrow at ten o'clock sharp."

Bullock straightened and smoothed the front of his waistcoat over his belly. "Thank you, sir. Thank you. I shall see you tomorrow, then." He nodded toward Ellie, and the look he gave her was only slightly condescending. "Good evening, Miss Law."

Ellie managed to contain her ire until Bullock was out of earshot, then she whirled back to "Henri" and pinned him with a look that could have pulverized rock.

"What on earth are you playing at?" she hissed. "You are *not* Charles King. In fact, I very much doubt you're Henri Bonheur either. Explain yourself, sir!"

Chapter Three

The scoundrel's lips curved upward at her fury.

"We can't talk here. Come on." He caught her elbow and steered her gently through the crowd.

Ellie went willingly, but as soon as they reached a quiet corridor beyond the ballroom, she tugged her arm from his grasp and whirled around to face him.

He shook his head, silently indicating a group of women to their left who were talking and fanning themselves as they took a break from the dancing.

"Still too many people."

With a growl, she marched along the corridor, opened a door at random, and stepped into a small study. The elegant furniture, pale pink walls, and proliferation of porcelain figurines suggested it was a room favored by the lady of the house.

Ellie turned to face her tormentor as he closed the door behind him with a click.

"Of all the outrageous, presumptuous, dishonest—"

His laugh made her stomach somersault. "You have an excellent vocabulary, Miss Law. Are words with three syllables your favorite?"

Ellie glared at him. "Not at all. In fact, here are some shorter ones: Explain, you fraud."

He sank gracefully into a comfy-looking armchair on one side of the fire, and with a sweep of his hand indicated its pair, opposite. "Please, sit down."

She complied with a huff, arranging her skirts so as not to crease them, then raised her brows in regal indication that she was waiting for him to speak.

"You're right," he said, "Henri Bonheur is not my real name. Neither, of course, is Charles King. Because, as we both know, Charles King doesn't exist."

Ellie's heart missed a beat, but she schooled her expression to hide her alarm. "Why on earth would you think that?"

"Because I've been trying to make his acquaintance for some time. And while plenty of people know him by reputation, I've failed to find a single one who's actually met him in person. Every one of his previous clients have been dealt with by his able 'assistants': yourself, the Duchess of Wansford, and Dorothea Hamilton."

"He's a very busy man," Ellie lied.

"He's a very *fictional* man," he countered with a chuckle.

Ellie pressed her lips together, stubbornly refusing to either confirm or deny his theory. Who was he? And why had he been trying to find Charles King? Was his plan to blackmail them with the threat of revealing the truth about their female-led agency—and thereby ruin the business? Why would he do such a thing? Was he a competitor? Or was it purely for money? He seemed rich enough. Then again, appearances could be deceiving.

"What *is* your real name?" she demanded.

His shoulders lifted in an elegant shrug. "I wish I could tell you. I was orphaned at a young age, and whatever records were made at the time were lost."

"That sounds just as much of a fairy tale as 'Puss in Boots,' my Lord Carabas," she said acidly.

"Ah, you caught that reference, did you?" His dimples flashed. "I thought you might. Nevertheless, it's true. I've had many names because—and I trust I have *your* complete discretion on this, Eleanor—for the past ten years I've had an extremely successful career as a criminal."

Ellie blinked. "That's a risky thing to confess to the daughter of England's Lord Chief Justice."

"Perhaps. My best work has been on the Continent, in Italy and France, although I can't say I haven't broken a few laws here in England too."

"What sort of crimes?" Ellie's heart pounded against her breastbone. She was usually a fair judge of character. Had she made a terrible mistake and allowed herself to be lured into a private room with a murderer? A rapist?

His lips curved as if he knew precisely the direction of her thoughts.

"Nothing too dreadful, I promise you. A little burglary, some light pickpocketing. A heist or two. I can crack a safe, pick a lock, cheat at cards, and forge a variety of documents. Perhaps you read about the disappearance of Raphael's *Madonna and Child* from the archbishop's palace in Rome?"

"That was you?"

He gave a pleased nod. "I held it for ransom until the archbishop paid for its safe return. And in my defense, he was a thoroughly unpleasant individual who'd bribed and blackmailed his way to the top and very much deserved the aggravation. I donated all but a small percentage of the proceeds to a foundling hospital in Venice."

"Why are you telling me this? And why are you here, in London? Are you planning another crime?"

He crossed one long leg over the other, resting his ankle on the opposite knee, and studied her intently. Ellie felt her body heat.

"Quite the contrary. I've decided to go straight."

"Because you've realized the error of your ways?"

"Of course not. I'd do precisely the same again, given the chance." He sent her an unrepentant grin. "But a good player knows when it's time to quit the game. One can possess extraordinary talent, but the element of chance can never be discounted. A single, unexpected event can ruin the best-laid plans, which is why the most successful criminals are the ones you've never heard of. They're the ones who stopped before they were caught, whose executions never made the news sheets, who lived out their days in blissful obscurity."

Ellie shook her head, even as she smiled. "You've decided to stop before your luck runs out?"

"Precisely. I have no desire to be the richest man in the cemetery. Wise men do it for the money. Dead men do it for the fame."

"But why are you here?"

"For the same reason you're working for 'Charles King.'"

"Which is . . . ?"

"Stimulation."

Her brows shot up and he chuckled. "Let me clarify that. You, Ellie Law, have a brilliant, enquiring mind. You need to fill your days with something challenging, something rewarding, or you'll go completely mad."

Ellie's heart gave an odd little twist. This man was a stranger, a criminal, the complete antithesis of everything she stood for, and yet he could read her as easily as if she were an open book. She felt exposed, *seen*, as if he'd delved into the deepest part of her soul and pulled out all her frustrations and desires, her drive and ambition, and laid them out on the floor.

His lips curved as he watched her face, and he tilted his head. "And besides, you need me."

She didn't hide her instinctive snort. "How have you arrived at that conclusion?"

"I'm sure you've heard the phrase 'it takes a thief to catch a thief'?"

"Of course."

"It comes from an Ancient Greek chap called Callimachus. He said, 'Being a thief myself, I recognize the tracks of a thief.'"

"You're very well-read, for a criminal."

"The two are not mutually exclusive. I'm sure you're very well-read, too, for an investigator. Either way, you must see there are obvious benefits to having an ex-criminal by your side in a professional capacity. Someone who knows every trick in the book."

It was Ellie's turn to laugh. "You want to work with me? At King and Company?"

"Precisely. You're successful now, but just think how much *more* successful you could be with my help."

"So you want a job? A salary?"

He waved his hand in an elegant, dismissive gesture. "Pfft, no. I've enough money to last me two lifetimes. Three, probably. What I need is a vocation. A reason to get up in the mornings."

"You could do what most other rich, bored gentlemen do. Buy a stable of racehorses, join a club like White's or Brooks's, spend a fortune at the tailors and bootmakers on Bond Street."

He indicated his beautifully fitted boots. "I *already* spend a fortune on Bond Street. Horse racing is dull. And most of the men who drink and game their days away in the clubs are even duller."

"With your particular skills, you should become a politician," she said cynically.

"And be surrounded by even more crooks? No thank you. I might as well take lodgings in Newgate."

He sent her a pathetic, pleading look, like that of a puppy begging for a morsel of ham. "Think of me as a re-habilitation project. If I'm not helping you solve crimes, I'll be so bored I'll start committing them again, which is not a good outcome for anyone."

Ellie rolled her eyes at his ridiculousness.

"Saving me from a sticky end on the gallows would be an act of mercy," he pressed. "Employing me would practically be a public service. You'll be preventing as many crimes as you'll be solving."

She gave an inelegant snort. "Why choose King and Company? Why not approach the Bow Street runners, or any of the other private investigative firms in town?"

"Because I believe we can come to a mutually benefi-cial arrangement. Admit it, there is no Charles King, is there?"

Ellie weighed her options. He'd already guessed their secret, and in admitting his criminal past he'd already entrusted her with plenty of incriminating information. She might as well reciprocate.

"Very well, you're right. We made him up. Daisy, Tess, and I run King and Company."

He nodded, unsurprised. "As someone with a fictional name myself, I feel a particular kinship with Charles King. It's almost like fate brought us together. I'm in need of a new start, a new name. You're in need of some-one to embody your fictional employer in order to deal

with fools like Bullock. Why refuse five hundred pounds
when a simple solution has presented itself?"

Because the thought of working with someone as hand-
some as you makes my stomach flutter.

No, she couldn't say that.

Ellie frowned. "The past has a nasty way of catching
up with people. What if someone who knew you in Italy
or France comes to London and recognizes you? You'll
be revealed as a fraud and jeopardize the case."

"It's a risk, of course, but there are risks involved in
any endeavor. It's low enough to be acceptable, in my
view."

"I'm not the only one who makes the decisions at
King and Company. I'll have to discuss your proposition
with my partners."

"Of course. I'm sure they'll see the benefits of having me around." He uncrossed his legs and stood, and
Ellie did the same, trying not to notice how beautifully
proportioned his long, lean body was. Or how tempting
his lips were.

She'd *kissed* those lips. She still couldn't believe it.

He reached into his jacket pocket, pulled out a large
gold-cased pocket watch on a thick albert chain, and
held it out to her. "Here."

"What's this?" She took it from his outstretched hand
automatically, then frowned as she read the monogram
engraved on the back. *WB.*

"Just a trifle, to prove how useful I can be. It's Bullock's."

"You *stole* it?"

"Just now. From his pocket, while he was talking with
us." His eyes gleamed with devilry. "You can return it to
him when he comes to your office tomorrow. It will put
him in a good mood."

"And how will I explain it being in my possession?" Ellie demanded, aghast.

"Say you saw him drop it when he walked away, but by the time you'd picked it up, you'd lost him in the crowd."

Such sleight of hand was annoyingly impressive, but Ellie sent him a disapproving frown. "Let me make this quite clear, Mr. whatever-your-name-is. I do *not* condone using illegal means of *any sort* to solve a case. Is that understood?"

"Of course. Completely. I simply wished to give you some proof of my claims. In case you thought I was a charlatan."

"You *are* a charlatan. By you own admission."

He shrugged. "A talented, useful charlatan."

The watch was still warm from his body heat. She slipped it into her skirt pocket with an unwelcome shiver of awareness.

He gestured toward the door. "If that's all, we should both get back to the ball. I'll be at King and Company tomorrow morning at nine o'clock sharp, to see what decision you and your colleagues have made. Bullock is coming at ten, don't forget."

It was hard to look businesslike when his physical attractiveness was so distracting. The elegant severity of his coat emphasized the breadth of his shoulders, and his form-fitting breeches made it surprisingly difficult to concentrate.

"I want you to swear to me that you won't tell anyone what we've discussed."

His smile made her pulse flutter. "Trust goes both ways, Miss Law. You could have me swinging from the gallows before the week is out, with the things I've told you about myself."

"*If* they're true," she said cynically.

"Oh, they are. But if it puts your mind at ease, then I also give you my word. Both as a gentleman, and as a thief."

"Fine. That is acceptable." She cleared her throat. "I promise not to send *you* to the gallows."

He nodded, but she saw his lips twitch in amusement as he gestured toward the door. "You go first. I'll wait a few moments so we're not seen together."

"Yes, heaven forbid we should do anything that causes a scandal." Ellie injected a little acid into her tone. "Good evening, sir."

His smile made her remember their kiss again, and she bustled out into the corridor to hide her blush. His *"Good night, Eleanor,"* floated behind her like a ghost.

Chapter Four

"Henri Bonheur" smiled as his unwilling new accomplice closed the door behind her with a distinctly irritated click.

Eleanor Law was everything he'd been hoping for, and more, and his heart pounded against his ribs at the prospect of crossing swords with her again. She was, for want of a better word, invigorating.

He hadn't planned on kissing her—not tonight, at least—but since the perfect moment had presented itself, he'd seized the opportunity. Fortune favored the brave, after all. Or the brazen, in this case.

The shocked look on her face had been delightful; her expressive features had betrayed first incredulity, then an unexpected flush of desire, and his body hardened at the memory of her soft pink lips beneath his own.

He'd kissed scores of women in his time, for countless reasons, but none who'd been so unsuspecting, nor so innocent. The experience had been deliciously novel, and for the first time in a long time he'd found it hard to remember the plan. The urge to keep on kissing her had been that strong.

He wondered, idly, if he should be worried.

When he'd first arrived in London and started investigating King & Co., it had been because he liked to know the nature of those he was considering working with. Forewarned was forearmed, after all. Whether his accomplices were crooks or honest men made little difference—both were equally predictable—although he steered clear of those with violent tendencies. Knowing someone's true nature meant he could plan accordingly.

In Charles King he'd expected to find a man with a strong moral code and an even stronger dislike of socializing, but what he'd found instead was three remarkably clever women running a delightfully subversive deception.

Their ruse was one he could thoroughly appreciate. After all, being economical with the truth and lying by omission were things at which he himself excelled. He could only applaud the way they'd twisted society's expectations and forged their own path.

Tess, the Duchess of Wansford, was undeniably beautiful, but not to his personal taste; he could admire her pleasing features as one might enjoy those of a classical statue. Plus, she seemed entirely devoted to her besotted husband.

The stormy, wilder attractiveness of Dorothea Hamilton hinted at a restless spirit a little too similar to his own, but the instant attraction he'd felt on seeing Eleanor Law had been an unexpected shock.

At first glance she appeared almost plain. Her physical beauty was subtle, as if she was deliberately hiding the full strength of it for fear of drawing unwanted attention, but he was a man accustomed to spotting a single diamond among a mountain of paste.

Ellie reminded him of a Roman coin he'd once found

in a field in Tuscany. It had appeared dull, almost unin-spiring, but a quick rub on his shirt had revealed its true nature: glistening, breathtaking gold.

The fact that she clearly possessed brains, as well as a sharp wit and even sharper tongue, gave him a moment of disquiet. He'd never wasted much time thinking about his "ideal" woman, but if he *had*, then she had many of the attributes he'd doubtless desire.

Which was foolish. Love at first sight was as much of a myth as the name he'd given her. *Lust* at first sight, however, certainly existed, and exploring his attraction to her while they worked together for the next few weeks was something he was looking forward to with a great deal of anticipation.

Chapter Five

Ellie found Daisy as soon as she reentered the ballroom.

"Can we go home now?"

The two of them had shared a carriage with Devlin, one of Daisy's three older brothers, which technically satisfied the need for a chaperone and had the added convenience of him being the most inattentive of companions.

Daisy made a comical pout of displeasure. "But the night is still young!"

"It's after midnight. I need to send a message to Tess to tell her to meet us at the office first thing tomorrow. Mr. Bullock's coming at ten o'clock."

"You managed to convince him he doesn't need to see Mr. King?"

"Not exactly, but it's a long story. I'll explain tomorrow. Can you be there at eight?"

Daisy rolled her eyes in horror. "*Eight?* You just said Bullock's not coming until ten. Not even the birds are up at eight o'clock."

"Someone else is coming at nine, but I need to speak to you and Tess before then."

"Ooh, a mystery!" Daisy grinned. "Say no more. I'll go and drag Devlin away from the card tables." She disappeared into the crowd.

Unlike Tess and Daisy, who both lived in Mayfair, Ellie and her parents lived relatively close to the Lincoln's Inn Fields office, in Bloomsbury, near the British Museum. Her father, Baron Ellenborough, had eschewed the more fashionable parts of town in favor of being closer to the Royal Courts of Justice. The three girls had only met thanks to their common attendance at Miss Honoria Burnett's Ladies Academy.

As soon as she arrived home, Ellie dashed off a brief note to Tess that was guaranteed to pique her interest.

New job. Urgent.

P.S. Just kissed Charles King.

Tess's recent marriage to Justin Thornton, Duke of Wansford, had sent ripples through the *ton*, but the two of them were blissfully happy. Daisy, Tess, and Ellie had already arranged to meet for dinner tomorrow night, but Ellie sent the note to Tess's town house in Portman Square to urge her to come to the office in the morning. Then she went to bed, her brain whirling with memories of her unexpectedly eventful evening.

When morning arrived, she dressed with care and arrived at the office to find Daisy pacing the room with barely suppressed energy, and Tess seated calmly behind her desk, drinking a cup of tea.

Daisy's eyes grew wide when Ellie described the events of the previous night.

"He kissed you? Right there in the ballroom, where anyone could have seen?" Her tone was one of astonished awe. "No wonder you were blushing. What a risk!"

"And then he pretended to be Charles King to Bullock

and accepted the case," Ellie confirmed. "Without even knowing what it was about."

Daisy shook her head in wonder, and all three of them stared at Bullock's gold watch, which Ellie had deposited on the desk. It was clear that "Henri Bonheur" had risen dramatically in Daisy's estimation: not merely a handsome rogue, but a capable thief too.

Daisy's criteria for what made a man attractive was incomprehensible.

"Well, apart from the fact that we don't know who he is," Daisy said, "his suggestion isn't bad. Having a man around is sometimes quite useful."

"For opening tightly sealed jars of jam?" Ellie snorted. "Reaching hard-to-access shelves?"

"I meant for solving cases. A physically intimidating specimen like him could be useful when questioning male suspects. And if you ever need personal protection, he'd make an excellent bodyguard."

Ellie's body heated at the memory of that particular hard body pressed against hers in the alcove. How had something that lasted less than three seconds left such an indelible impression?

"But he's a self-confessed criminal. The antithesis of everything we stand for: justice, order, and the rule of law."

Tess took a leisurely sip of her tea. "True, but haven't you heard the phrase 'a reformed rake makes the best husband'? This is the criminal version of that: a reformed thief makes the best thief-taker."

"That's just what *he* said," Ellie groaned. "But wouldn't we be foolish to trust a man like that? How do we know he's not just using us for his own nefarious ends?"

"Like what?" Daisy scoffed.

"Tess is rich," Ellie said. "And so is your father. Maybe he's trying to inveigle his way into a position of trust so he can rob you both?"

"If he's as good as he claims, he wouldn't need to go to all that bother." Tess took another sip of tea. "He'd have already broken in and stolen whatever he wanted to steal."

Ellie frowned, reluctant to admit that her friend had a point. "Well, perhaps he means to ruin the business. Perhaps he's been employed by someone we've annoyed to close us down."

"Most of the people we've annoyed are either dead, in prison, or have fled abroad in disgrace," Daisy said with satisfaction.

"I think his explanation makes perfect sense," Tess added. "He's intelligent enough to stop thieving before he's caught, but too young to retire and sit quietly by the fire. Who can blame him for wanting a little excitement?"

"So you think we should agree to let him work on the Bullock case?" Ellie asked.

"Why not? We can tell him it's a trial. If he's useful, we'll consider letting him work with us on a more permanent basis."

"He's unpredictable, unethical—"

"—charming, confident, suave," Daisy finished with a chuckle. "Better to have him on our side, don't you think?"

Ellie gave a groan of defeat. In truth, the thought of seeing "Henri Bonheur" again made her heart beat strangely in her chest.

A sharp knock on the back door made all three of them jump. Tess stayed where she was, but when Daisy started for the door, Ellie waved her back. She took a steadying breath and went to open it herself, and found the man in question lounging negligently against the doorframe, looking just as handsome as he had the night before.

A navy overcoat hung from his shoulders, a matching top hat perched on his head at a jaunty angle, and a silver-topped walking cane completed the ensemble. It was tucked beneath his arm, however, since he held before him a large terra-cotta pot filled with a green, leafy plant.

"Morning, Ellie, my sweet." He smiled, and the dimples made an appearance. "You look rather studious."

Ellie cursed silently. She snatched the offending spectacles from her nose and thrust them in her pocket; she'd forgotten she was wearing them. Painfully conscious of the way her cheeks were heating, she swung the door wide to usher him in.

"I come bearing gifts." He thrust the pot and its leafy contents into her hands.

Ellie backed up, careful to avoid contact with his muscular frame. "What's this?"

"A gift. For you."

The delicious scent of his cologne enfolded her in an olfactory embrace as he stepped past her, and she closed her eyes, praying for strength. The man smelled irresistible. Perhaps he was some kind of sorcerer—a genie, capable of bewitching unsuspecting victims into doing his bidding.

To protect herself, she sniffed the plant, trying to identify the scent, and frowned at his back as he preceded her into the front office and made his own introductions.

"Lady Dorothea, it's a pleasure to see you again. And I assume I have the honor of addressing Her Grace, the Duchess of Wansford?" He removed his hat and bowed to both Daisy and Tess.

Daisy sent him a pleased, intrigued smile, while Tess nodded regally and finished pouring a second cup of tea. "You do indeed."

"Henri Bonheur, your most humble servant."

Ellie deposited the potted plant on her desk with a thump.

"You've bought us a present?" Tess asked.

"I have. In Italy, it's traditional to give basil to bring good luck and ward off poverty."

"How kind." Tess smiled, delighted.

"Plus," he continued, "the name 'basil' derives from the Greek word 'basilius,' which means 'king.' It seemed rather fitting, considering the name of your agency."

Ellie frowned. The man was already ridiculously handsome. Did he have to be considerate and well educated too?

As if aware of her silent irritation, he sent her a teasing smile. "Cut flowers only last for a few days. With this, you'll have a constant reminder of me."

Ellie couldn't decide if that was a blessing, or a curse. Daisy sent an envious glance at his silver-topped cane. The handle was modeled as a lion's head, with a shaggy mane and snarling mouth.

"Is that a sword stick?"

"It is indeed." He held it forward obligingly, and Daisy inspected it with obvious delight.

"I've been thinking about getting one of these. How do you release the blade?"

"There's a catch, beneath the lion's jaw. Press it."

Daisy did so, and revealed the slim two-sided blade that had been hidden inside the stick with a satisfying hiss. "How marvelous!"

He removed it from her avaricious grip and slid the dangerous-looking weapon away. "It's come in handy a time or two, certainly. The element of surprise is always useful."

"Ellie told us about your meeting last night," Daisy said. "I must say, it was extremely impertinent of you to pretend to be our Mr. King and accept a case. We don't usually investigate burglaries."

He shrugged. "It was a calculated risk. But one I'm hoping has paid off. Money is money, after all, and five hundred pounds is not to be sneezed at. Are you willing to let me be of assistance with Mr. Bullock?"

Ellie leaned against the edge of her desk and crossed her arms. Her father always berated her for the pose, saying it made her look like a fishwife, but she didn't care. "Henri Bonheur" made her feel extremely combative. She sent a silent look at first Tess, then Daisy, and noted their almost imperceptible nods.

"We are," she said firmly. "But only on a probationary basis. If you prove useful in this case we'll consider you for further collaboration, but if you do *anything* to jeopardize the investigation, we will end our association with you immediately."

His face creased into another of those devastating smiles. "Excellent. In that case . . ." He extended his hand toward Daisy in formal greeting, "Charles King, Esquire, at your service."

Daisy shook it with an amused chuckle. "Delighted to make your acquaintance, Mr. King."

Tess sent him a wide, genuine smile, the kind that usually had men tripping over their feet and forgetting their own name, but Henri, astonishingly, merely smiled back. Perhaps, since he possessed the male equivalent of Tess's beauty, he was immune.

Ellie ignored his tomfoolery, childishly determined

to burst his bubble of confidence. "You're named after a dog, you know."

His brows shot up. "I thought you chose King because it sounded regal. Trustworthy. Capable."

She shook her head. "I'm afraid not. We chose it in honor of the one male all three of us adore: Daisy's dog, Montgomery. He's a King Charles Spaniel. King Charles. Charles King. Voilà."

His face fell in comical dismay. "A dog. How very lowering."

"I'm afraid so," she said with mock solemnity. It was difficult not to laugh. "We'll call you Charles in front of Bullock, but you're going to have to provide us with a name to call you in private, when we're not on the case. I refuse to call you Henri Bonheur, or the Comte de Carabas. What do your friends call you?"

His lips curved at her echo of his own words from the previous night. "My old tutor called me Harry. You can call me that, if you like. It's as good a name as any."

Ellie gave a businesslike nod, and Tess rose from her seat.

"Perfect. Now, Mr. Bullock will be here soon, but there's no reason for all of us to see him. I've promised to go shopping with Justin. Ellie, you and Harry can find out what his problem is, and go from there." She shot Ellie a look so sweetly innocent that Ellie was immediately suspicious. "Daisy, my love, you can come to Bond Street with me. Ellie will be perfectly fine on her own."

Daisy, the little agitator, immediately nodded. "Of course, I *adore* shopping."

The shameless lie slipped effortlessly off her tongue as she shot Ellie a wicked grin behind Harry's back.

Ellie almost rolled her eyes at their monumentally

unsubtle attempt to matchmake. She reached into her skirt pocket for her glasses, so she could glare at them both in perfect focus, but her hand clasped around nothing.

"Looking for these?" Harry asked cheerfully.

Ellie glanced up with a frown, and her mouth dropped open as she recognized her spectacles held aloft in his large, tanned fingers. How on *earth* had he managed to swipe them from her skirt pocket without her noticing? Had he done it when he'd passed her in the hall?

The man was a menace. Still, as Tess would doubtless say, he was *their* menace.

She plucked them from his grasp with a myopic glare, which he returned with a smile that reminded her of a well-fed crocodile.

Tess, on her way out of the door, gave a throaty chuckle. "Why, Mr. King, that is a remarkable talent. I look forward to seeing you employ your other skills on our behalf."

Harry grinned at her, but his gaze rested on Ellie when he answered.

"It will be my pleasure, Your Grace."

Chapter Six

Tess opened the front door just as a postboy with a letter in his hand ascended the steps. Daisy took it and scanned the contents.

"It's from Mr. Bullock. He's asked you to meet him at his museum, instead of here."

"The Egyptian Hall, in Piccadilly?" Ellie asked.

"Yes."

"We can take my carriage."

Harry's voice came from directly behind her, and she stiffened. The man was as silent as a mouse!

He placed his top hat on his head at the same jaunty angle as before and gestured down the street, to where a handsome equipage waited, drawn by two perfectly matched grays. The liveried coachman was dressed as smartly as one of the king's own servants, and Ellie squinted to see the painted crest adorning the door panels. It was not one she recognized, consisting of three lions rampant on a red shield with a gold chevron, and she wondered briefly if it was a fanciful decoration created purely for the "Comte de Carabas."

"That's not a stolen carriage, is it?" Daisy asked, a faint note of hopefulness in her tone.

"Of course not," Harry said with mock dignity. "I'm merely borrowing it from a friend."

Tess smiled. "Is your friend *aware* of that fact?"

"He is indeed." Harry's dimples deepened in appreciation of her wit. "Fear not, Your Grace. Sweet Ellie and I shan't be arrested by Bow Street's finest on our way to Piccadilly."

Ellie frowned, but Daisy sent her a delighted smile as she stepped up into Tess's carriage. "In that case, best of luck. Ellie, you can tell us all about it when you get back."

Tess joined Daisy in their carriage, and the two of them pointedly ignored Ellie's narrow-eyed glare for abandoning her to the dubious charms of Harry-No-Name.

They clattered away, and Ellie resigned herself to sharing a coach with her unwanted new accomplice. He gallantly stepped aside as she headed back into the office to retrieve her coat and gloves, and by the time she emerged he was settled comfortably in his own carriage that had drawn up outside.

The coachman handed her up the step, and she sank onto the plush velvet seat across from Harry while trying not to look impressed by the luxuriousness of the interior.

The horses set off. Harry appeared completely at ease, unaffected by the erratic bouncing of the wheels over the cobbles. His big body was fluid and athletic, his legs stretched at an angle to accommodate their length, and Ellie drew her own heels back against her seat, beneath her skirts, to avoid brushing his ankle.

Oddly, despite his size and undoubted masculinity, she didn't feel threatened by his presence. He seemed to possess an enviable ability to make his companion feel at ease. She was, however, acutely aware of his proximity, and the delicious scent of his cologne that seemed to permeate the carriage and sent her pulse rate soaring.

"I can see why the three of you have been so successful," he said presently.

"What do you mean?"

"Well, you're all clearly in possession of above-average intelligence, which is something most men will have failed to notice, I'm sorry to say. Gentlemen rarely think of women as anything other than ornamental, especially when they're as beautiful as you and your friends. Many will have underestimated you, at their peril."

Ellie blinked at the casual way he'd just called her beautiful. Men used the word to describe Tess on a daily basis, and Daisy, too, but she herself was more often overlooked. Her curly brown hair and hazel eyes were not the height of fashion, and her studious air of detachment—the inevitable result of vainly refusing to wear her spectacles in public—usually made men head in the opposite direction.

Harry didn't seem to notice her self-conscious flush, however. "I suspect there are times when one of you provides the most wonderful distraction, while the others do what needs to be done. It's like three-card monte."

"A what?" Ellie frowned.

"It's a card trick. A ruse, based mainly on sleight of hand. The mark—the person who's being conned—is so busy watching the money card, the Queen of Hearts, for example, that they ignore everything else."

Ellie nodded. "That's certainly true on occasion, but there are also plenty of times when a woman can be almost invisible. Men tend to ignore female servants—as long as they're not too pretty—and often speak freely in front of them, as if they were a piece of furniture."

"Have you ever disguised yourself as a servant?"

"Once or twice. It's quite useful for overhearing gossip in the cloakrooms at parties."

"We're not so dissimilar, then. We've both assumed roles for the purposes of subterfuge."

"It's not the same at all," Ellie countered sternly. "*I've* never donned a disguise to commit a crime. Only to foil them."

He seemed amused, instead of chastened by her scolding. "That said, there are places where respectable women *can't* easily go. The gentlemen's clubs, for one. And gaming hells. One hears a great deal when the members have been at the claret. I may be of use to you yet."

Ellie managed a disdainful sniff. "That remains to be seen."

Luckily for her peace of mind, they arrived at the building that housed Bullock's museum in short order. The Egyptian Hall was one of the most recognizable landmarks in Piccadilly, and probably in London too. Bullock had commissioned it a few years previously, at the height of Egyptomania, when Bonaparte's voyages to the country, and the subsequent discoveries of its treasures, had created a fascination with all things Egyptian.

Some called the building an eyesore, but Ellie secretly loved the unashamed flamboyance of the place. Two huge, fluted pillars flanked the door, their tops shaped like tulips, both painted in a gaudy array of colors. Above them, a pair of huge stone statues stood guard, each wearing the traditional headdress of the pharaohs. One was a female, representing Isis, the Egyptian goddess of healing, holding a palm frond, the other an improbably muscled male depicting Osiris, the god of fertility, cradling a small crocodile. An array of carved sphinxes, scarab beetles, winged suns, and all manner of other exotic embellishments enlivened the rest of the exterior.

The sight of Osiris made her wonder what Harry looked like beneath *his* clothes, and heat rushed to her cheeks. What was wrong with her?

"Perhaps I should wait in the carriage," she said suddenly. "If someone sees us together, without a chaperone, we'll start all sorts of rumors."

He rolled his eyes, as if he had no time for such propriety.

"My parents know that I work with Daisy and Tess at King and Company," she explained, "but they think I just sit in the office and read witness statements and sift through potential evidence. They have no idea that I sometimes go out undercover. They certainly wouldn't approve of me going somewhere with an unmarried gentleman. I should have come in disguise."

"If anyone recognizes you, you can introduce me as your long-lost, distant Italian cousin, and I'll pretend I don't speak a word of English."

"And what if they already know you as Henri Bonheur?"

"We'll cross that bridge if and when we get to it. Come on."

Chapter Seven

The inside of the museum was hardly less fantastical than the outside. Harry magnanimously paid the entrance fee of one shilling each, and together they started through the exhibition rooms.

Rows of glazed cabinets held curiosities from around the world, including those brought back from the South Seas by Captain Cook, and large naturalistic displays showed such wonders as taxidermy kangaroos, birds, and giraffes.

"I came here a few months ago," Ellie said, "to see Napoleon's carriage. Bullock had a special exhibition. It was a terrible crush."

"A pickpocket's dream," Harry said with a smile. "Scores of people all pushing and shoving, paying no attention to their personal belongings."

"I wouldn't know," Ellie said primly.

The Grand Hall, lined with even more pillars, was (according to Ellie's guidebook) a replica of the avenue of the sphinxes at the Karnak Temple, near Luxor, and included an alabaster sarcophagus from the tomb of an Egyptian pharaoh.

It was there that Bullock met them, and after a brief greeting, he got straight down to business.

"You're here, Mr. King, to investigate a brazen theft," he said, directing his attention to Harry. "This way, if you please, and I'll show you the scene of the crime."

He led them into a smaller, considerably less crowded part of the museum and unlocked a door hung with a sign that read EXHIBIT TEMPORARILY CLOSED.

Ellie immediately saw the issue: the glass to one of the cabinets had been smashed, leaving a hole with jagged edges. She and Harry both stepped closer to investigate.

"That's odd," she murmured.

The case contained several gold brooches, a carved medieval chess piece, and some silver Roman coins, but only one label seemed to be lacking a corresponding artifact. "The thief left quite a number of precious items behind. Perhaps he was disturbed before he could steal it all?"

Harry shook his head. "A good guess, Miss Law, but I'm afraid that's incorrect."

Ellie raised her brows. "Oh, really?"

He sent her a beatific smile that made her want to stamp on his foot. "May I present my theory?"

"Please do," she said with false sweetness, conscious of appearing subservient to her "employer" in Bullock's presence. "I bow to your superior knowledge of such things, Mr. King."

His lips twitched at her dig.

"This is a very inelegant theft," he said. "It is *not* the work of a professional." He gestured at the broken glass with a disapproving shake of his head. "A professional would have been more careful, more subtle. This is brutal. Amateur work."

He turned to Bullock. "I tell you, Mr. Bullock, all the

artistry has gone from thieving nowadays. People are so impatient. Nobody cares to learn the beauty of picking a lock, or to become expert at anything, because it takes a huge amount of time and dedication. To cheat at cards, for example, takes hours in front of a mirror learning sleight of hand: how to hold the cards correctly, how to palm them, to deceive the watcher, all accompanied by a seamless flow of conversation and witty repartee to distract and entertain. It's a lost art."

Ellie snorted. "You sound as if you admire such things."

He turned to her with a smile. "I admit I have a certain professional respect for an *elegant* thief. I once encountered a man in Italy who stole a silver tea service, but tipped the contents of the sugar bowl out onto a napkin instead of emptying it out on the floor, so as not to make a mess."

"How considerate," Ellie said drily. She was sure the thief he was talking about was himself. "But wouldn't it have been more considerate not to steal the silver in the first place?"

"Of course," he agreed amiably, turning back to Bullock. "This may have been a crude smash-and-grab, but our thief was no opportunist. This was a targeted burglary. He or she wanted that one particular item. What exactly was stolen?"

Ellie bent closer to the cabinet in an attempt to read the writing on the little card, then cast vanity to the wind and fished her spectacles from her reticule and put them on.

"It says it was a jeweled Book of Hours once owned by the French king François the First, Henri the Fourth, and Cardinal Mazarin," she read aloud.

Harry turned to Bullock. "There are thousands of items here in your museum, Mr. Bullock. Why would someone steal this particular book? Was it very expensive?"

"Well, yes, it was." Bullock frowned. "It had a gold cover decorated with jewels and precious stones—rubies and turquoises and whatnot. And inside it was very pretty, with colored pages and little paintings in the borders. But it was quite small, maybe six inches by four. There are plenty of other things here in the museum worth considerably more."

"Perhaps the small size made it appealing to the thief? Easy to hide in their clothes," Ellie suggested. "Maybe they plan to remove all the jewels from the cover and sell them?"

"Perhaps," Harry said, but he still sounded skeptical. "Certainly, something so rare would be difficult to sell on the black market, because it's so recognizable."

"It could have been stolen to order, for some avid rare-book collector who wants it in their own collection," Ellie countered. "How did it come to be in your possession, Mr. Bullock?"

"I looked back at my purchase notes this morning to check that very thing," Bullock said, "and it turns out it once also belonged to Napoleon Bonaparte himself. I bought it from a military man, who said he'd got it in Russia. His regiment captured the emperor's personal baggage train when he retreated in such haste from Moscow, and the book was found inside."

"Ah," Harry murmured. "Now we could be getting somewhere. What else did the soldier say, about it, Mr. Bullock? Can you recall?"

Bullock's bushy brows knitted as he considered the

question, then he gave a laughing snort. "Ha! He actually said the damn thing was lucky! Fat lot of lies *that* turned out to be."

"Lucky in what way?"

"He said the book was Bonaparte's lucky charm, that he never went anywhere without it. And you know, perhaps it was true, because everything started to go wrong for Old Boney almost as soon as it left his possession, didn't it? His attempt to conquer Russia was a disaster, and he ended up losing everything to Wellington at Waterloo."

Bullock shrugged. "Don't see what that has to do with it being stolen, though. My guess is it was just someone who saw something shiny and expensive-looking and took it."

Harry nodded thoughtfully. He slid his fingers into the breast pocket of his coat and withdrew a silver quizzing glass, then raised it to his eye and leaned in, toward Bullock's cravat.

"Speaking of shiny and expensive, that is a very fine tiepin, sir."

Bullock puffed out his chest at the compliment. "Why, thank you. The diamond belonged to Napoleon too. A stash of 'em were hidden in a tea caddy in his carriage when it was seized at Waterloo. The carriage itself is on display right now in the other room, along with all manner of other items, but I bought this diamond from Mr. Mawe, the diamond merchant in the Strand. He got it from a Prussian, Baron Von Keller. I had him fashion this pin for me."

"A lovely piece," Harry murmured, and as he tucked his quizzing glass away, Ellie shot him a sideways glare that clearly said *Don't you even think about stealing it.*

His dimpled smile was hardly reassuring.

Ellie turned back to Bullock. "Oh, that reminds me. I have your pocket watch, sir."

"You do? How? I thought some devil had pickpocketed me at Lady Chessington's last night."

She reached back into her reticule and handed it to him. He turned it over, opening it to make sure it was, indeed, his.

"You dropped it as you walked away from me last night, but by the time I'd picked it up, I'd lost you in the crowd." She sent him a sheepish look and gestured at the spectacles she still wore. "I'm afraid I'm as blind as a bat without these, but I don't like wearing them in public. They make me look too much of a bluestocking."

Bullock accepted this shameful fabrication with genial condescension, as if foolish female vanity was entirely expected of her.

"Thank you, Miss Law. You are a credit to your employer." He sent a jovial smile to Harry. "Not that I needed proof that an employee of King and Company would be anything other than trustworthy."

Ellie almost rolled her eyes at the irony and managed a sweet smile. "You're very welcome, Mr. Bullock." She turned to Harry. "Shall we go, sir?"

Harry offered his arm. "Indeed."

With one last glance to make sure Bullock's diamond tiepin was still there—it was—she allowed Harry to lead her from the room.

Chapter Eight

As soon as they were out of sight of Bullock, Ellie removed her hand from Harry's distractingly muscular forearm and turned to him.

"All right, tell me your thoughts."

"About life, love, and the universe in general?" he teased. "Very well. All in all, I'm in favor of—"

"About the *case*," she said testily. "Why do you think it was a targeted attack?"

He turned and pretended to admire a large stuffed ostrich, so their backs were to the room. "I think that particular book was stolen because it was rumored to be lucky."

"That's ridiculous."

"No more ridiculous than all the other superstitions people put their faith in on a daily basis. Admit it, I bet even you, a rational, educated woman, do some superstitious things. Do you walk under ladders?"

"No," she said. "But that's just common sense. I don't believe I'll be disturbing evil spirits or ending my days on the gallows if I do. I'd just rather not be hit on the head if the person up the ladder drops something."

He sighed, as if disappointed by her pragmatism. "I bet there's something. Do you toss salt over your shoulder if you spill it? Or think that breaking a mirror brings you seven years' bad luck?"

"I do not."

He sent her a skeptical look, eyebrows raised, and she gave a disgruntled sigh and gave in.

"Fine. I'm polite to single magpies. I always say, 'Hello, Mr. Magpie, how's your wife and children?' if I see one."

"Ha!"

"But that's only because magpies are known to mate for life, so seeing a single one makes one hope that their partner is somewhere about, or that they'll find a mate soon. Wishing them well is just good manners."

"Of course," he said soothingly. "And nothing to do with the belief that a single magpie brings bad luck: one for sorrow, two for joy, and all that?"

"Not at all."

"Hmm. My point is," he continued, "that the world is full of people believing in things, and not even the most intelligent people are immune. Almost every profession has its own superstitions. In the theater, for example, it's traditional to say 'break a leg' on opening night, and bad luck to whistle backstage. It's even worse luck to say the word 'Macbeth' unless one is actually working on the production and the script requires it. At all other times it's referred to as 'the Scottish play.'"

Ellie smiled ruefully. "To be fair, I do know one barrister who wears the same shirt for the whole length of a trial, and another who refuses to have his hair cut until the verdict is read out."

"There you go. My point is, believing that something is lucky is a powerful motivating force. I think the

monetary value of that book was of less importance than
the fact that Napoleon himself believed it to be lucky."

"You think the person who stole it wants some of that
luck for themselves?"

"I do." Harry tilted his head. "And believe me, as a
former criminal, I have an excellent understanding of the
power of making people believe in something—even if
it isn't true. In three-card monte, for example, the skill
lies in making the mark believe they're cleverer than all
the other players, making them think they can win easy
money because they can follow the money card better
than anyone else."

"Hmm," Ellie said, still unconvinced.

"It's the same with holy relics," he continued. "I've
lost count of the number of churches I've been to that
house the finger bone of saint somebody-or-other.
You could make at least twenty full skeletons of Saint
Francis of Assisi with all the body parts strewn around
the Continent. And I'm sure that in the back of their
logical minds, people know this, but they don't care,
because they all think *their* finger bone is the *real*
true finger bone, and that it will cure their goat of
scrofula."

Ellie chuckled.

"And because they believe," he said, "they do everything they can to make it happen. They visit the veteri-
narian and make the goat take its medicine, and feed it
better food, and lo and behold, the goat recovers. And
they attribute it to the lucky finger bone, instead of their
own good sense or actions."

"Are you saying there's no such thing as luck?"

"I'm saying it doesn't matter whether there is or not.
What matters is if someone *believes* in that luck, and it
starts to affect their actions."

"So things began to go wrong for Bonaparte when he lost the book because he didn't believe he'd be lucky anymore?"

"Exactly. With it, he imagined himself invincible and destined for greatness. But without it, defeat became almost inevitable. As soon as a man starts questioning his own judgment, and feeling that nothing he does will succeed because good fortune's deserted him, failure becomes a self-fulfilling prophecy."

"That's quite a theory," Ellie said. "But I fail to see how it's going to help us catch Mr. Bullock's thief. Bonaparte is locked up on Saint Helena, so I don't think we can add *him* to our list of suspects."

"True." Harry turned back to her, and Ellie was surprised to discover how close they'd been standing. She still couldn't determine the exact color of his eyes: depending on the light they appeared green, blue, or even hazel, and the inability to define them was becoming mildly annoying. Still, she couldn't keep staring up at him like a simpleton.

His own gaze lingered for a moment on her lips, and she felt her blood heat. Why did such a scoundrel have to be so appealing?

Suddenly self-conscious, she slid her spectacles from her nose and folded them neatly into their velvet-lined filigree holder.

"Well, I suppose we'd better be getting back to the office."

They walked side by side through the remaining rooms, and when they finally stood on the street outside, she peered left and right to see where his carriage was waiting.

Harry, however, paused on the steps, staring intently at something across the road.

"What is it?" Ellie squinted with little success in the vague direction he was looking.

"Something else I learned as a criminal, Eleanor, is to take note when something seems out of place."

"What do you mean?"

"Do you see that beggar, in the doorway across the street?"

"No," Ellie said bluntly.

He glanced down at her with a smile. "Oh, put your spectacles back on, you ridiculous thing. You're wrong about thinking they make you look less attractive. You're gorgeous either way."

Ellie's mouth dropped open at the unexpected, off-hand compliment. She snapped it shut and willed the blush in her cheeks to subside as she delved back into her reticule. Spectacles back on, she glanced across the street.

"Now I see the beggar. The one with a dog?"

"Yes. Do you notice anything unusual about him?"

Ellie considered the question. The man was sitting in the doorway of a disused shop, his legs stretched out in front of him, a scruffy black mongrel curled up on the step next to him. His face was partly obscured by a military cap, and a large blue overcoat covered the rest of his form.

"He's wearing a military hat. Which might suggest he's a veteran who's fallen on hard times," she ventured.

"True. But his overcoat doesn't make sense. The cut and the cloth are of the highest quality, the collar is velvet, and unlike those trousers of his, and his boots, there's not a hole or a patch anywhere on it. It's pristine. Which means he only recently acquired it."

"Maybe some kind soul gave it to him? Or do you think he stole it?"

"The poor wretch looks too skinny to have been able to steal it. A stiff wind could knock him over. And it's a damned fine coat to give away, even out of pity. So the question must be asked, where did he get the money to buy it?"

Harry took her arm and led her down the steps, then across the busy road, dodging carriages and milk carts as they went. The dog heard their approach and lifted its head, but didn't growl. The man, who had been dozing with his chin on his chest, started awake with a jolt.

Harry touched his hat in greeting, and the man squinted up at him in obvious surprise.

"Good day, sir. Charles King." He nodded at the man's ragged cap. "Do I have the honor of addressing a former member of the rifle brigade?"

The man's face lost its suspicious look and his bearded jaw widened in a smile. "Indeed, you do, sir. Sergeant John Morris, Ninety-fifth Regiment of Foot. At least I was, until a musket ball broke me collarbone and I was invalided home."

He extended his hand and Harry shook it, showing no disdain for the man's grubby fingernails or generally unkempt state.

"Was you in the Rifles too?" Morris asked. He got to his feet a little unsteadily, and Ellie felt a flash of pity. The man was barely a decade older than herself, but he seemed frail and malnourished.

"I'm afraid I didn't have that glory," Harry chuckled. "My contribution to His Majesty's cause was a little more—how shall we say?—*clandestine*."

Morris's eyes widened at the inference. "You mean you were a spy?"

"A mere gatherer of gossip." Harry waved his hand

in an airy, dismissive gesture. "Now happily returned to England, and doing what I do best, investigating crimes in our fair metropolis."

Morris's face fell. "Oh?"

"Is this your usual spot, Mr. Morris?" Ellie asked gently.

Morris crossed his arms in a defensive gesture. "Maybe it is."

"Then perhaps you might be able to help us. A rather valuable book was stolen from Mr. Bullock's museum over there a few days ago. I don't suppose you happened to notice anyone loitering about or leaving the place in a hurry?"

"I never saw nobody do nothin'," Morris muttered.

"That's a pity." Harry let out a sigh. "Because I pay extremely well for useful information."

Morris bit his lip, looking indecisive, as if he wanted to say more but was holding himself back, but Harry didn't press him. Instead, he bent down to stroke the dog, which was rubbing itself against his shins in a shameless demand for attention.

"Who's this little rascal?"

"That's Mutton."

"Hello, Mutton." Harry glanced up. "Now, my assistant here may be interested in gathering information for the case, but I for one am much more interested in learning where you purchased that exquisite coat."

Morris glanced down at his chest and stroked his hand down the front, enjoying the texture of the cloth. He opened his mouth to say something, but Harry straightened and indicated his own beautifully crafted outfit before Morris could speak.

"No, no. Don't tell me! Let me guess!"

He took a step back, and tilted his head to study Morris's coat with a critical eye.

"Anyone with a keen eye for fashion, such as myself, immediately recognizes the work of one of London's finest tailors." He tapped his lips as if deep in thought. "The cut is excellent, equal to that of Weston, but the style is too severe to be his. The straight lines and deep blue color might suggest Stultz, but Stultz favors fabric-covered buttons, and those are gilt."

Morris was looking at him in a kind of dazed wonder.

Harry retrieved his silver quizzing glass from the pocket of his waistcoat, and leaned in for a closer look.

"Wool broadcloth, but not the work of Gieves and Hawkes, Lord Wellington's favorites." He pursed his lips, then let out a whistle. "I have it! That silk velvet trim on the collar can only have come from Schweitzer and Davidson on Cork Street. Am I right?"

Morris's forehead wrinkled in confusion. "I couldn't tell you, sir. I never bought it myself."

Harry raised his brows. "That doesn't surprise me at all, Sergeant Morris. That coat was clearly made for a gentleman of far larger proportions than yourself. It practically hangs off you."

Morris gave an unhappy sniff. "Doesn't matter. It keeps me warm at night. That's why I asked him to throw it into the deal. A warm coat, and enough coin to buy Mutton a beef pie."

"In exchange for stealing a book from the museum." Harry nodded, his tone gently understanding.

Morris's eyes grew wide. He shook his head, silently denying the accusation, then seemed to crumble under Harry's intense gaze. His face fell and his shoulders lowered in a defeated slump.

"How could I refuse an offer like that? Mutton was starving! And I damn-near froze last week, when it snowed. The gent said 'e'd pay me ten guineas, plus this 'ere coat, if I just went in there"—he pointed across the road at Bullock's place—"an' brought 'im back some dusty old book."

Chapter Nine

Ellie tried to hide her shock. Morris was their thief! But how on earth had Harry suspected that he was involved? She'd have bet money on the perpetrator of the crime having long-since fled the scene, not remained encamped less than fifty paces from the front door.

Despite having confessed, Morris seemed to have no intention of trying to escape. He slumped back against the doorframe with a weary, defeated sigh.

"I s'pose you're going to cart me off to Bow Street now, ain't you? I'll be up before the magistrate, and they'll hang me, for sure. Who'll look after old Mutton then, eh?"

"Oh, I don't think we need to complicate things by involving the authorities at this stage," Harry said easily.

Morris looked up, a faint glimmer of hope in his eyes. "Sir?"

"Can you tell me the name of the gentleman who gave you this coat?"

Morris shook his head. "I can't. We never used names. He approached me here, late on Thursday night, and asked if I ever went in the museum. I told 'im I went in there almost every day, to stay warm and get out of the rain. When he told me he wanted some fancy book, I almost said no. I felt bad, stealin' from an honest gent like Mr. Bullock, who's never been nothin' but kind to me, but I didn't 'ave no choice. Mutton 'ere was wastin' away."

"I understand," Harry said soothingly. "*Extremis malis, extrema remedia*, and all that."

Morris's brow furrowed in confusion. "What?"

"Desperate times call for desperate measures," Ellie translated, earning her an impressed, sideways smile from Harry that shouldn't have made her feel as warm as it did.

"Exactly," Morris said, relieved.

"Can you describe the man?" Harry asked. "Judging from that coat, he was fairly tall and broad."

"Never seen 'im 'round these parts before," Morris admitted. "He was English. Older gent, maybe sixty years, with black hair goin' gray at the temples. 'ad a fancy pair o' boots—like yours—and a stick like yours too. Only his 'ad a bird as the 'andle."

"Any particular type of bird?"

Morris shrugged apologetically. "Dunno. One with a beak. Crow? Raven? I didn't get a good look."

"Mind if I take a closer look at that coat?"

Morris obligingly shrugged out of it, revealing a rumpled bottle-green military jacket and pair of ragged trousers beneath.

"Are you hoping the previous owner left a calling card in one of the pockets?" Ellie asked as Harry inspected it.

"I am, but unfortunately there's nothing here to help us." He glanced up at Morris, but instead of giving him back the coat, he handed it over to Ellie. To her amazement, he started to remove his own handsome topcoat.

"I tell you what, Sergeant Morris. Let me take this coat, and I'll give you mine in exchange. We're of a similar size, and you'll do far better in a coat that fits you. This, might I add, is by far the superior garment. The finest cashmere twill, made from goats, not sheep, produced by Ternaux of Paris, and lined with a silk-wool blend." He held it out to Morris, who stroked the sleeve.

"Gawd," he murmured, his tone almost reverent. "That's softer than a whore's—" He snapped his mouth closed, belatedly realizing he was in the company of a lady, and a red flush crept up his neck. "Beggin' yer pardon, miss."

Ellie smiled serenely, having heard such terms, and worse, while investigating some of her previous cases. "Softer than a kitten's fur?" she suggested wryly.

"Aye."

Giving into temptation, she removed her own leather glove and touched the coat herself—something she'd wanted to do from the very first moment she'd seen Harry at her door. The fabric was as outrageously luxurious as it looked, and she marveled at the carelessness with which he surrendered such a treasure.

Perhaps, since his was ill-gotten wealth, it was easily gained, and easily lost, but if *she* owned such a beautiful thing, she'd have fought tooth and nail to keep it.

Morris threaded his arms into the sleeves and tugged it up over his shoulders, then gave a pleased nod at the better fit.

Harry gave him a jovial slap on the shoulder. "There. An almost perfect fit."

That wasn't entirely true—the ex-soldier was demonstrably slimmer than Harry, both at the shoulders and the waist, and since he was also shorter, the coat reached to his shins, instead of falling just below the knee. It was, however, far better than the mysterious criminal's coat, which Harry folded over his arm.

He reached into his waistcoat pocket and pulled out a guinea, which he pressed into the sergeant's hand.

"Thank you for your help, Sergeant Morris. Much appreciated. And if you make your way over to Feather Court, in Covent Garden, behind the Drury Lane Theatre, ask for Long Meg at the Traveler's Rest tavern. Tell her you're a friend of Ambrose Cox, and she'll give you a hot meal and a place to stay until you can get back on your feet."

Morris stared at him in disbelief. "What about Mutton?"

"He'll be welcome too. Meg loves dogs."

"Ambrose Cox." Morris nodded, half to himself, as if to remember the name. "I'll do that sir, thank you. Gawd bless you."

Harry waved off his gratitude. "No more stealing, agreed? It's a sorry end for a man, dancing the Tyburn jig."

"I swear to you, sir. Never again. You 'ave my word. Come on, Mutton. We're off to Feather Court. Good day miss, sir."

When Morris had loped off, Harry headed back toward the carriage and Ellie trailed in his wake, buffeted by conflicting emotions.

The scoundrel's observational skills were impressive, but she'd been equally touched by the kindness he'd exhibited. Instead of shaming the ex-soldier for his crime, he'd made him feel understood, and his no-nonsense compassion had left the man with his battered pride intact. He'd made accepting charity easy, instead of humiliating.

Ellie huffed to herself. It was one thing to disapprove of a selfish, unscrupulous scoundrel. It was much harder to dislike a man who showed consideration for others. If she wasn't careful, she might be in danger of *liking* the man.

Harry tossed the greatcoat inside the carriage, helped her up the step, then clambered in himself.

"Cork Street, please, Carson," he called up to the driver.

Chapter Ten

"Who's Long Meg?" Ellie asked, as soon as they set off. "A courtesan?"

Harry's dimples flashed. "No. She's an old friend."

"I'm not even going to ask how you became acquainted with her," she said primly, ignoring an inexplicable flash of jealousy that washed over her.

He sent her an amused, chiding glance. "Not that kind of 'friend.' If you must know, she was the best fence in London until a few years ago, with a shop on Petticoat Lane, but she gave it all up when she fell in love with a Bow Street runner. They run a boardinghouse for veterans now. She's completely reformed."

Ellie smiled in sudden recollection. "When Tess's first husband, the awful old duke, died, we said she should do something charitable with her new fortune. Daisy joked we should open a home for wounded veterans, reformed harlots, and stray dogs. It seems your Long Meg is catering to at least two of those groups."

"Oh, she caters to the soiled doves too, but in another boardinghouse around the corner."

How many of them were his "friends"? Ellie refused

to voice the question. His amorous escapades were none of her affair. Even if she *was* inordinately curious.

"That was a very kind thing for you to do for Sergeant Morris," she said instead.

He shrugged, but she was intrigued to see the faintest flush of pink sweep across his cheekbones. He was embarrassed!

She bit her lip and sternly told herself not to find that attractive.

"It was nothing. Morris was injured defending this country. It's shameful that the government isn't providing enough help for him now that the war's over and he's struggling to find honest work."

"Giving up your beautiful coat was a noble sacrifice to the case," she said solemnly.

Again, he waved off her thanks, as though uncomfortable with it. "It was a fine coat, but I was about to get rid of it anyway. I'd never have been able to look George Brummell in the eye if I'd worn it for a second season."

Ellie shook her head at his ridiculousness.

"So, we're off to Cork Street because you think the tailors who made that coat will be able to tell us who it was made for?"

"Schweitzer and Davidson," Harry said. "And yes, exactly. A man's coat is as individual as the wooden last made for his shoes. They also keep a record book of every coat they've made, with details of the type, and cloth, and cost. I've no doubt they'll be able to tell us the man we're looking for."

Ellie studied him curiously. "Was it true, what you told Sergeant Morris? Were you really a spy during the war?"

His dimples deepened. "That depends on your definition of spy. I certainly heard a number of interesting tidbits as I was traveling around the Continent. And it's fair to say that I passed on any information that might have been of interest to Lord Wellington. I was never officially employed by the government, though. More of a free agent."

"Did you ask for payment for your 'services'?"

He grinned at her obvious disapproval. "Of course not. I may be many things, but a traitor to my country isn't one of them. And while I very much enjoy French tailoring, cheese, and wine, I don't believe we'd all be better living under Bonaparte's thumb."

Ellie nodded, satisfied. "How did you know to question Morris?"

"To acquire knowledge, one must study; but to acquire *wisdom*, one must observe."

"That's very profound."

"Isn't it?" He leaned back in his seat, effortlessly elegant. "Morris stood out on that street in the same way a gold sovereign would stand out in a pile of copper pennies. He was awash with inconsistencies—which to an observer of human nature like myself was immediately intriguing."

"'Observer of human nature,'" Ellie scoffed. "You mean *crook*."

He didn't seem the least offended. "Of course. Every thief needs the ability to read his potential target. Why waste time breaking into the house of a man who has nothing to steal? Why take the purse of a woman whose jewels are obviously paste? I never steal from anyone who can't afford to buy it back. You'd be surprised at how many people only pretend to have money."

"A disappointment in your line of work, I'm sure," she said drily.

"*Previous* line of work," he reminded her. "Like Meg, I'm completely reformed."

She raised her brows. "What about Mr. Bullock's gold watch?"

"Ninety-nine percent reformed," he conceded. "And now all those ill-gotten skills are yours to command. Book learning can only get you so far, Eleanor. There's no substitute for practical experience. Reading about how to do a card trick and understanding how it works, for example, is not the same as becoming a master at it yourself. No book can let you know the exact weight of the cards in your hands, their thickness, how slippery they are, how easy to bend, how it feels when you toss one over another. Nor can it give you the elation when someone falls for your trick and you win their money."

"True. But book learning won't land me on a ship bound for transportation either."

Her tart answer made him chuckle, and her blood heated. He really was a charming scoundrel.

"Is Ambrose Cox another of your aliases, Monsieur le Comte?"

"Actually, it's one used by my mentor, the man who introduced me to a life of crime when I was a bright young lad of sixteen."

"Is that his real name?"

"Goodness, no. But he's a wonderful chap, the closest thing I have to family in this world. Who knows, perhaps one day you'll get to meet him."

"Is he here in London?"

"I haven't the foggiest idea. The last time I saw him was on the arm of a delightfully wealthy widow at the Venice Carnevale, but he's a man who likes to travel. He could be anywhere." He glanced out of the window as the carriage bounced to a stop. "Ah, Cork Street."

Ellie accepted his hand as he helped her down, ignoring the tingle in her fingers, and studied the wares in the window of Schweitzer and Davidson with interest. She'd never been inside a gentleman's tailors before.

The proprietors were suitably impressed when Harry introduced himself as the Comte de Carabas, complete with an ever-so-slight Italian accent inflecting his perfect English. In no time at all he'd got them to agree to helping his "friend" Miss Law, of King & Co.

No sooner had he handed over the overcoat he'd exchanged with Morris, than an assistant was sent to retrieve a large leather-bound ledger from the back room. Mr. Davidson himself came to assist them, and in less than ten minutes, they had their answer.

"The gentleman this coat was made for is John Patmore, Lord Willingham."

Ellie sent the tailor a warm smile. "How wonderful. I'm so glad we'll be able to return it to him."

"May I ask where he misplaced it?"

"Oh, my friend Tess, the Duchess of Wansford, held a ball a couple of weeks ago and this was left behind in the cloakroom," she lied blithely. "Since there were over three hundred guests, it wasn't practical to write to them all individually asking about a lost coat, so we waited to see if anyone asked after it. When nobody did, I promised to look into the matter for her."

Harry raised his brows in silent congratulation of her quick thinking, and she reminded herself sternly that she shouldn't be so pleased by his approval.

She turned to leave, but Harry, it seemed, was in no hurry to go.

"Would you mind waiting just a few moments longer, Ellie, my sweet?" he purred. "Mr. Davidson here has been so helpful that I feel the urgent need to purchase a new topcoat."

The tailor's face lit up at the prospect of a wealthy new client.

Ellie sent Harry an impatient glare behind Davidson's back, which he ignored completely.

"If I could just take Monsieur's measurements?" The tailor helped remove Harry's perfectly fitted jacket, and made a point of complimenting the cut of his waistcoat, which forced Ellie to notice the neat tuck of his waist and the impressive breadth of his shoulders.

She sank begrudgingly into a chair at the edge of the showroom and became an unwilling voyeur as the tailor took various measurements, including chest, neck, and arm length.

When Harry turned his back to her, his beautifully proportioned rear was at a level with her eyes, and try as she might, she couldn't stop herself from admiring the fit of his buckskin breeches as they hugged the strong curves of his thighs and buttocks with loving faithfulness.

She tried not to listen as the two men discussed cut and fabric choices, but when the probable cost of the garment was discreetly mentioned she sucked in a horrified breath. She'd never spent so much on a single item of clothing in her life!

Harry, she was sure, was well aware of her disapproval, and promptly ordered a new riding jacket, too, to be delivered the following week.

"And where shall your purchases be sent, sir?" Davidson asked.

Ellie pricked up her ears, desperate to know where "Henri Bonheur," charlatan extraordinaire, was pretending to live. Perhaps he'd cite the King & Co. offices as his abode?

"You may send them to Cobham House, Thirty-one Norfolk Street."

Ellie stored the information away for future investigation, and was pleased when Harry finally escorted her out of the shop. They walked a little way down the street in companionable silence, waiting for his carriage to return. The driver must have taken the horses for a short walk to prevent them becoming impatient.

"So, now we know Lord Willingham is behind the theft of the lucky prayer book," Ellie said. "That was excellent work."

"Do you know him?"

"I've never met him personally, but I've seen him at various social events. He's a friend of Lord and Lady Holland, who've been quite vocal in their support of Bonaparte over the years. A month or so ago the newspapers reported that they were preparing to send him an ice maker, of all things, to Saint Helena to make his incarceration more bearable."

Harry shook his head. "Some people just can't accept when they're beaten." He glanced down at her. "Out of interest, where do you get *your* clothes made?"

Ellie bristled immediately in suspicion that he was critiquing her attire. "By Miss Macdonald, of Wells Street. Why, is there something wrong with them?"

He tilted his head, the way he'd done when assessing Morris's coat. "The fit of that dress is acceptable and the style is certainly fashionable."

"I'm sure Miss Macdonald would agree."

"But cotton's such a boring material."

"It's practical," she said, through gritted teeth. "We can't all have coats made from goat beards."

"And that blue . . ." He shook his head sadly. "Too insipid. With your coloring, you should be wearing something more striking."

"In my line of work, it's better to blend in than stick out," she said testily.

"Yes. You do seem to enjoy the role of wallflower. That's what you were doing last night, at Lady Chessington's: hiding away in that alcove, content to watch the world dance by, instead of taking part yourself."

"Is this more of your 'doing something is better than watching it' philosophy? What happened to acquiring wisdom by observing? I *wanted* to dance, if you must know. But nobody asked me."

She sounded peevish, even to her own ears.

He shook his head with an amused smile. "It's perfectly understandable. Deception is an extremely common tactic in the animal world. Blending into one's surroundings, making yourself next to invisible, is extremely valuable. Believe me, you're talking to an expert. But there's also something to be said for allowing yourself to *live,* instead of merely survive." His dimples deepened. "I'll dance with you next time, Ellie."

Her heart gave an uncomfortable thump at the promise.

They stopped walking, and he gestured to the window of the shop next to them. It belonged to the seamstress Madame Lefèvre, who'd made dresses for Tess, and Daisy, too, but Ellie had never felt flush enough to order one for herself.

The small glass panes displayed three of the most beautiful dresses she'd ever seen, all far more daring and colorful than she'd ever worn. It was impossible not to

secretly imagine herself sweeping down a grand staircase to a round of appreciative murmurs.

She shook her head to dislodge the foolish daydream.

Harry pointed to the most gorgeous dress of the trio,
a shimmering emerald-green silk with a neckline that
looked scandalously low. "You would look ravishing in
that."

"It's far too revealing."

"Not at all. One only needs the confidence to wear it.
Every man who saw you would fall instantly at your feet."

Ellie snorted to hide her embarrassment. "I'd be the
one falling over, without my glasses on. And besides, it's
grand enough for a Royal ball. When would I ever get the
chance to wear it?"

He shook his head, disappointed yet again by her
practicality, and when his carriage appeared at the end
of the street, he hailed it with a whistle. It clattered to a
stop, and he let down the step and helped her in.

"Was the address you gave to the tailor your real address?" she asked, when they got settled.

"It was."

"Is there no Lord Cobham who wishes to use his family
town house?"

"There may well be, but he hasn't been seen for over
a decade."

"You mean he's a recluse?"

"No, I mean he's *lost*. Disappeared somewhere on the
Continent years ago. But since there's no definitive proof
that he's dead, his relatives have been renting the place
out in his absence. It's fully furnished and extremely
convenient."

Ellie sniffed. "You'd better hope he doesn't make a
sudden reappearance and throw you out."

Harry shook out the cuffs of his shirt. "Considering

how long he's been missing, I'd say that is a very remote possibility indeed."

"As soon as we get back to the office, I'll ask Tess and Daisy what they know of Lord Willingham."

"I'd be happy to go and investigate his town house, if you can find out his address."

"If by 'investigate' you mean 'break into and search illegally,' then no, thank you. We'll do this without breaking any laws."

He groaned. "But doing things by the book takes *so much time*. Don't you ever get impatient to see justice done?"

"Of course I do, but two wrongs don't make a right."

He groaned again, like a petulant child, and she suppressed a laugh.

"You clearly don't have the creative mindset needed to be a successful thief." He sighed. "You're far too encumbered with morals and principles."

She chuckled. "Yes, it's most inconvenient."

"I suppose it was inevitable, considering your family name is Law. You were bound to be tiresomely honest. Have you noticed how often you meet people whose name matches their job? Like a turnkey named Locke or an executioner named Hackett."

"You may be on to something. I once met a gravedigger called Mr. Bury."

"It happens all the time."

"Is that why you chose 'Henri Bonheur'?"

He nodded. "Better to be 'Happy Henry' than 'Simple Simon' or 'Boring Bartholomew.' Do you know the name Eleanor comes from ancient Greek? It means 'sun ray,' or 'shining light.'"

Ellie smiled. "I like to think I brighten people's days. Where does Harry come from?"

"It's short for Henry, of course. Which is a good, solid, kingly name. I believe it means 'ruler.'"

"Rather like Charles *King*, then."

He lifted his chin and adopted a regal pose. "I like it. It suits me."

She snorted back a laugh. "You have such an elevated opinion of yourself."

"On the contrary, I know my own worth. Which is something you, Ellie dearest, constantly fail to do."

His gaze rested on her face, and she suddenly felt very warm indeed. His propensity to go from teasing to saying something quite profound in a heartbeat was incredibly disarming.

"You shouldn't underestimate yourself, or your abilities," he said softly. "You are remarkable. Never forget it."

The interior of the coach had suddenly become strangely intimate. Heat tingled in her cheeks at his praise, but she was saved from having to answer as they pulled up in front of King & Co.

She pushed open the door as soon as the carriage rocked to a stop, and jumped down without bothering to wait for help.

Harry leaned forward in his seat. "I won't come in. I'll let you and your colleagues start to investigate Willingham. I'll be in touch soon." He blew her a kiss. "*Au revoir, ma belle.*"

Harry started to whistle under his breath as the carriage pulled away. All in all, that had been a very successful morning.

They'd made excellent progress on the case, and Ellie

had been a delightful companion. He'd relished the opportunity to see her at work.

He'd thoroughly enjoyed their verbal sparring, too, and the way she tried to hide her reactions from him was highly entertaining. She liked to think of herself as logical and unemotional, but he hadn't missed the way her cheeks flushed and her eyes had lingered on his body when he'd stripped for the tailor, nor how she bristled at his attempts to get under her skin.

The devil in him couldn't resist teasing her, just to get a reaction. He loved the way her eyes sparkled and her lips parted in exasperation. Unfortunately, that inevitably led to thoughts of how *else* he could make her eyes sparkle and her lips part—with desire.

Kissing her beneath that mistletoe might have been a mistake. Because now whenever he looked at her mouth, all he could think of was the softness of her skin and the tiny gasp she'd made when their lips had touched.

He wanted to hear it again.

Chapter Eleven

Tess and Daisy were impressed by their successful sleuthing.

"We need to find out as much as we can about Lord Willingham," Daisy said. "Is he still in London, for a start? And where does he live when he's here?"

Ellie went to the bookcase and pulled down a copy of Boyle's *Fashionable Court and Country Guide and Town Visiting Directory*.

Since her own desk was still taken up with Harry's ridiculous plant, she placed the book on Daisy's desk and turned the pages until she found the correct entry.

"Ah, here we are: Patmore, John, T. Honorable Lord Willingham. He lives at Twenty-two Gloucester Square."

"That's just to the north of Hyde Park," Tess said.

"If he stole the book because it's valuable, and plans to sell the gold and jewels, then he'll have to go to a jeweler or pawn shop to do it. We should put a watch on his house and follow him if he leaves," Daisy said.

"And we should look into his financial situation," Ellie added. "Perhaps he has gambling debts or a crippling mortgage that means he needs the money? I can ask my cousin Reg to see if he's heard any rumors at the gentlemen's clubs."

"And I'll ask my brothers if they know anything," Daisy said. "One of them might have been sober enough to have taken note."

Her tone indicated she didn't hold out much hope of that possibility, and since all three of her elder brothers were known to be scandalous reprobates, it was probably a well-founded belief.

"But if Harry's theory is right, and Willingham wants the book because it's supposed to be lucky, then he won't be looking to sell it at all," Tess said. "He'll want to keep it close by, either at one of his properties, or maybe even on his person. I doubt he'll hide it away in a bank vault or deposit box."

"What if he stole it for someone else, though?" Daisy mused. She perched on the edge of her desk, one leg swinging back and forth as she thought aloud. "Maybe it's intended as a gift to bring luck to the recipient." She glanced over at the plant on Ellie's desk. "Like that basil."

Ellie glared at the unwanted greenery. She picked it up, and moved it to a side table near the window. "Do either of you know the Willinghams socially?"

Tess shook her head. "Not really. They're more our parents' generation."

"I've seen them a few times around town, but never spoken to either of them," Daisy said. "My father knows them, though. I'm pretty sure they've attended some of his drunken gatherings at Hollyfield. Lord Willingham likes to hunt. And drink."

"We need an excuse to get into the house and look for it. Do you think they'll be holding a party soon?"

"It's possible, given the festive season. The difficulty will be getting an invitation."

"Harry would happily forge us some," Ellie said tartly. "Or steal some. He seems to think that small crimes are permissible if executed in pursuit of foiling a larger one."

"I agree with him," Daisy said. "Needs must, and all that."

"You would," Ellie groused. "You have a highwayman's soul."

Daisy grinned at what she perceived as a compliment. "Didn't that fortune-telling hermit we visited at Vauxhall Gardens say my ideal match would be with a highwayman?"

"I think the actual wording on your scroll was 'meet your true match on a dark highway,'" Tess reminded her. "But fortunes are notoriously open to interpretation."

"He accurately predicted that *you'd* be happy," Daisy countered. "He said you'd receive undying fidelity from your husband, and you only have to look at Justin to know that's true. The man's besotted with you."

Tess smiled, and a tinge of pink swept her cheeks. "Well, that was probably a lucky guess. But yes, he is. And I with him."

Ellie wrinkled her nose. "He said *I'd* marry a mysterious stranger."

Her pulse did an odd little skip as an image of Harry formed in her mind, but she dismissed it with an impatient shake of the head. He was *not* the stuff of happily-ever-afters.

Daisy hopped down from her desk. "I'll be off to try to find my brothers, then. Do you have any idea when we'll see Harry again?"

"He said he'd 'be in touch.'" Ellie shrugged. "But if we need to contact him, he's staying at Cobham House, on Norfolk Street."

Tess raised her brows. "That's just off Hanover

Square. Lovely part of town. Is he a guest? I've never heard of a Lord Cobham."

"That's because he disappeared some years ago, apparently. Nobody's quite sure if he's dead or alive, but in the meantime, Harry's renting the place from one of the man's relatives."

"Ah." Tess nodded, satisfied. "Very well. Let's meet back here at noon tomorrow to discuss what we've managed to find out. Justin and I are attending the Levensons' soirée tonight, but if the Willinghams are in attendance, I'll try to get an introduction."

"I'll call on my other cousin, Edward, the barrister, tomorrow morning. He might know if the Willinghams have ever been involved in any court cases." Ellie stood and rounded her desk. "See you both tomorrow."

Chapter Twelve

Ellie's cousin Edward suggested a walk in Hyde Park when she called on him the following morning, and she readily agreed. The weather was cold and crisp, but the sky was blue—typical of December—and she laughed at the way her breath made dragon puffs of "smoke" when she exhaled.

Unfortunately, Edward had no useful information to tell her about Lord Willingham, other than the fact that they were both members of the same gentlemen's club, and that Willingham and his wife, Cassandra, were known to have been vocal supporters of Bonaparte before his defeat.

They were just walking beside the northern section of the carriage drive, discussing William Garrow's sponsoring of a parliamentary bill to prevent animal cruelty by proposing increased penalties for riding horses until their severe injury or death, when a familiar figure appeared from a side-path.

Ellie's stomach did a foolish little somersault, even as she let out a sigh of resignation as Harry sauntered toward them, the silver top of his sword cane glinting in the sun.

She reluctantly made the introductions.

"Edward, have you met Henri Bonheur? He's recently arrived in London after some years on the Continent. Monsieur Bonheur, this is my cousin, Edward Hussey."

The two men shook hands, and Edward sent her an intrigued glance. The two of them had practically grown up together—his mother being her aunt—and they'd always been more like siblings.

"And how are you two acquainted?" Edward asked Harry. "Ellie's never mentioned you before."

Harry sent her a smile. "Oh, we met on a professional basis. I recently found myself in need of King and Company's services. Your cousin has been a wonderful source of assistance."

Edward was too polite to inquire further into what he surmised were unfortunate circumstances, but Ellie was sure his sharp gaze was assessing Harry's expensive clothing and drawing his own—incorrect—conclusions; namely, that a man as wealthy as Harry had probably been the victim of a crime, instead of the likely perpetrator.

Appearances could truly be deceptive.

She was reluctantly admiring Harry's dove-gray coat and wondering how many of the things the blasted man owned, when an incongruous detail caught her eye. A lone leaf dangled from the shoulder of his otherwise immaculate sleeve, and she reached out and brushed it off without conscious thought.

Harry looked down at her in obvious surprise, and she felt her cheeks heat at the impulsive, intimate gesture.

"You had a leaf," she said quickly. "It must have fallen from a tree."

All three of them glanced up at the leafless branches above them, and Harry let out an amused laugh.

"It would appear not. It's far more likely I picked it

up when I was rolling around on the ground with Lord Willingham a few moments ago."

Ellie gaped at him, and his dimples deepened in delight at her obvious shock.

"What do you mean?" Edward demanded with an astonished laugh.

"I'm afraid I made the poor man's acquaintance in the most unfortunate manner. It was my fault. I bumped into him, quite literally, just over there by the duck pond."

Harry gave a vague wave in the general direction of the Serpentine, and sent Edward a self-deprecating shrug. "I was so busy thinking that I really *must* commission a waistcoat the exact green of the feathers on a mallard's head, that I failed to look where I was going, and barreled into poor Willingham. We both took a tumble."

Ellie sent him a narrow-eyed look of suspicion, which he returned with an innocent smile that fooled her not one bit. He'd clearly engineered the encounter with Willingham to effect an introduction.

Or worse.

"I thought I'd managed to restore my usual sartorial elegance, but apparently not." He made a great show of smoothing his cravat and checking the tails of his coat for additional debris.

Ellie shook her head. "Edward, I hope you don't mind, but I have some news for Mr. Bonheur about his case. Mr. Bonheur, if your carriage isn't far, you may give me a lift back to Lincoln's Inn Fields."

Edward nodded in easy agreement, while Harry said, "I'd be delighted."

Ellie took his arm and the two of them started along the path, but as soon as Edward was out of earshot she turned to Harry with a glare.

"All right, out with it. What did you do to Willingham? Steal his wallet? Pilfer his house keys?"

His chuckle was hardly reassuring. "Nothing of the sort. I merely took the chance to see if he had our missing book concealed on his person. He did not, by the way."

"That was a very risky thing to do," she scolded.

"Not if you're as skilled as I am. Willingham didn't suspect a thing. He accepted my profuse apologies, of course, and I'm pleased to say that in the ensuing conversation we discovered a shared interest in vingt-et-un."

"Of course you did." Ellie rolled her eyes.

"Not only that, but he kindly extended an invitation to a festive little gathering he's hosting tomorrow evening. Deep play guaranteed."

Ellie let out a frustrated growl. "I don't know whether to scold you for interfering, or commend you for getting the invitation. How on earth did you know that Willingham would be here in the park at this hour? Was it just a lucky guess?"

Her hand was still nestled in the crook of his arm, and he patted the back of it with teasing condescension.

"Of course not. You know how I feel about luck; it's far better when it's helped along. I spent last evening enjoying a few pints with His Lordship's stablemaster and footman, Albert and George."

"As Henri Bonheur?"

He shook his head and affected an entirely different accent, one that made him sound as if he'd lived his entire life without ever leaving the bounds of London.

"Gawd no, love. As plain 'Arry Smith, rat-catcher and knife-grinder from Covent Garden."

"In far less expensive clothes, I assume," she sniffed.

"Too right," he said, still with his accent. "The scratchiest shirt and worst-fitting jacket you ever saw in yer life. We won't even mention the boots. Still, old 'Arry bought a round or two of drinks and it didn't take long to learn that old Willingham takes a morning constitutional at ten o'clock every Thursday to avoid his wife's sisters when they visit."

"Good sleuthing," Ellie said begrudgingly. "As long as you made yourself unrecognizable."

"Oh, me own mother wouldn't 'ave known me," he chuckled. "I didn't shave, and I even added a gold tooth"—he tapped one of his straight white incisors with his finger—"right 'ere."

"You must have looked like a pirate," she scoffed, even as the unbidden and annoyingly alluring image of him as a roguish buccaneer swam in her brain. The cold was clearly affecting her ability to think rationally.

She tried to tug her hand from his arm, but he tightened his grip, and she resigned herself to the not-unpleasant warming effect his proximity had on her body.

It was a relief to see the crested panels of his carriage waiting just beyond the park railings.

"Willingham said I was welcome to bring a female guest," Harry said, reverting to his usual voice as he handed her into the conveyance.

"I can't attend as myself," Ellie said. "Not with you. Perhaps Daisy and I can dress as servants and—"

He shook his head, and his eyes crinkled at the corners. "Oh, I didn't introduce myself to Willingham as Henri Bonheur. I told him my name was Enrico Castellini."

"You pretended you were Italian?" Ellie said, aghast. "For Heaven's sake! Why?"

"Why not?" he chuckled. "Variety is the spice of life. And I haven't been the Visconti di Modrone for a long time."

"You're mad."

"Maybe. But there's method in my madness. Enrico Castellini is a slightly eccentric, clearly rich and bored nobleman on his first visit to London. Willingham's arrogant enough to think him a plump pigeon ready to be plucked; hence the invitation to play cards for 'proper stakes.'"

"Well, I still can't go with 'Enrico' either. Not unless Tess comes with us as a chaperone."

"Eleanor Law isn't invited," he said, and Ellie tried to hide the sudden wretched swoop of disappointment that pitched her stomach.

"I told him I'd bring my paramour."

She forced a polite smile. "Oh. And who is that?"

Harry was so handsome that she shouldn't be surprised that he had a lover. Would it be one of the beautiful actresses or opera singers who trod the boards at Drury Lane? Or some lucky society widow or wife?

"Her name's Carlotta. She's also Italian, from Venice, and she barely speaks a word of English."

A wicked flash of envy stabbed her heart. "Oh."

"I've already arranged a dress for you."

Ellie frowned. "What?"

His raised his brows. "To wear when you're Carlotta. I can't imagine you've anything remotely suitable in your own wardrobe. Carlotta wouldn't be seen dead in cotton. She barely deigns to wear silk."

For a moment Ellie was too stunned to utter a word. "You've bought me a dress suitable for an *Italian courtesan*?" she said finally. "How? From where? It can't possibly be the right size."

"Of course it can. I told Madame Lefèvre to get your measurements from Miss Macdonald. You're going to look delicious."

"I can't possibly—"

"You can," he said firmly. "It's a necessary prop for the role you need to play. Unless you trust me enough to go and search Willingham's house alone . . ."

Ellie sent him a narrow-eyed glare. He knew exactly how to hook her. There was absolutely no chance she'd allow him free rein without her there to supervise. Heaven knew what mischief he'd get into.

"A provocative dress isn't going to be enough of a disguise if I see someone I know."

"Which is why you'll also make use of the wig I'm having sent over. You said you've disguised yourself for past investigations. This is no different."

"As a maid," she said hotly. "Or a washerwoman. As people who blend in. *Not* as someone who makes a spectacle of themselves."

"I have every faith in you," he said bracingly. "I'm sure your friends can help you with makeup and such forth." His eyes twinkled as he sensed her silent, if unwilling, capitulation. "I'll have it delivered to King and Company tomorrow. Be ready for ten tomorrow night. I'll come to collect you."

Chapter Thirteen

"I can't wear it!"

Ellie gazed down at the emerald-green dress that had been delivered to King & Co. in dismay. It was, almost inevitably, the outrageously beautiful silk gown that she'd seen in the window on Cork Street.

She refused to think of how much Harry had paid to get it adjusted to her particular measurements in such a short space of time. Nor how much it had cost to buy in the first place.

"It's magnificent," Tess countered, stroking her fingers over the near-invisible stitching on the bodice. "Madame Lefèvre is a genius."

"Go on, put it on," Daisy prodded.

With a helpless sigh, Ellie lifted the garment from its tissue-paper-lined box and stepped into the back office to change.

Ever impatient, Daisy rapped her knuckles on the door after only a few minutes. "Come on, stop hiding in there. Let us see."

"It's dreadful," Ellie moaned. "Even worse than I feared."

"Doesn't it fit?" Tess asked through the door. "That's a surprise. Madame's usually so—"

"It fits *perfectly*," Ellie wailed.

"And that's a disaster, how?" Daisy asked, confused.

"Because it's a scandalous, low-cut, harlot's dress and I was completely prepared to hate it, and . . . it's the most beautiful thing I've ever worn."

"You like the silk, then?" Tess said drily.

"I never want to wear any other fabric for as long as I live. It's ruined me for cotton forever. It's a *disaster*. I can't afford to like it."

Daisy's snort of amusement echoed through the wood. "Come out, you goose."

Ellie opened the door and even without her glasses on, she was close enough to see the stunned delight on her friends' faces.

"Eleanor Law, you look incredible!" Tess breathed. "Why have you never bought a dress that color before? It's perfect for your eyes and your hair."

"And when did you get breasts so big?" Daisy gaped.

Ellie clapped her hands self-consciously over her bosom. The daringly low cut of the neckline made her feel as though the entire top half of her chest was exposed.

"It's not me!" she breathed. "It's this dress. There's some kind of magical corsetry sewn into the bodice that pushes them up and together. They've never looked this impressive before, I swear."

Tess laughed. "All your other dresses have been far more conservative."

"Modest," Ellie groaned. "Appropriate."

"Unremarkable," Daisy said decisively. "That this is by far the most flattering thing you've ever worn. Even if it is a little risqué."

"I look like an opera singer."

"Perhaps that's 'Carlotta's' profession?"

Ellie snorted. "If I take one deep breath to sing an aria, my breasts will pop out of this bodice."

Daisy giggled gleefully. "Come on, sit down and we'll help you with your hair."

True to his word, Harry had sent a wig to add to her disguise. In keeping with the rather flamboyant style of the courtesans who graced the demimonde, it was a striking red shade, the color of garnet, with curls arranged in an artful froth on the top and spilling down over one shoulder.

Ellie sat stoically as Tess pinned her brown locks flat to her head, secured the wig, and added some tasteful embellishments. Madame had sent three silk flowers, made from the same green fabric as the dress, for just such a purpose.

"I've borrowed some beauty products from my friend Mary, who works in the Drury Lane Theatre," Daisy said.

A pink fluid from a bottle labeled "Liquid Bloom of Roses" was used to give a heavier-than-usual blush to Ellie's cheeks, and the addition of some vermilion paste to her regular almond-oil lip salve painted her lips a deep red.

"Close your eyes. I need to line your lashes," Daisy commanded.

Ellie squinted at the small pot and paintbrush Daisy brandished in her hand. "What *is* that?"

"A mix of lamp black and a little oil. Don't worry, it'll wash off. Probably."

Tess took care to protect the outrageous dress with a cloak while Daisy added a final dusting of powder to Ellie's shoulders and face with a shimmery mixture that made her skin glimmer with the luster of a pearl.

When they were finally done, Ellie looked at herself in the mirror and barely recognized the bold, brazen woman who stared back at her. Her eyes glittered with excitement, her cheeks were flushed as if she'd recently risen from bed, and her body was an extraordinary combination of womanly curves.

She didn't look like herself. She didn't *feel* like herself, either, and a thrilling pulse of anticipation warmed her blood.

Perhaps she did have it in her to be a little bit wicked after all.

"*Bellissima!*" Daisy kissed the tips of her fingers, like a chef. "Time for me to get ready."

"I'm glad you're going too," Ellie said as Daisy lifted her own outfit from the chair and slipped into the back room.

Few households employed enough permanent staff to cater for large parties, and most people hired additional servants from a reputable agency whenever the need arose. Thanks to the busy time of year, and an old school contact, Daisy had managed to secure a place as a temporary maid for the Willinghams' event.

Tess hadn't received an official invitation, and since she was the most recognizable of the three of them, she was reluctantly remaining at home.

In contrast to Ellie's exuberance, Daisy transformed herself into an unremarkable maid, complete with white apron and demure mob cap covering her hair. The same cosmetics added an ashen pallor to her smooth, blemish-free skin, and created dark circles under her eyes. Nobody seeing her would guess she was the healthy daughter of a duke. She looked tired and over-worked.

"I look perfectly hideous!" Daisy cackled in glee when she saw her reflection. "Even the most lecherous drunk-ard wouldn't give me a second look. But for the final touch . . . Ellie, do you have a spare pair of spectacles?"

Ellie obligingly found a pair in her desk, but when Daisy put them on, she uttered a squawk of horror.

"Dear God! Is this what the world's like when you *don't* wear glasses? Everything's all blurry."

"It is," Ellie confirmed.

"It's like that time we pilfered a bottle of Father's ap-ple brandy and got foxed down by the river at Hollyfield. Everything's swimming."

Ellie reclaimed her glasses. "I remember it well. It was a horrid sensation. I thought my brain was going to fall out of my skull. Never again."

"Forget the spectacles," Daisy said. "I need to see what I'm doing."

A knock at the front door made Ellie's stomach som-ersault, and she braced herself to see Harry, but it was a deliveryman instead.

"Is there a Carlotta Pellegrini at this address?"

Tess grinned and pointed toward Ellie. "That's her. The famous Italian contralto herself."

Ellie rolled her eyes, but accepted the package the man held forward. She gave him a gracious nod, careful not to dislodge her wig.

"*Grazie*," she murmured—the only Italian word she knew.

When the man departed, the three of them gathered around as Ellie untied the string and peeled open the un-assuming brown paper wrapping.

Tess let out a low whistle when she saw the flat, red-leather box within.

"That's from Rundell, Bridge and Rundell. Justin's always buying me things from there. Even when I tell him he shouldn't."

"Oh, the misfortune of having a rich, besotted husband," Daisy teased. "Would that we were all so afflicted!"

Tess stuck her tongue out at her.

Ellie flipped the metal catch and lifted the lid, and all three of them stilled. Inside lay the most dazzling necklace, earrings, and bracelet she'd ever seen.

"Are those emeralds? And diamonds?"

"It would seem so," Tess breathed.

Daisy gave a little hum of approval. "Scoundrel or not, your Monsieur Bonheur has impeccable taste."

"He's not mine," Ellie murmured. "And these had better not be stolen."

With shaking hands, she donned the jewels. The smooth cabochon emeralds matched the green of her dress perfectly, while the faceted diamonds sent rainbow flecks of light onto her skin.

"You look like a princess," Daisy said.

"Or a very expensive whore," Ellie said.

"You're going to be the envy of every woman who sees you tonight." Tess's eyes shone with pride.

"And the object of desire for every man," Daisy added with a grin. "Wallflower you are definitely *not*."

Ellie groaned, but the door knocker interrupted her protest.

"Courage!" Tess said bracingly. "You'll find that book if it's hidden at Willingham's, I know it. Now, go and have some fun!"

Carson, Harry's coachman, stood on the step, and

Ellie quashed another stab of disappointment. Did Harry mean to meet her at Willingham's?

She drew her evening cloak around her shoulders, covering her dress completely, and was about to climb up into the carriage when a gloved hand emerged from the dark interior, and she glanced up into Harry's handsome face.

He took her fingers, and the firm touch made her pulse rate double as she climbed in and sat opposite him.

"Are you wearing the dress I sent you, beneath that cloak?" There was a hint of suspicion in his tone, as if he expected her to have chosen something less revealing.

"I am."

He gave a satisfied nod, and she took her time studying his own outfit. His coat was in the Italian style: a pale blue silk with floral embroidery at the sleeves, cut to perfection to emphasize his broad shoulders. His white shirt held a profusion of ruffles, its lace-edged cuffs peeking out from his sleeves, and a frothy cravat was secured with an aquamarine pin impressive enough to have been "borrowed" from the crown jewels.

"You look like a dandy," she said.

On any other man, the ensemble would have looked ridiculous, almost feminine, but on *him* the flamboyant clothes only served to accentuate his intense masculinity.

The paradoxical contrast of hard muscle and soft silk, the impeccable contours of his thighs beneath his pale buckskin breeches, produced a swooping, quivery sensation in her stomach.

Ellie glanced down, fully expecting him to have jeweled heels on his shoes, like a gentleman of the last century, but his black court shoes were unadorned save for a pair of silver buckles.

His lips curved in a self-mocking smile. "*Buonasera, mia bella.*"

The sound of his sinfully deep voice made her toes curl.

"I'm afraid I don't speak Italian. Only a little French."

"I said 'good evening,'" he translated. His eyes studied her face and ridiculous hair. "It's a shame you dislike the name Nell. You put me in mind of Nell Gwynn."

"King Charles the Second's mistress? The orange seller?"

He nodded, pleased by her knowledge of history. "An infamous courtesan. But she was also a fine actress, praised by Samuel Pepys for her performances on the stage. Pretty, witty Nell."

"I'm going to need all my acting ability to be Carlotta the Courtesan," Ellie huffed. "I'm not as well-versed in deception as you are."

"You'll be perfect."

She had no time to worry about it, since they arrived at the Willinghams' town house in short order and she pushed aside her nerves as Harry escorted her up the steps.

A liveried footman took her cloak and she glanced at Harry as her outfit was finally revealed, keen to see his reaction.

For the briefest of moments, he seemed at a loss for words. His eyes roved her from head to toe in a hot sweep that made her entire body flush, and his lips parted on what she hoped was shocked inhale.

Just *once* in her life, she wanted to rob a man of breath.

"I am very much regretting my promise to give up crime," he muttered softly.

She frowned. "How so?"

Those wicked dimples appeared. "Because I want to steal you away from here and keep you all to myself."

Ellie blushed, and took his offered arm, and together they ascended the stairs.

Chapter Fourteen

Ellie pressed close to Harry as they entered the crowded ballroom, her stomach churning with dread that she'd see someone she knew, and be recognized. The room was a blur without her spectacles, so she wouldn't even see if potential disaster was coming her way until it was too late.

"Smile," Harry whispered, leaning close to her ear. "You're a goddess with the power to render men speechless with desire, remember?"

Ellie forced a smile, wishing it was true.

"It seems the Willinghams have some interesting acquaintances," he commented, raking the crowd with his gaze.

"They're not regarded as the best *ton*," Ellie murmured. "Willingham's a bit of a boor, and their support of Bonaparte didn't help their popularity, so now you could say they linger at the edges of fashionable society."

Harry nodded. "Shall we dance?"

He guided her onto the dance floor and swept her effortlessly into a waltz, and Ellie threw caution to the wind. Professional pride demanded that she play her part well, so tonight she would be Carlotta, a woman so confident of her own appeal that she had men eating out of the palm of her hand.

She lifted her chin, straightened her spine, and sent Harry a glittering smile.

His fingers tightened on hers. "Perfect," he murmured.

The room blurred even more as they swirled around in perfect unison.

"Please tell me these jewels I'm wearing aren't stolen," she said breathlessly.

He clucked his tongue in a chiding sound. "Of course not. We're just borrowing them for the night."

"With the owner's permission?" she pressed, suspicious of his ability to skirt the truth.

"Of course. They belong to a friend. He's not yet married, so he's glad they're getting some use, instead of sitting in a dusty bank vault."

Her skin grew warm as his hot gaze traveled over her throat and chest. "You're certainly doing them justice tonight. I'll have to be careful someone doesn't steal you away. 'Beauty provoketh thieves sooner than gold.'"

Ellie tried to place the quote. "Shakespeare?"

He nodded. "*As You Like It.*"

A bubble of happiness swelled in her chest. The waltz was her favorite, but she'd rarely danced it in public, and the music made her feel reckless and wild and free.

Perhaps Harry was right about needing to *live*, instead of just existing.

She didn't for a moment believe his flattery was serious—he probably complimented his horse and his valet with equal fluency—but still, it was nice to feel attractive for once.

His warm palm pressing the lower curve of her back felt ridiculously intimate, while the muscles of his shoulder flexing beneath her hand made her stomach somersault. His chest was mere inches from her own, but she leaned closer still, to bring him into focus, inhaling the delicious scent that always clung to him.

She stared into his eyes, studying him intently, and his dimples reappeared.

"Are you pretending to be a love-besotted fool? Or is it just because you can't see without your glasses?"

"Your eyes," Ellie said, ignoring his teasing, "have been vexing me for some time."

"How exciting. Haunting your dreams, I hope?"

She gave an unladylike snort. "I couldn't tell if they were blue or green or even hazel, and now I see why. They're two different colors. It's extraordinary."

His teeth flashed in a smile. "Ah, yes. A curiosity, is it not? There's a fancy Latin name for it, but I forget what it is."

He stared back at her, allowing her to look her fill, and she tried to ignore the sensation that she was falling into his gaze. Or under his spell.

"If you look closely," he said softly, "you'll see that both eyes are blue, with gold and brown flecks. But my left eye has so many flecks it appears hazel—more brown or green."

He blinked, and she noticed with a stab of envy how long his eyelashes were.

"I can't tell you how useful it's been in my previous career," he smiled. "Whenever people tried to describe me to the authorities, they could never agree on what color they were. It made them far less credible as witnesses. And made me far less susceptible to prosecution."

"A very convenient quirk of nature."

He shrugged. "In some cultures, having mismatched

eyes is thought to be a sign of witchcraft. Some think it means I have the ability to see both heaven and earth."

"Have you found that to be the case?"

"Sadly not. My talents for trickery have all been gained through tedious practice and dull repetition. Nothing as exciting as making a pact with the devil, I'm afraid."

His eyes still held hers, and the butterflies in her stomach increased at the intensity of his regard. It would not be difficult to imagine him a sorcerer, with the ability to read her mind, or steal her heart.

"*Your* eyes are the color of caramel," he said. "Or toffee. I can't decide. Something sweet, at least. *Hai un bell'aspetto da mangiare.*"

Ellie frowned. "What does that mean?"

"You look good enough to eat."

Heat scalded her cheeks as her unhelpful brain provided a scorching image of him teething her neck, pressing little nibbling kisses to her shoulder and collarbone.

"Scoundrel!" she muttered, pinching his arm.

He chuckled.

"Out of interest, how many languages do you actually speak?"

"Fluently? Only a handful. English, obviously. Plus French, Spanish, Italian. I have a smattering of Russian and Portuguese. And I can swear impressively in at least a couple more." His lips quirked. "Perhaps I should teach you a few useful Italian phrases. Just in case someone tries to talk to you tonight. Repeat after me: *Harry è l'uomo più bello in questa stanza.*"

"What's that?" she asked suspiciously.

"Harry is the most handsome man in this room."

She rolled her eyes.

"Here's another: *Vorrei che Harry mi baciasse.*"

"Meaning?"

"I wish Harry would kiss me."

Ellie laughed at his cheeky presumption. "You are ridiculous."

Those dimples appeared. "I live in hope. Perhaps, when we get that book, my fortunes will change and you'll throw yourself into my arms."

Ellie snorted. "Perhaps pigs will fly. It'll take more than a lucky book to win my kisses, signore."

The music came to an end with a final flourish of violins, and she pulled out of his embrace. They were here to work, not to flirt, and she'd been too easily distracted.

Harry tilted his chin toward a tall, broad man standing at the entrance to the cardroom. "That's Willingham. Let's go and say hello."

Chapter Fifteen

Ellie pulled back in alarm. She would have avoided their host entirely, but Harry clearly had other ideas.

"Come on, Carlotta, stop stalling. You know what they say: procrastination is the thief of time. Take a deep breath."

"I don't think I *can* in this dress," she grumbled.

The subtle pressure of his arm was inescapable, so she imagined herself a sultry Italian temptress.

"Willingham!" Harry made an elaborate bow in front of the Englishman, then straightened. "Your 'little party' is magnifico! I was expecting twenty people. Instead, you 'ave two 'undred."

The older man smiled, clearly flattered. His rather protruding eyes swiveled to Ellie—or rather, to her cleavage; he barely spared her face a glance. "Glad you could come, sir. Who's your charming companion?"

Harry tugged her closer to his side in a clear display of possession. "May I present Carlotta Pellegrini. In Italy she is famous contralto." He turned adoring eyes on her. "To 'ear her sing is to 'ear the sound of the angels."

Ellie smothered her instinctive laugh. To hear her sing

was more akin to listening to dogs howling, but she managed to look suitably self-important and disdainful, as befitted a goddess of the stage.

She took a deep breath so her breasts swelled above the neckline of her bodice, and watched in satisfaction as Willingham's gaze followed the movement. She was beginning to see what Tess meant when she said that most men were easily manipulated by showing a bit of skin.

Willingham kissed her hand for a second longer than was polite. "Enchanted, madame."

Ellie tugged her fingers back, and sent him a scornful look.

Willingham was undeterred. "Perhaps the lovely Carlotta will treat us to an impromptu performance this evening?"

Ellie pretended not to understand, but trod on Harry's foot beneath the concealing folds of her skirts.

"Carlotta speaks no English," Harry said easily. "But I can answer for her. Alas, she must save her voice for a special, private performance for the prince regent tomorrow evening."

Willingham's face fell. "Ah well, another time perhaps." He waved a hand to indicate the baize-topped tables in the room behind him. "There are few good games of vingt-et-un and hazard on the go. Perhaps we can play a hand or two a little later?"

His eagerness to fleece Harry was painfully obvious, but Harry sent him a wide, guileless smile. "Of course. But first I 'ave promised to dance with *amore mio*."

He bent and pressed a casual kiss to Ellie's neck, just below her ear, and it took all the acting ability she had not to gasp in shock.

Luckily, Willingham was paying more attention to her jewels than her face.

"Of course," he murmured, his eyes lingering on her emeralds with an avaricious gleam. "One should never disappoint a lady."

His emphasis on the final word indicated he thought the term "lady" was generous, for an opera singer who was clearly also Harry's paramour, but Harry ignored the unsubtle snub and patted the older man on the shoulder.

"Until later, then."

He ushered them away through the crowd, and Ellie let out a relieved sigh when they left the main ballroom and found a relatively secluded corner in one of the smaller salons.

Her neck still tingled from the touch of Harry's lips, but she forced herself to concentrate on the business at hand. He'd only done it to make their performance more believable. It had been an act, nothing more.

"Daisy's going to look for the book downstairs," she said. "Which means it's up to us to search upstairs. Do you think we can sneak up there without being seen?"

Harry looked down at her, and her heart did an odd little flip. He really was stupidly handsome.

"Oh, I'm sure we can."

He reached up and straightened a stray curl that had escaped from her coiffure, and the brush of his knuckles on the side of her cheek made her knees a little weak. Everything inside her seemed tight, on edge.

Did he know the effect he had on her? Was he doing it on purpose? And if so, to what end? Did he just like the added frisson of danger that flirting on the job provided?

"Just to be clear, if we find the book, we're going to steal it, yes?" he whispered.

"*Reclaim* it on behalf of the rightful owner," she corrected.

His eyes twinkled at the prospect of a spirited discussion. "Aha! So, we're allowed to steal something that's already been stolen, as long as we're planning on returning it to the right person?"

Ellie narrowed her eyes at him, certain she was walking into a verbal trap. "In this particular instance, yes."

"Which would make it a case of two wrongs actually *making* a right."

She sighed at his inversion of her previous logic. The man had a brain as sharp as a defense lawyer's. William Garrow would have hired him on the spot.

"I'm willing to bend the rules just a little in this instance," she conceded.

His delighted laugh warmed her insides. "Ha! You're about to do a bad thing, for a good reason. You're practically Robin Hood. You're halfway to scoundreldom already."

She wrinkled her nose at him. "Scoundreldom isn't a word. And I wouldn't celebrate just yet. This isn't the start of a glittering criminal career; we're simply giving justice a helping hand."

"If that's how you want to think of it." His shrug and raised brows indicated his skeptical amusement.

He took her arm and ambled toward the nearest doorway, which led into an even quieter corridor. A few couples lingered about, clearly taking the opportunity for a little privacy, and Ellie averted her eyes as they passed a couple kissing in a curtained alcove.

Harry took her hand, threading his fingers through hers, and when she glanced down in surprise he whispered, "We need to look like an amorous couple trying to find somewhere for a tryst."

She nodded. "I think we should search the bedrooms.

Willingham won't have hidden the book anywhere guests might venture, like the library, or the drawing room."

"Agreed. He and his wife keep separate apartments, on the floor above."

"How on earth do you know that?"

"Rule number six: *Always talk to the servants.*"

"You have rules?"

"For thieving? Of course."

"What are the others? How many are there? Do all thieves have them, or just you?"

He tapped her fondly on the nose. "So many questions, Miss Law, but now is not the time. I'll tell you another day."

The sound of music grew fainter as they ventured farther along the hall. A footman carrying a tray laden with wineglasses rounded the corner, and they ducked into a room containing a billiard table to avoid being seen.

They reached a second stairway without encountering anyone else, and Ellie lifted her skirts as they ascended the stairs, careful not to trip on the beautiful green silk.

The upper hallway was clear, but her heart pounded with the threat of being discovered. Harry opened the second door on the left and slipped inside, drawing her behind him, and she breathed a sigh of relief when the door closed behind them with a satisfying click.

The room was dark, and empty; the doorway to an adjoining room was faintly visible in the pale gray moonlight.

As her eyes became accustomed to the gloom, she could see the walls were lined with shelves of leather-bound books. A few gilt-framed paintings hung in the gaps, and a heavy wooden desk was positioned at an angle to the door.

"This is Willingham's private study," Harry whispered. He released her hand, and she mourned the loss of warm contact. "His bedroom's through there."

"I'll—" Ellie froze as a soft, yet very distinct *thud* sounded from the adjacent room.

She shot wide, panicked eyes at Harry. Someone was in there!

Harry clearly thought the same. But instead of retreating, to her horror he slipped silently through the doorway and disappeared into the gloom.

A succession of more muffled thuds followed, then a faint crash, as if a wordless altercation were taking place. Ellie glanced around the study, desperately looking for something to use as a weapon, and snatched up the brass fire poker that stood to the side of the fireplace. She rushed through the doorway to see Harry and a dark-clad figure wrestling in the moonlight.

Harry's arms were wrapped around the stranger's head, but the other, stockier man had him around the waist. As she watched, the man issued a grunt, swept his leg around the back of Harry's knee, and the two of them toppled sideways onto the mattress of the four-poster bed that stood in the center of the room.

Harry let out a low growl of frustration. His assailant twisted his ear in a painful-looking move, but Harry retaliated by tugging the man's hair, then elbowing him in the stomach.

Ellie didn't dare try to help. The two of them were rolling around so much, they were just a blur of limbs; she was just as likely to accidentally strike Harry as she was to hit his opponent.

"Oof! Get off, Harry, you great popinjay!"

Ellie stilled at the unexpected sound of the stranger's

deep voice, as did Harry. The fight on the bed came to an abrupt end.

"Hugo?"

Harry released the man and sat back, astonishment evident in his tone.

The stranger pushed himself off the bed and stood, panting with exertion, then, to Ellie's amazement, he started to laugh.

"Damn me, I must be getting old if the likes of you can ambush me! You've still got a cracking right hook, my lad."

Chapter Sixteen

Ellie glanced from one man to the other in confusion.

"Harry, do you *know* this man?"

The stranger was shorter and broader than Harry, with curly brown hair lightly dusted with gray, upswept eyebrows, and a rounded face that made him look like a slightly naughty cherub.

Harry's face broke into a grin. "I do indeed." He slid off the bed and enfolded the man in a crushing, jubilant hug. "I didn't think you were coming back to England, you old rogue."

The older man shrugged. "You clearly haven't been reading the obituaries. Peregrine Barclay is dead!"

Harry seemed to understand the relevance of this strange information. "*Finally*. That's excellent news. What did he die of?"

"Ill temper and gout, I expect."

Ellie frowned. Belatedly realizing she was still brandishing the poker like a rapier, she lowered it to her side. "Could someone explain what's happening here, please?"

Harry sent her a laughing glance. "Of course, I'm

sorry. Ellie, may I present the one and only Hugo Ambrose, sometimes known as Ambrose Cox."

Ellie's brows rose as she recognized the name Harry had given to Sergeant Morris. "Your mentor?"

"The very same," the older man said. "Although several inept law enforcement agencies simply refer to me as The Harlequin."

He straightened his rumpled dark jacket, shot a glance at the poker in Ellie's hand, and addressed Harry.

"Who is this delightfully bloodthirsty creature? She clearly subscribes to rule number three. I'm glad you didn't brain me with that poker, my dear."

"Rule number three is, *never go anywhere without a weapon*," Harry explained. "Hugo, this is Eleanor Law. Daughter of the Lord Chief Justice."

The man's eyes twinkled with a devilish amusement. "Chief Justice, eh? You always liked to live dangerously. I do hope you're not breaking rule number four?"

Harry's dimples appeared. "Not yet. Although I can't deny the temptation has been almost overwhelming."

Ellie pressed her lips together. No doubt rule number four was something along the lines of *never murder your accomplice*.

Hugo kissed her hand with a flamboyant bow and she smiled; he was, without doubt, a charming, irrepressible rogue. It was easy to see where Harry had learned his scoundrelly ways.

"Why have you only returned to England now that somebody is dead?" she asked.

"Ah. Because of a foolish duel I was involved in over a decade ago," Ambrose replied.

"Did you kill your opponent?"

He gave a dismissive snort. "No. But the man I was meeting fired early. When he realized he'd missed me, he turned to run, so instead of knocking his hat off his head, as I'd planned, I accidentally took off the lobe of his ear."

Harry shook his head. "Needless to say, Barclay was livid. Despite the fact that it was his fault, the dishonorable sod."

"He told me to leave the country, and vowed to have me arrested and tried for attempted murder if I ever set foot in England again," Ambrose continued. "And since his father was a viscount with some dubious political connections and plenty of blunt, he had the means to carry out his threat, so I decided to make myself scarce for a while."

He smiled, and a pair of dimples almost as pronounced as Harry's appeared in his cheeks. "Luckily, there is much to enjoy on the Continent for a gentleman as enterprising as myself."

"Like helping wealthy, bored widows enjoy their fortunes to the fullest." Harry smiled.

Ambrose inclined his head in wry acknowledgment. "Happy days! And when those activities palled, I found other, more exiting ways to spend my time."

"More illegal ways," Harry elaborated. "Like stealing and gaming. Hugo taught me everything I know."

Ellie turned to Ambrose. "I assume you couldn't return until Barclay was dead because, unlike France, England doesn't have a statute of limitations on the prosecution of crimes?"

He shot her an approving look. "Clever girl. That's exactly it. I never doubted that he'd make good on his threat if he ever heard I'd returned."

"That explains why you're back in the country," Harry said. "But why are you *here*, in Willingham's bedroom?"

Ambrose reached into the inner pocket of his dark jacket and pulled out a handful of glittering jewels.

"I'm relieving Lady Willingham of her rather vulgar diamonds."

Ellie took a step back. "That's stealing! I can't be party to this!"

"It's justice," Ambrose countered. "Willingham was Barclay's second for the duel. He could have denounced Barclay as a cheat, and exonerated me, but instead he kept his mouth shut when Barclay paid him off, and let me be unfairly exiled for years."

He held a necklace up into a patch of moonlight, where it glittered softly. "This setting is extremely ugly. It doesn't do the diamonds justice. Lady Willingham can buy something nicer to replace it, and the inhabitants of the Traveler's Rest will be most appreciative of her generous donation."

He tucked the jewels back into his coat.

Ellie frowned, torn between wholehearted disapproval and reluctant admiration for his twisted—yet overall commendable—morals. She'd often decried the inequality of wealth in the world, but she'd never done anything quite so drastic about it.

"What are *you* doing here, Harry?" Ambrose asked. "If it's not breaking rule number four?"

Harry opened his mouth, but the other man raised his hand, exactly as Harry had done to Sergeant Morris.

"Wait! No, don't tell me! Let me guess. I bet it involves that rather lovely prayer book Willingham has stored in his safe." He waved toward the darkened study they'd just entered. "Through there."

Chapter Seventeen

Ellie's mouth dropped open in shock.

How on earth did Ambrose know about the book?

"Your reputation for omnipotence is as impressive as ever." Harry grinned. "And yes, you're right. I'm just surprised you're not after it yourself."

"I want nothing to do with it," Ambrose said. "Willingham's working for Bonaparte's brother, Joseph—the one who went over to America. When I paid Willingham a little social visit last week, he actually tried to *hire me* to travel all the way to Saint Helena and deliver it, in person, to Bonaparte himself!"

"But why?" Ellie asked.

"The emperor thinks it's his lucky charm, apparently. Joseph's sure that if the book's returned, his brother will escape his imprisonment and return to conquer Europe again, just as he did from Elba two years ago."

Harry sent Ellie a look that clearly said *I told you so.*

"That's extraordinary," she muttered.

Ambrose shrugged. "People have the strangest fancies. I told Willingham I wasn't interested. Do you know how far Saint Helena is? Four thousand, seven hundred miles, give or take. I looked it up on a map. If old Boney was still on Elba, I might consider a nice trip around the Mediterranean, but I've no wish to spend weeks at sea, getting tossed around like dice in a cup."

"So the book is still here?" Harry asked.

"As far as I know. Unless Willingham's managed to find someone else to deliver it."

"We're being paid to return it to the owner, William Bullock."

Ambrose swept his arm in a gesture for Harry to precede him into the study. "Have at it. Annoying Willingham and thwarting old Boney will combine revenge and patriotism very neatly. I'll let you discover the safe yourself."

Harry stepped into the study and peered around while Ellie wished she'd brought her spectacles so she could see better in the dark. It wouldn't do to light a candle in case someone saw the light beneath the door and came to investigate.

Harry crossed to the glazed bookcases and studied the contents, presumably to see if Willingham had concealed a safe behind a row of books or a wooden panel.

Ellie, however, stopped in front of one of the paintings, a rather indifferent seascape, and inspected it closely. The frame was dusty.

"Willingham clearly doesn't let the servants come in here often to clean," she said. "Presumably because he values his privacy. But that's a mistake, because it means he's left his finger marks in the dust here, on the frame."

She pointed at the telltale marks, then reached out and lifted the picture from the wall. A small iron safe was set into the paneling behind it, and her heart gave a triumphant leap. Her father had something very similar in his office at home.

Harry came to stand beside her. "Impressive."

"Is rule number seven *always carry a set of lock-picks*?" she whispered.

His lips twitched. "No. Rule number seven is, *If it looks too good to be true—*"

"*—it probably is,*" Ambrose finished succinctly, and the two men shared an amused, conspiratorial smile.

"Besides," Harry said, "no need to go to all the bother of picking the lock when I have the key right here." He reached into his waistcoat and held up a small, iron key.

"Where did you get that?" Ellie sighed.

"Willingham had it in his pocket when we met him earlier. I assumed anything he had on his person was something he probably wanted to keep safe. Like the key to his wife's jewelry box. Or this safe."

Ambrose snorted. "Good lad."

"I'm going to pretend you haven't told me that," Ellie said sternly.

The lock opened with a smooth click, and the door swung open to reveal a small, rectangular object wrapped in cloth. Harry took it, and Ellie couldn't hold back her gasp as the tiny, jewel-encrusted gold cover was revealed.

Even in the partial moonlight from the bedroom it looked impossibly opulent.

"How lovely!"

Harry nodded in satisfaction. "Time to go. We can look at it more closely when we're away. Ellie, put it in your pocket. Your skirts will conceal it."

Ellie took the book with reverent hands. It was even smaller than she'd expected, perhaps only six inches high, and the gold metal cover studded with precious stones felt cold and bumpy against her fingers. She slipped it through the slit in her skirts and into the pocket she wore underneath, secured with a ribbon around her waist.

A heady thrill of excitement made her blood pound.

Harry closed the safe and replaced the painting, then turned to Ambrose. "I'm staying at Cobham House."

The other man smiled. "Oh, I know. I'll pay you a visit in a day or two." He patted his pockets. "As soon as I've dealt with tonight's little windfall. Miss Law, it has been a pleasure. I hope to see you again soon."

Ellie smiled, unsure whether she ought to return the sentiment or not.

Harry put his ear to the door, and when he judged the coast was clear, he turned the knob and ushered her out into the corridor.

She glanced back, to see if Ambrose was following them, but he tilted his head toward the bedroom window.

"I'll make my own way out," he whispered with a wink. "The same way I came in. Over the rooftops."

Harry closed the door, and together they hurried to the top of the stairs. A peek over the bannisters confirmed there were no guests below, so he took her hand again and drew her down the steps.

Her skirts clung to her legs, and the book bumped against her thigh with every step. Ellie was sure her face was pink with guilt, but she followed Harry's lead as they turned the corner.

Another couple was there, clearly sneaking off for a little *amour*; the woman's giggles and the man's staggering gait indicated neither was particularly sober. They disappeared into a side room just as a larger group could be heard approaching.

Ellie panicked; she pulled on Harry's hand and tugged

him into an alcove partly hidden by an enormous flower arrangement.

His big body followed hers, and she let out a wheeze as his solid chest came into contact with her own. He ducked his head, enclosing her with his body, shielding her from view, and Ellie inhaled the magical scent of him; a heady mixture of skin and his unique cologne that made her senses swim.

She wanted to press her nose into his cravat and fill her lungs with the smell.

The excitement of the evening was clearly addling her brain.

The men grew closer, their voices loud and obnoxious, and to her dismay she recognized Willingham's nasal tones.

"The billiard room's this way, Larkin," he brayed. "Ten pounds says I beat you."

"Done," another replied.

She shot a desperate glance up at Harry. She could barely see his face in the semidarkness, but she could sense his amusement at her panic.

"Shhh!" His soft whisper tickled the hair by her ear, more vibration than sound. "Let them pass. Keep looking at me."

The buttons on the front of his jacket pressed into the bare skin of her décolletage every time she sucked in a rapid breath, and the warmth of him heated her blood. His left leg was pressed between her own, and the intimate sensation, with him almost full-length against her, made her stomach somersault with more than just nerves.

"Pretend to kiss me!" she hissed. "Quickly!"

"With pleasure," he grinned. "*Si, mio caro. Baciami.*" He raised his voice and groaned the words, loud enough for those approaching to hear. *"Voglio scoparti contro questo muro finché non urli il mio nome."*

A cacophony of jeers and ribald comments ensued as the men caught sight of them and unanimously assumed they were interrupting a tryst.

"Looks like the Italians have a new way of waltzing," one man chuckled. "One that involves tongues!"

"She's an opera singer, isn't she?" another guffawed. "Maybe he's checking her tonsils are in good working order?"

Harry brought his arms up on either side of her head, his elbows resting against the wall to shield her face. His breath tickled her temple and his nose brushed hers as he bent lower.

"Breathe," he commanded softly.

Ellie's heart was pounding with a heady mix of fear and desire. Harry's lips hovered so close to hers that his warm exhales mingled with her own shallow breaths.

There was scarcely an inch between them.

And then there wasn't any space at all.

She wasn't sure which one of them moved, but Harry's lips touched hers, and she almost swooned in delight.

The kiss was tentative, almost a question. He paused, as if to gauge her reaction, and without thought she pushed herself up on tiptoe, closer, silently encouraging him to do it again.

He muttered something under his breath, possibly in Italian, then leaned in and kissed her again, harder this time, tracing the seam of her lips with his tongue.

Ellie opened her mouth instinctively, and when she did, he took full advantage. He slanted his head and his tongue swept inside to tangle with her own, and she gave a soft, incredulous groan at the delicious sensation.

It was possession, pure and simple. A hot, lush exploration, and she closed her eyes, kissing him back, surrendering completely. She'd *dreamed* of this—who cared whether he was just playing a part?

The world around them dissolved, narrowed to his touch, his lips. As she slid her hands up to squeeze his shoulders, his hand came round to cradle the back of her head, tilting it back, holding her in place as if he never wanted to let her go.

Ellie whimpered. In the back of her mind, she was vaguely aware of Willingham and the other men passing by, but that knowledge was of little import when Harry's breath was in her mouth and the taste of him was making her brain swim.

More. Harder. Please.

Time ceased to exist. Every wicked lick, every slow delve of his tongue, caused a corresponding tug in her belly, an ache between her legs. Her blood felt thick, like treacle.

And then it was over. With one last playful tug of her lower lip, Harry raised his head, breaking the contact.

Ellie sucked in a cool lungful of air as he moved back, and the loss of his body as a support almost made her stagger. Heat swept over her skin as embarrassment replaced desire, and the reality of their situation reasserted itself.

Harry cleared his throat and tucked a stray curl behind her ear. His eyes appeared almost black, but a dimple creased his left cheek as he sent her a lopsided smile.

"Excellent distraction, Miss Law. First rate."

Ellie took some comfort from the fact that his voice sounded far more gravelly than usual, and that his chest was rising and falling almost as rapidly as her own. She felt hot, and restless, but managed a brisk, businesslike nod, as if kissing men senseless against walls was all in the line of duty.

She reached up and wiped her finger over the corner of his mouth. His questioning gaze met hers, and she sent him a rueful smile. "You had a smudge of red. From my lip rouge."

His lips quirked. "Time to go."

They stepped fully apart. Harry straightened his cuffs and smoothed his still-impeccable coat, and she patted the prayer book in her pocket to make sure it was still there. A servant appeared at the far end of the hallway, and Ellie realized with a start that it was Daisy, carrying two bottles of wine.

Daisy's delighted expression clearly indicated that she'd witnessed at least some of their interaction, and she sent Ellie a wide-eyed smile.

Ellie pointed to her pocket to indicate they'd found the book, and Daisy nodded her understanding before she turned left and disappeared into the billiard room.

Ellie gave an inward groan. She would have some explaining to do when she got back to King & Co.

Chapter Eighteen

Ellie could scarcely look at Harry as they stood on the Willinghams' front steps awaiting his carriage. She was desperate to get the prayer book home, and so full of restless, nervous energy that it took all her control not to hop from one foot to the other.

She'd been on successful missions before, with Daisy and Tess, but she'd never felt so terrifyingly alive as she did now, in Harry's presence. Excitement and daring seemed to fizz in her blood.

The cold wind whipped at her cloak and brought a sheen of moisture to her eyes, and she was glad when Carson finally drew the horses to a stop at the front of the queue. She threw herself down on the seat with a theatrical sigh, and smiled up at Harry as he settled across from her.

"We did it! I can't believe it! What a night."

He returned her grin, his eyes glowing with good humor. "Feels good, doesn't it? Admit it, Miss Law. Sneaking around can be fun."

Ellie laughed. "Sneaking around can be *terrifying*. So many things could have gone wrong."

"Ah, but they didn't. Luck was on our side. And talent. We make a good team."

She shook her head with a wry chuckle. "We still committed a crime. I can't believe I've stooped so low."

He shot her a mocking, commiserating look. "Yes, guilty of aiding and abetting a known criminal. What a naughty girl you are."

The way he said it brought the heat back to her cheeks. He sounded more approving than anything else.

She *felt* like a bad girl.

Not for the stealing, but because she wanted another kiss. Quite desperately.

He sat back, his arm resting along the back of the seat, the picture of masculine ease, and she squirmed as she tried not to look at his mouth and remember the taste of it.

He'd been acting. Playing a part. Nothing more. She had to pull herself together.

"If it's any consolation," he said lightly, "you're in excellent company. Most of the great artists and composers were thieves, too. They all copied one another, stealing ideas and techniques. Michelangelo started his career by faking ancient Greek statues. He buried them in the ground to artificially age them, and when the Italian cardinal he sold them to as 'antique' discovered they were new, he was so impressed by Michelangelo's talent for imitating that instead of prosecuting him, he invited him to Rome, and became his patron."

Ellie rolled her eyes. "That's an exceptional case. You only have to look at the trials at the Old Bailey to know that the vast majority of crimes are punished, not rewarded."

"I happen to think that *everyone* is capable of becoming a thief, given the right circumstances. For example, stealing a painting just because it would look nice in your drawing room is undoubtedly bad. But is stealing that same painting to sell and feed your starving family equally wrong?"

"The law would say yes. Stealing is stealing, regardless of the motivation."

"Pfft. People aren't so clear-cut. We're all a mass of contradictions."

Like you, Ellie thought.

Harry had so many facets to his personality she wasn't sure what to believe. She didn't even know his real name, and yet she felt closer to him, more attracted to him, than to any other man she'd ever met.

How was that possible?

"What did you do with the key to the safe?" she asked instead.

"Dropped it on the floor by the billiard room as we left. Willingham will assume he mislaid it."

Ellie nodded approvingly. "Do you mind if I take off this wig? The pins are sticking into my skull."

"Go ahead."

With a relieved sigh she removed the elaborate hairpiece, and began to pull out the numerous hairpins that Tess had used to secure her own hair. She did it by feel, since the carriage lacked a mirror, patting her hands over her head and releasing her curls one by one until they fell around her shoulders in an unruly brown cloud.

Harry watched her efforts with unconcealed amusement, and when she finally shook her head, free of the last pin, he gave a silent nod, despite the fact that she probably looked an absolute fright.

"That feels *so* much better," she breathed.

"You look delightfully rumpled." His eyes looked

almost black in the shadows, and there was a roughness in his voice that made her spine tingle.

They traveled in silence for a few minutes, then he glanced at her again.

"Do your parents expect you home tonight?"

"No. I told them I'd be staying with Daisy, but you can drop me off at King and Company. I'll put the prayer book in our safe, and sleep on the cot in the back office."

He tilted his head and his gaze burned into her. "Do you really think you'll be able to sleep, after so much excitement? I doubt I will."

Her breath caught. "What are you suggesting?"

"Come back to my house."

She sent him an arch look. "And . . . ?"

"We'll have a drink and inspect our ill-gotten gains." His eyes dropped to her thigh, where the tiny book rested beneath her skirts, and her body tingled. Just the way he looked at her made her heart miss a beat.

His gaze traveled inward, to the wrinkled silk in her lap, then up, over the exposed skin of her chest, lingering in the shadowed cleft between her breasts, and a dull, aching throb pulsed between her legs.

She wasn't naive. Harry wasn't simply inviting her in for a nightcap. If she said yes, she'd be tacitly agreeing to so much more.

If he kissed her again, she'd kiss him back—willingly.

And if he wanted to do more than kissing, well . . . she wanted that too.

She wanted *him*.

"And after that?" she asked softly.

His brows rose. "I'll show you how to run three-card monte, if you like. In case you change your mind about pursuing a life of crime."

"It never hurts to have a backup plan." Her voice sounded scratchy, hoarse. "Will you take me back to Lincoln's Inn Fields after that?"

The look in his eyes made her stomach somersault.

"If that's what you want. But, Ellie, if you *still* weren't sleepy . . . then I suppose I could kiss you."

Her pulse stuttered, but she couldn't resist teasing him. "To pass the time? Or because your kisses make ladies want to go to sleep?"

He raised his brows. "Did you feel remotely sleepy when I kissed you earlier?"

She bit her lip. "No."

"I didn't think so." He uncrossed his legs. "You could kiss me back. And then I'd strip off that dress you're wearing—the one that's been driving me slowly insane all evening—and I'd do what I've been dreaming of since the first moment I saw you, which is to take you to bed and make love to you until we were both so exhausted, we'd *have* to sleep."

Her bodice was definitely too tight. He wasn't even touching her, and she felt like she might go up in flames.

"Oh," she managed weakly.

His dimples flashed. "Oh, indeed. So, what's your answer?"

Chapter Nineteen

A thrill of excitement speared through her, but caution still tugged at her brain.

How many times had Harry made the same offer to a woman? She surely wasn't the first.

Still, there was something refreshing about his honesty. He wasn't luring her to his home under false pretenses, as so many men might have done. He'd put all his cards on the table and was leaving it up to her to make the call. That in itself was liberating.

She still didn't entirely trust his motives for being in London. Did he truly want to leave his life of crime behind, or was working with her just a ruse to cover some larger scheme he had planned? She had no idea, but reason warned her not to expect too much, or to involve her heart.

Men like Harry stole hearts as easily as they picked pockets, and she was too sensible to allow herself to be duped.

Oddly, she *did* trust him when it came to the rest of her body. For all his criminal ways, he was a gentleman, and she knew that if she refused his offer, he'd see her safely back to King & Co. with no hard feelings. Several other men of her acquaintance had sulked and then ignored her when she'd politely rejected their advances, but Harry was both more sophisticated and more pragmatic than that.

Tess and Daisy had both enjoyed bedsport—Tess with her husband, Justin, and Daisy with Tom Harding, a childhood friend who'd been tragically killed at Waterloo two years ago. They both talked in the most glowing terms of the pleasure that could be had with a man who knew what he was about.

Harry was a scoundrel, certainly, but she had no doubt that he could bring her physical pleasure. Her attraction to him was like a simmering furnace beneath her skin, and the thought of *not* seizing this moment, of returning to the cold and empty offices of King & Co. alone, seemed like the height of foolishness, something she'd regret forever.

After all, what was she waiting for? At two and twenty she was almost on the shelf, and the few men who'd shown an interest in her had usually done so to impress her father, rather than because of any real attraction. Her independent spirit was regarded as something to be frowned on; she'd have done far better to pretend to be a malleable, empty-headed featherbrain if she truly wanted a husband.

Harry wasn't matrimonial material, but why shouldn't she grasp this chance for a reckless, imprudent fling? Provided they took the necessary precautions against pregnancy, there was little danger of her being ruined, and she was aching to know if lovemaking really was as wonderful as it sounded.

She met his gaze, decision made.

"I'm not sleepy yet."

His pupils darkened and her heart thumped erratically in her chest. Amazed at her own uncharacteristic daring, she looked out of the window, at the darkened streets rushing by.

Harry stayed silent, and in no time at all they pulled up outside a neat white stone mansion.

"Welcome to Cobham House."

A liveried servant opened the front door and Ellie looked around in interest as Harry took her cloak and removed his own coat. The marble-lined hallway held an array of expensive-looking mirrors, paintings, and gilt sconces.

He indicated a staircase with a wooden banister that curved upward. "My study's upstairs. Come on."

The room was decorated in rich burgundy tones, and she crossed to warm her hands in front of the fire that crackled in the grate. Harry poured two glasses of red wine from a decanter on a side table, and she took a sip to steady her jittery nerves.

"So, this is your lair," she said. "It's very nice."

"Thank you. I was delighted to discover the place was furnished. I believe credit for the decoration should go to the Earl of Cobham, but he seems to have been a man with excellent taste. We clearly share a love of beautiful things."

His eyes rested on her face and, flustered again, Ellie reached up and unfastened the emerald necklace at her throat.

"Speaking of beautiful things, here—have these back before I lose them." She slipped the bracelet from her wrist, tugged the earrings from her ears, and thrust them toward him. "Please thank your friend for letting me borrow them. They made me feel like a princess."

Harry held out his hands and received the glittering mass with a solemn smile. "They made you look like a princess. And thank you. I'll tell him."

The loss of the jewels made Ellie feel oddly naked; she became incredibly aware of the expanse of skin displayed by the low neckline of the dress, and Harry's slow sweep of her cleavage didn't help her feel any less exposed.

She cleared her throat and cast around for something to say as he deposited the jewelry in the drawer of his desk.

"Let's see the book, then," he urged, and she blinked. She'd actually forgotten the entire reason for the evening!

She dug in her pocket, slightly surprised that he hadn't already removed the book with those magical, thieving fingers of his, and held it up to the light.

Both the front and back covers were made of solid, beaten gold, warm to the touch now from being pressed against her body. Smooth, circular jewels were set in a thick band all around the edges, with more bordering a raised image of the Virgin Mary chased in gold in the center.

Ellie traced her fingers over the green emeralds, blue sapphires, and bloodred rubies. Some of them were a little skewed, and irregular in shape, indicating the age of the piece.

She let out a reverent breath. "This must be worth a small fortune."

"It's called a treasure binding," Harry said. "In years past, certain gems were believed to possess magical properties. Diamonds were for healing. Emeralds protected against devils. Sapphires guarded against poisoning."

"It seems whoever had this book made wanted as

many protections as possible," Ellie smiled. "Maybe that's where its reputation for being lucky came from?"

She opened it, and was amazed at the brightness of the painted illustrations within. Considering it was several centuries old, it was remarkably well-preserved.

Fantastical borders of colorful flowers and plants decorated the edges and encroached onto the beautiful medieval script. Huge gilt letters filled with dragons and angels, soldiers and birds added to the incredible richness.

"Can you feel good fortune seeping into your body?" Harry teased with a smile. He slid his finger over a page depicting a great feast, brushing her thumb as he did so, and her heart missed a beat at the seemingly innocuous contact.

Nothing he did was an accident.

Oh, he was wicked, bringing her to a slow boil.

"Put it somewhere safe," she urged, pushing it toward him.

He crossed to the bookcase behind her and, after a moment's perusal, selected a large, leather-bound book that appeared to be a weighty treatise on agricultural practices. It opened, however, to reveal a hollowed-out space within, where the central parts of the pages had been removed to create a hiding place the perfect size for the jeweled book.

He placed it inside with a wry glance at her, then put the book back on the shelf.

Ellie had to admire the simple but effective strategy. The brown leather binding blended perfectly with the other books. Finding it would be like trying to locate a needle in a haystack.

"There. Now, I promised to show you how to cheat at cards. Still interested?"

He indicated two chairs set on either side of a green baize-topped card table. She sat, and watched in awe as his nimble fingers picked up a pack of cards and shuffled them with such dexterity and speed that it was as if they came alive in his hands.

"I first saw this done in Venice, when I was just sixteen," Harry said. "In Italy it's known as *gioco delle tre carte*. In France it's called *bonneteau*. There are several variations on the theme, but the important thing is the way the three cards are held and tossed on the table."

He selected three cards from the pack, two black jacks and the queen of hearts, then turned them over so the backs were uppermost. He picked up one of the cards in his left hand, and two in his right, and showed her the queen as the bottom card of the pair. "Now, watch closely."

He tossed what appeared to be the bottom card— the queen—onto the table, then followed with the other two, laying them down in a straight line in front of her. He then moved the three cards around, switching their positions until he stopped and looked expectantly at Ellie.

"Where's the queen?"

Ellie pointed to the card she was sure was the right one. He turned it over to show a black jack.

"What?!"

He chuckled at her astonishment. "I made it look as though I threw down the queen first, but in truth I discarded the upper card, the jack. Watch again."

He picked up the cards and repeated his movements extremely slowly, using exaggerated motions to show how it was done. He curved the cards slightly in his hand, his big palms making it look easy. Then he repeated the trick at full speed, his hands moving so quickly that it was impossible to detect the substitution. Ellie chose the incorrect card again.

"It takes a lot of practice to be able to deceive people," he said, when she shook her head.

"But surely the person you're fooling occasionally chooses the queen, just by sheer luck."

"True. And when that happens, they win the pot. The frequency with which that happens, though, is very small. The odds are strongly in the dealer's favor."

"Don't you feel the slightest bit guilty for conning people out of their money?"

"Why should I? It's their greed and foolishness that makes them enter the game. They take part with the absolute certainty they're going to win. It's their choice. Shouldn't such arrogance be punished?"

Ellie frowned, unwilling to debate the point, but still stubbornly determined to beat him. "Give me one more chance."

His dimples appeared. "Think you're going to win?"

"Now that I know what you're doing, perhaps."

He laughed. "Very well. Let's make a bet. If you win, and find the queen, I'll kiss you."

She shook her head at his shameless maneuvering. "That's very magnanimous. And what if I lose?"

His eyes dropped to her lips, and she waited for him to say something like *Then you'll kiss me*.

Instead, he said, "If you lose, and select a jack, I'll take you straight back to King and Company."

She blinked, convinced he was joking, but he appeared completely serious.

Her spirits sank. He was so skilled at this game that

the chances of him winning, and her losing, were extremely high. Had he changed his mind about wanting to
bed her? Was he looking for a way out?

She didn't want to leave. Now there was the possibility of *not* kissing him, she wanted it more than anything
in the world.

"So, you're leaving it up to luck," she said, pleased that
her voice didn't betray her disappointment.

"I prefer to call it fate." His dimples appeared, dispel-
ling his stern look, and the wicked glint in his eyes al-
layed her fears a little. He definitely still wanted her, but
he was enough of a gambler to enjoy these heightened
stakes.

"Very well. Go ahead."

He'd been shuffling the cards as they talked, but he
showed her the red queen in his hand before he started to
move them around on the table. Ellie wrinkled her brow,
watching his hands with fierce concentration. When he
stopped moving, she was certain the queen was the center card, but knowing his skill, she deliberately pointed
to the left-hand card in the row. If the central card was
unlikely to be the queen—simply because that was where
she'd been led to believe it was—then she had at least a
fifty percent chance of it being on the left.

His brows rose. "That one? Are you sure?"

He would be an excellent poker player. His expression
didn't betray a thing. She couldn't tell if he was pleased,
or disappointed.

She bit her lip and nodded.

Instead of turning the left card over, he inverted the
one on the right, and she breathed a silent sigh of relief
when it revealed a black jack. His hand hovered over the
central card, deliberately teasing her, and she scowled
at him.

Impatient, she reached for the central card herself, and flipped it over. The jack of clubs stared back at her, and her heart skipped a beat as he turned the queen of hearts over on the left.

His odd eyes met hers, one blue, one brown.

"You win."

Chapter Twenty

Ellie pushed back her chair and stood, her heart beating wildly in her throat.

"If you want me to leave, you just have to say. Really. It's fine if you don't want to kiss me."

He stepped out from behind the table, and she took a nervous step back. "I mean, you can't have possibly known I'd choose that card," she continued breathlessly.

His lips quirked as he shook his head. "You think not? I'm disappointed you have such a low opinion of my skill."

He took another step, and she retreated until her bottom hit the bookcase behind her. "We could have played that game ten times over, and you'd have chosen the red queen nine times out of ten."

She didn't know whether to be relieved, or suspicious. He must have manipulated the cards so that she'd win. But how had he induced her to choose the queen? It seemed far-fetched, ridiculous, but she was beginning to think there was nothing he couldn't do, no end to his cleverness.

"If I'd chosen the jack, would you really have taken me home?"

His hot gaze held hers. "We'll never know, will we?"

Ellie pressed her shoulders back against the bookcase. "So, you *do* want to kiss me?"

"I do." His dimples appeared as he came closer still, stalking her. "So much that I'm willing to break rule number four."

That was the rule Ambrose had mentioned at Willingham's. "Which is . . . ?"

He leaned in. "Never mix theft with seduction."

"That sounds like a very sensible rule," she murmured.

His lips were so close to hers she could smell the delicious scent of his skin.

"Sometimes being sensible is overrated."

He pressed his lips to hers and Ellie closed her eyes with a sigh of surrender. His hands came up to cradle her face, his long fingers stoking her jaw, and she reveled in the taste of him, so exciting and yet also strangely familiar.

He wasn't acting now. There was no one to deceive, no ulterior motive, and the fact that he wanted her, *truly*, made excitement bloom inside her like a fiery glow.

She kissed him back with wholehearted enjoyment, stroking her tongue against his, loving the deep groan of approval that rumbled from his chest at her enthusiastic participation.

His lips left hers as he kissed below her ear, then down her neck. His hand slid to her waist to tug her closer, and she tilted her head back with a gasp as he pressed a line of kisses along the neckline of her bodice, pressing his nose to her décolletage. The slight scrape of his evening beard on the tender skin of her breasts made her shiver in delight, and she threaded her fingers through his hair to hold him in place as he licked and nipped the exposed curves.

"This is a wicked dress," he murmured. "And you are a wicked woman, to tease a man so. I could barely concentrate enough to pick Willingham's pocket with you standing there, looking so tempting."

Ellie let out an incredulous laugh. "It's your own fault. You chose it."

His hand squeezed her hip as he reclaimed her mouth. "True," he murmured. "I must be a glutton for punishment."

He kissed her long and hard, a thrilling statement of intent, and Ellie melted against him, weak-kneed. When they finally pulled apart, she was pleased to see his breath was as choppy and uneven as her own.

"Feeling sleepy?" he panted.

She shook her head with a gleeful laugh. "Not even a little."

"Good."

In one swift move he bent and lifted her against him. He carried her through a doorway, across the hall, and into what was clearly his bedchamber, and her heart fluttered in excitement.

God, she really was doing this! She'd always fantasized about being a wicked, wanton rebel, but she'd never imagined she'd truly get the chance. Yet here she was, in the room of a gorgeous scoundrel, determined to enjoy the miraculous experience to the fullest.

Harry deposited her on the edge of the bed with a bounce, kissing her again so quickly she didn't even have time to look around the room. Ellie put her arms around his neck and tried to drag him down onto the bed with her, but he pulled back with a deep chuckle.

"So impatient, Miss Law," he chided. "Surely as an investigator you know the importance of not rushing into an unfamiliar situation? One must take stock, observe. Be patient."

He stepped back and stripped off his waistcoat with a carelessness that almost made her protest, then untied his cravat and tossed it onto a chair in the corner of the room. His white shirt opened in a deep V at the front, revealing a deliciously tempting expanse of tawny skin, and her cheeks heated as she leaned back on the bed and studied him.

He really was ridiculously handsome. Maybe that book really *had* brought her luck?

"I must admit, I've never been in this particular environment before," she said. "I'm willing to bow to your superior knowledge of the terrain."

She studied his face, worried that her lack of experience would count against her, but the hot look in his eyes dispelled her fears, as did the prominent bulge visible in the front of his breeches. He definitely desired her.

"That's very sensible," he said. "I'd be delighted to show you how this particular investigation should be conducted."

He stepped closer, between her bent knees.

"I thought you said being sensible was overrated?"

His lips curved up. "Stop being so clever."

He rested his hands on her knees, then slid them slowly up her thighs, bunching the emerald-green silk with his palms as he went. Ellie shivered in anticipation.

Instead of kissing her again, he dropped to his knees and caught the hem of her skirts. There was no resistance from the slippery silk as he pushed it up to reveal her white silk stockings and garters, inch by inch, and Ellie let out a scandalized breath as the cool air wafted against the bare skin of her inner thighs.

"A sensible thief—I mean, *investigator*," he amended drily, "always takes time to do plenty of reconnaissance. Open your legs."

Ellie sucked in a breath at his unexpected command. From her position, she could see his wicked face and broad shoulders between her thighs. Desire made her body throb, and she bit her lip as she held his gaze and slowly did as he asked.

Heat flushed her cheeks. She wasn't wearing any drawers. The dress had come with the sheerest of muslin shifts to wear underneath, and even the corset was built in to the bodice itself.

Harry lowered his gaze, and she squirmed in embarrassment as he pressed her knees even wider. Could he see everything? Or did the froth of her skirts and the shadows still hide her from view?

She tensed as he encircled her ankles with his long fingers, then drew his hands up her stockinged calves with deliberate slowness.

"I need to make sure you're not hiding any weapons under here," he murmured, and the gravel in his voice made her toes curl. The paradoxical combination of teasing rogue and stern instructor was playing havoc with her senses.

"I'm not, I swear," she gasped. "But by all means satisfy yourself that I'm telling the truth."

His dimples flashed. "Oh, I intend to satisfy *both* of us, my sweet. Lie back on the bed."

The butterflies in her stomach were almost insupportable, but Ellie slid her hands back on the soft coverlet and lay down. She gasped as he caught her hips and dragged her even closer to the edge of the bed, then let out a little yelp as he pulled off her shoes, draped her knees over his shoulders, and leaned in.

His warm palms slid up under her skirts, and he pressed a kiss to the bare skin on the inside of her leg, just above her garter.

"Oh!"

He kissed her again, even higher, and she wriggled in combined mortification and excitement. Tess had once shown her a naughty etching of a man kissing a woman between the legs, and the knowledge that Harry was about to do the same thing to her made her core clench and throb.

"No obvious daggers," he whispered, "but let me double-check."

Another kiss, so close to the slick, wet center of her that she could barely breathe. And then his mouth was there, his tongue probing at the entrance to her body, and she tensed her stomach, curling up toward him automatically to grab his hair.

"God," he groaned, and the word was a vibration against her skin. "Ellie, you taste so good."

Ellie closed her eyes in amazement. His wicked tongue lapped and teased, alternating between slow, languorous licks and harder, quicker stabs, and jolts of pleasure shot through her body like fireworks.

Just when she didn't think she could enjoy it any more, his clever fingers joined his mouth, his thumb sliding over the sensitive pearl between her folds, then sliding to her entrance and pushing in, just the tiniest amount, before he withdrew.

"Again. Oh, please!" she begged.

She was beyond embarrassment now. She clutched at his head, pushing him closer in a wordless demand for him to continue, and his breath fanned over her as he chuckled at her ferocity.

"Wicked girl."

He slid his finger inside her, then did it again, and the sensation was so delicious, so addictive, that she arched up into his touch. Every muscle in her body grew taut; he kept hitting a spot somewhere inside her that made her catch her breath.

She pushed down, matching his rhythm, and suddenly the pleasure became too much. He curled his finger, and the tension that had been building suddenly broke like a wave. Ecstasy rolled over her in great shuddering pulses, a dizzying release, and she choked out a cry that was almost a sob.

"Harry!"

Chapter Twenty-One

Ellie collapsed back on the bed, every muscle limp.

Harry rose, and when she peeked at him from below her lashes he was standing at the foot of the bed. He'd removed his shirt, and her mouth grew dry at the sight of his wide shoulders and the smooth curves of his biceps.

So *this* was what he'd been hiding under those elegant clothes. She bit back a sigh. However expensive his tailoring, it was a crime to cover a body as beautiful as his with fabric. Her gaze moved lower, over tawny male nipples and the strong ridges of his stomach, then down to the intriguing line of hair that ran from his navel and disappeared into the top of his breeches.

"Feeling drowsy?" he teased.

"Not yet."

Might as well be hung for a sheep as a lamb.

"Perhaps you should take that dress off, then. Make yourself more comfortable."

She smiled. "It isn't easy sleeping in a bodice. But I don't have a maid to help me with the laces."

His expression turned wolfish. "Allow me. Roll over."

She turned onto her stomach and buried her face in

the coverlet. The woodsy scent of him clung to the luxurious blue satin and made her belly flutter. The mattress dipped as he rested his knee beside her thigh, and she felt the tug on the laces that fastened her bodice at the back.

Her heart began to pound.

The constriction of the inbuilt stays loosened in tiny increments, and she sucked in a deep breath, glad to be released from the stylish imprisonment. The back of the dress opened fully, revealing her muslin chemise beneath, and his warm fingers traced the bumps of her spine through the sheer fabric.

"Turn over and sit up."

Ellie did so, careful not to crush the delicate silk. She slid to the edge of the bed and stood, holding the loose fabric of the bodice to her chest as she looked up into his face.

"Dresses like this should be illegal." He reached out and smoothed her hair back over her shoulder. "They're a threat to public safety. They cause accidents in the street, make sane men lose their senses. Step out of it."

She forced her fingers to release their grip, and the treacherous silk slid down her body like water. It caught momentarily on her hips, but a little wiggle freed it again, and the whole thing pooled at her feet like a mossy green puddle.

Heat scalded her cheeks. The chemise Madame Lefèvre had provided stopped just above her knees, and was scandalously transparent; her peaked nipples must be clearly visible to his roving gaze.

"Ready to turn in?"

His teasing growl bolstered her confidence. He wasn't entirely unaffected, no matter how cool he pretended to be. She bit her lip, and was pleased to see a hungry look flash across his face.

"Not quite yet. Perhaps you could tell me a bedtime story?"

A muscle ticked in his jaw. "Very well."

She sat down on the edge of the bed and glanced up at him expectantly. He came to stand in front of her, his long fingers resting teasingly on the top button of his falls. "Once upon a time there lived a thief."

"A handsome, wicked thief?"

He nodded and undid the first button. "Very. One day this thief met a studious female investigator, and, for the first time in his life, he got a taste of his own medicine."

Ellie gave a fake gasp of shock. "She *stole* something from him? Surely not!"

"I'm afraid so." He popped the second button and sent her a look from beneath his brows. "She wasn't nearly as innocent as she seemed."

"What did she do?"

"She stole the breath from his lungs with a scandalous dress. And then she kissed him, and stole the wits from his head, as well."

Her heart gave a joyous little flutter, even though she knew he was only being flippant. He'd probably used the same words on half a dozen women.

"Serves him right," she said stoutly. "He probably deserved it."

He released another button with a smirk. "Oh, don't worry. He got his revenge."

Ellie pressed her lips together to stifle her laugh. "How? By stealing her innocence?"

He shook his head, his mismatched eyes hooded and dark. "Oh, no. *That* she gave willingly. There was no stealing involved."

"What, then?"

"He stole something even better. Her heart."

"The scoundrel!"

He leaned closer, deliciously menacing. "And he never, ever gave it back."

Before Ellie could come up with a suitable retort, he released the fourth and final button. His cock sprung free, and she lost her train of thought, watching in fascination as he wrapped his fingers around it and gave it a gentle squeeze.

She'd never seen an aroused male before. Not in the flesh. Tess's naughty engraving had shown an erect phallus, true, but it had been two-dimensional, black and white, merely theoretical, whereas Harry was right here in front of her, thick and long and very real.

"I think you were right about book-learning," she breathed. "There's no substitute for practical firsthand experience."

"Does *your* hand want to experience it?" His jaw clenched as he stroked himself again, slowly up and down, and she nodded.

She reached out and trailed her fingers over the hard ridges of his stomach, then stroked down to the tangle of curls. With a growl of impatience, he caught her hand and wrapped her fingers around his length, covering them with his own, and she gasped, fascinated by the paradoxical combination of rigid muscle and silky-soft skin. He was *hot*.

He gave her fingers a squeeze, then pulled their joined hands away with a rueful sound.

"Enough of that, or our joint investigation will be concluded very quickly."

She knew what he was referring to. Tess and Daisy had explained the mechanics of lovemaking in helpfully graphic terms. Men experienced the same pleasurable convulsions as she herself had just received from his hand, but when they did, they released a fluid that could impregnate a woman if he happened to be inside her.

Ellie bit her lip. Courtesans, presumably, had frank discussions with men all the time, but she was unsure how to delicately phrase her request.

"I know this isn't the most convenient moment, but . . . I can't risk conceiving a child."

Harry reached forward and cupped her jaw, stroking his thumb over her lips in a slow caress that made her shiver.

"I didn't dream that you'd be here with me tonight, so I don't have anything prepared. Sheaths need soaking before they can be used. But if you trust me, there are other things we can do. I can take my pleasure, and give it to you, without risking your reputation."

Ellie caught his hand and interlaced their fingers. "I trust you."

It was true. At least partially. She trusted him with her body, if not with her heart. And her body was clamoring for more.

He let out a slow exhale, as if he'd been braced for rejection, then leaned forward and kissed her with a passion that took her breath away.

His knee pressed the mattress near her hip and she lay back on the bed as he crawled over her. His mastery was thrilling, irresistible, and she surrendered to it with a needy moan.

"God, Ellie, I want you so much. Please, let me touch you."

His hands slid into the curve of her waist, then down, over her chemise and bare thighs. Desperate to feel her skin against his, she lifted her hips, helping him pull the chemise up and over her head in a blur of movement, hardly breaking their kiss.

She was left in just her stockings and garters.

Her breasts came into contact with the warm skin of his chest, but she barely had time to register the sensation before he slid down her body and fastened his lips over her nipple. His wicked tongue licked and flicked the peak, while his left hand cupped her other breast, stroking it with a kneading rhythm that made her blood feel like molten lava in her veins.

"I've wanted to do this since I first saw you," he murmured. "I wanted to spirit you away and do precisely this."

She threaded her fingers through his hair and pulled his head back up, shocked by the intensity of the pleasure. He captured her mouth again, sharing her breath, his hips rocking against hers. The hot length of his cock pressed against her stomach, rigid, almost painful, and he let out an impassioned groan.

"So perfect," he whispered. "So perfect it's a crime. Open your legs for me, Ellie."

Chapter Twenty-Two

Ellie parted her thighs, and the weight of him slid down to settle between them. The smooth buckskin of his breeches was a delicious tease, and then she felt the slick head of his cock pressing at the entrance to her body.

They both stilled. Harry lifted himself up onto his elbows, relieving her of some of his weight, and she stared into his eyes—one blue, one green-brown—so close that she could make out the individual flecks of color that gave him such a unique look.

Her heart was pounding in her throat at the momentous step she was about to take, and for the briefest moment she was seized by an incredulous and utterly inappropriate desire to laugh.

She didn't even know his real name! This was madness, utter madness.

And yet, inexplicably, she *knew* him. Knew his essence, his soul. He was a reckless, wicked, wily scoundrel, and she wanted him, by whatever name he chose to use.

He raised his brows at her in silent question, as if checking that she wanted him to continue, and she lifted her hips in answer. Satisfied, he leaned down and caught her lower lip between his teeth, tugging gently, at the same moment as he pressed forward and slid into her.

Ellie gasped against his mouth as her body resisted the unaccustomed invasion. He kissed her, deeply, hungrily, and she forgot about the slight discomfort as his fingers tightened on her hip. He withdrew, then pressed again, and her inner muscles yielded to the pressure, welcoming him inside.

So this was what ruination felt like. A sweet, deep ache. Two bodies as close as they could possibly be.

She lifted her leg, wrapping it around the back of his thigh, and the change in angle made the sensations even better. This time, when he slid in, he stroked the spot inside her that his fingers had found before, and she bucked against him, eager to recapture that delicious feeling.

He increased the rhythm, sliding in and out with the perfect amount of friction, and Ellie closed her eyes as her head began to spin. Pleasure built, ratcheting higher and higher, and she clutched at his muscled back as she sought relief.

"Take your pleasure," he ground out hoarsely. "Steal it from me. That's it, beautiful girl. Take it. Now, Ellie. *Come.*"

Her body obeyed his command. Her inner muscles clenched down hard, and pleasure burst over her. It was overwhelming in the best possible way, as if she were being tumbled by a huge, unstoppable wave, and she let out a sob of relief.

With one last thrust, he withdrew from her body. Dazed, still bleary-eyed with her own climax, she watched him kneel between her legs and fist his cock. He pumped, his expression almost pained, and then with a groan he reached his own crisis. Hot, thick ropes of his seed lashed across her belly as he bent over her, supporting himself on one arm as his back bowed in ecstasy.

Ellie could barely move. Every limb felt like it weighed a hundred tons, as if she could sink down through the mattress, through the earth, but her skin was alive and glowing. She'd never felt better in her life.

Harry let out a long, satisfied sigh, and sat back between her legs. He pushed his hair back from his forehead, and his eyes roved over her naked body as if he were memorizing her curves for a future heist. He grabbed his shirt from the edge of the bed, and used the expensive material to wipe the evidence of his climax from her skin.

Ellie's stomach clenched at his gentle ministrations, and at the possessive, satisfied look on his face. She felt marked, somehow, as if what they'd done had left a permanent etching on her soul, an invisible version of the inked tattoos that sailors sometimes bore.

She shook her head to dispel the foolish notion. Her brain was too befuddled by the unexpected pleasure to think straight.

Harry slid off the bed and pulled back the sheets. "Get in. Unless you'd like to use the privy?"

She nodded, grateful for his consideration, and when she looked around for something to cover herself with, suddenly shy, he tossed her the coverlet that had been spread on the bed. The silky cashmere was as soft as a whisper, and he smiled as she wrapped it around her body.

"I suppose this is made from mermaid hair, or butterfly wings?" she teased.

"Why settle for second best?"

She collected her chemise from where he'd tossed it onto the floor, then went to investigate the adjoining bathing room. When she returned, feeling slightly less self-conscious in the chemise, he was lying in bed, the covers pooled at his waist. He looked thoroughly wicked and satisfied, and she slipped in beside him with a little shiver of delight.

His long fingers played with her curls, then stroked her cheek. "*Now* do you feel sleepy?"

Ellie yawned, perfectly on cue, and when he smiled, she had to resist the urge to reach up and trace those outrageous dimples.

"A little bit," she admitted. "Your plan to tire me out has worked."

He lay down and turned to face her on the pillows, and she shook her head with a rueful smile. "I don't even know your real name."

"'What's in a name? That which we call a rose by any other name would smell as sweet.'"

"Shakespeare, *Romeo and Juliet*," she said, identifying the quote. "That's an easy one."

He traced her eyebrow with the tip of his finger. "Do you know, some scholars argue that even Shakespeare was a fraud. He stole ideas from other sources. A few even claim another playwright wrote his works—or maybe a whole group of people."

His finger moved to her nose, running the length of it and back up. "But does it matter? Those plays have given audiences pleasure for hundreds of years. They entertain. They console. If the name of the man—or woman—who created them is wrong, who cares?"

"I know what you're doing," she said sleepily. His lazy touch was making her drowsy. "But names are important, especially in the *ton*. They show connections and relationships with other people. They prove how well we know a person, how formal we are with them. Addressing someone by their title is very different to using their surname. And using their Christian name, or a nickname, shows a closeness, a familiarity. I can be Miss Law, or Eleanor, or Ellie, depending on who I'm with."

"I work with Miss Law." He traced her top lip and she wrinkled her nose. "She's a formidable specimen. An excellent investigator."

"And Eleanor?"

"Ah. Eleanor is wallflower with a stubborn streak. I met her the night of the Chessingtons' ball. She needs to learn to live a little."

"And what about Ellie?"

His dimples made an appearance. "Ellie's my partner in crime. A wicked siren, impossible to resist."

She shook her head, denying the description, even as it secretly warmed her heart.

"Knowing someone's name feels like you *have* a little bit of them, somehow. Do you know, the ancient Greeks thought a person could achieve a kind of immortality by having their name spoken aloud, long after they were dead."

He caught her hand and placed it flat on his chest. His heart thumped, strong and steady, beneath her palm.

"The heart that beats in this body is the same, whether you call me Harry, or Henri, Enrico, or Charles King."

She shook her head, amused by his logic, but too tired to think of a counter-argument. "You were wrong about people living up to their names. Willingham's wife is called Cassandra. If she was named after the oracle in Greek mythology, she should have been able to predict the theft of her diamonds."

His lips curved. "I didn't say it was a perfect system. Only a general rule."

"Speaking of rules, do you really have your own set for thieving?"

"I do. Rule number one I've mentioned before. It's *never steal something from a man that he cannot afford to buy back.* Rule number two is *never rob an honest man.*"

"A thief with morals?" she snorted. "Isn't that a little contradictory?"

"Life's contradictory."

"Fair enough. Tell me the others."

"Hugo mentioned rules three and four at Willingham's. Rule number three is *never go anywhere without a weapon.*"

"And rule number four is *never mix theft with seduction.*" She smiled. "I remember that one."

"Which is closely related to rule number five," he continued. "*When it comes to women, jobs, and duels—one at a time.*"

"You told me rule number six yesterday," she said. "*Always talk to the servants.*"

He tapped her playfully on the nose. "Very good, Miss Law. You've been paying attention. Rule number seven is *if it looks too good to be true, it probably is.* And the final rule, rule number eight, is *what you take, you sell. What you're given, you keep.*"

Ellie yawned again. She was losing the battle against sleep, despite wanting to stay awake and talk.

"Those all sound very sensible. Can you add to the list, if you want?"

"Of course. It's an ongoing project."

He pulled the coverlet up over her shoulder and gathered her into his arms. Ellie tensed for a moment, unused to being held in such a way. She hadn't slept in a bed with another person since she, Daisy, and Tess had snuggled up together beneath the blankets at Hollyfield as girls, giggling and whispering beneath the covers.

No, that was wrong, she remembered sleepily. She and Ellie had kept Tess company at Wansford Hall two years ago, on the fateful night the old duke, Tess's first husband, had died on their wedding night and left Tess a wealthy, virginal widow.

This was a far more pleasant occasion.

The heat of Harry's naked body warmed her, and she slowly relaxed into his embrace, pressing her nose into his shoulder and inhaling the intoxicating musky scent of his skin.

A thousand thoughts jostled for attention in her brain. She was a virgin no more, technically ruined in social terms, but she couldn't seem to dredge up an ounce of regret. Even if she never married, never found another man to share such intimacies with, she'd always have this one, perfect night to remember.

Her eyes fluttered closed, but as she drifted off, she was sure she heard Harry whisper, *"What you're given, you keep."*

Chapter Twenty-Three

Henry James Charles Brooke, the twelfth Earl of Cobham, known to a select few friends as Harry, gazed down at the sleeping woman in his arms and sighed.

This had *not* been part of the plan.

But how could he possibly have foreseen the havoc that one shy, stubborn wallflower could wreak?

It was his own fault. He was more than accustomed to assessing the risks in any situation, and from the moment he'd set eyes on Ellie Law, he'd been drawn to her as to a priceless painting or an irreplaceable gem.

He should have known the danger he was in. Her cleverness and tenacity matched his own, and unlocking the passionate nature that lurked beneath her bluestocking exterior tonight had been both a pleasure and a privilege.

Her small, soft body curled trustingly into his and he tightened his arms around her as a strange protectiveness swept over him. He wanted to make love to her again. Once hadn't been enough, but he'd been very conscious of the fact that she was a virgin. It had taken every ounce of his restraint to go slowly, not to scare her, to make her first time enjoyable.

The pleased sounds she'd made as he'd kissed her, the silky feel of her skin, the way her eyes had widened in amazement when he'd buried himself inside her, were all burned into his brain.

His cock hardened just thinking about it. He'd fantasized about bedding her, but reality had surpassed even his fervent imaginings. He felt honored that she'd trusted him to introduce her to the world of pleasure, but there was still so much he had to show her. If she'd let him.

He didn't deserve her trust, of course. He was a liar and a thief. A charlatan and a scoundrel. The last thing he wanted was to hurt her, but it was almost inevitable, given the current situation.

He'd have to tell her the truth soon, of course, but the selfish part of him wanted to delay that moment for as long as possible.

He didn't want morning to come.

Chapter Twenty-Four

Ellie woke to the deliciously wicked sensation of Harry's hand stroking her thigh.

She must have turned over in the night, because his big body was curled around her, his chest to her back, and her bottom was nestled against the flatteringly hard rod of his cock.

It wasn't quite morning. The pale gray of dawn was just peeking through the heavy velvet curtains, and she smiled into the pillow as she wriggled provocatively against him.

Her chemise had rucked up, and his fingers inched it higher, pushing it up over her hip to bunch at her waist. His palm stroked the smooth curve of her bottom, then slid with cunning stealth between her legs.

Ellie bit her lip, feigning sleep, but Harry's soft laugh as he gently kissed her shoulder proved she wasn't fooling him one bit.

"Are you with me, sleepyhead?" he murmured. "You don't want to sleep through this." He paused, as if a new thought had occurred to him. "Unless you're sore? I can stop if you wish."

Ellie shook her head, even as his consideration warmed her. "I'm not sore."

She waited with bated breath for his hand to move higher, to touch her where she ached to be touched, and he didn't disappoint. She fisted the sheets beside her as he teased, his clever fingers sliding in the wetness of her body, but when she parted her legs in silent invitation, he withdrew his hand.

She groaned. "Tease!"

"Patience," he chided. "Good things are worth waiting for." He pushed her shoulder, gently guiding her to lie on her stomach, and she almost purred with pleasure as he stroked his hands over her thighs and spread her legs a little wider.

A flare of wickedness flickered inside her. Perhaps she was a secret wanton after all? Or maybe it was just this man who made her so.

"What did you say to me at Willingham's?" she murmured. "In Italian, in the hallway?"

He kissed the back of her neck. "I said, *Yes, sweetheart. Kiss me.*"

"You said something else too."

He chuckled at her tenacity. "I did. I said, *Voglio scoparti contro questo muro finché non urli il mio nome.*"

"And what does that mean?"

He moved over her and she caught her breath as the muscled length of him pressed her down into the soft mattress. His larger size was thrilling, his physical power undeniable, and the combination of threat and careful restraint made her stomach somersault with desire.

"It means, *I want to fuck you against this wall until you scream my name.*"

Ellie gasped, apparently not beyond being scandalized,

despite her non-virginal state, and he laughed against her ear.

"That was very rude."

"It was indeed."

"Did you mean it?" she whispered, blushing.

"Absolutely. And someday I'll show you exactly how it's done, but for now, I think we should make use of this far more comfortable bed."

His fingers slipped back between her legs, guiding the smooth head of his cock to her entrance, and she lifted her hips, bucking back against him eagerly. He entered her in one smooth thrust, and they both gasped at the glorious sensation.

"Better than stealing?" she whispered.

"Better than *anything*," he groaned. "Better than a royal pardon on the scaffold. God, you feel so good."

Ellie spread her arms wide, pressing them into the bed, as he set a slow, languorous rhythm. He seemed determined to push her to the very heights of frustration, to turn her into a begging, babbling mess.

He called her a good girl, a bad girl, a beautiful vexation. He fisted her hair and kissed her throat and stroked her skin as if it were the softest cashmere and he'd die if he didn't keep touching her.

By the time he finally took pity and quickened his pace she was almost delirious with desire. When her climax finally claimed her, it was a mercy, a shattering wave of pleasure that sucked her down into a glorious spiraling blackness then washed her up on a sparkling shore, breathless and reborn.

Harry stilled, still inside her, waiting until her last shudder had passed before resuming his torturously slow strokes. He didn't last much longer. His breathing grew choppy, his thrusts more frantic, and just when Ellie began to think he'd forgotten his promise not to spend himself inside her, he withdrew from her body with a fevered groan.

He angled his cock down, between her thighs, rubbing himself along her cleft without actually entering her body. She gasped at the delicious new friction, but Harry let out a hiss of frustration. Quick as a flash, he rolled her over onto her back, grabbed her wrist, and wrapped her fingers around his cock.

His fevered gaze locked with hers as he thrust into her hand, and she tightened her grip, determined to help him reach his own climax.

The sight of him above her, his sleek, powerful body flexing under her control, sent a heady shot of feminine power straight through her veins. She pumped her hand, sliding against him, acting on pure impulse, and was thrilled when he threw back his head and found his release.

When he finally caught his breath, he looked down at her with a wry smile. "I knew from the moment we met that you'd be trouble."

Ellie batted her eyelashes. "Me? I've never caused trouble in my life."

He shook his head and glanced at the small brass carriage clock on his nightstand.

"It's still early, but we need to get you back to King and Company before the streets get too busy."

Ellie bit back a little stab of disappointment. He was only being practical. No point risking her reputation by having someone see his coach depositing her at Lincoln's Inn Fields. That was how scandalous rumors started.

"You're right. If you'll let me use the bathing room, I'll get cleaned up and we can be on our way."

She slid off the bed and collected the green dress from where she'd discarded it the night before.

The mirror in the bathing room showed the full extent of her debauchery. Her hair, already a mess from having been pinned beneath the wig, was a riot of untamed waves. She looked thoroughly rumpled. But her skin was glowing with good health and her eyes held a suspiciously bright sheen. She looked exactly as she'd always imagined the phrase "well pleasured" would look.

Ruination clearly had its advantages.

She eyed the huge copper bathtub with envy. She would have loved the luxury of a hot, deep soak—she had aches in muscles she never knew existed—but Harry was doubtless keen to see the back of her and she was determined not to be gauche and unsophisticated.

The silk gown slid over her newly sensitive skin like a caress, and since she couldn't reach the laces at the back, she slipped back into the bedroom for Harry's assistance.

He was fully dressed, and for a disconcerting moment he looked like a stranger, standing across the room from her. And then he raised his brows, and smiled, and she pulled her hair over her shoulder and presented her back to him.

"Could you tighten my laces, please?"

He stepped close. "Of course."

His fingers were deft and sure, and she wondered with a pang how many other corsets he'd encountered in his life. She stepped back from him as soon as he'd finished, and he tilted his head at her.

"All good?"

She wasn't sure if he was asking about the tightness

of her laces, or her general state of wellbeing, but she smiled at him and tried to imagine what other, more worldly women would say at a time like this.

"All good, thank you. Shall we go?"

He swept his hand toward the door. "After you."

Chapter Twenty-Five

Harry did not join her for the journey to King & Co. and Ellie couldn't decide if she was relieved, or disappointed. So much had happened in the past twelve hours, but she wasn't quite ready to dissect it all just yet.

Neither Daisy nor Tess had arrived at the office, and she bolted inside with a brief wave to Carson, who gave her a friendly nod from his place on the box. The dress she'd worn the previous day still lay on the single bed in the back office, and she removed the green silk with a little pang of regret. Taking it off felt like the end of a beautiful dream, a return to the drab blue cotton of her normal existence, far removed from the glittering fairy-land of diamonds and daring of last night.

With steady hands she brushed out her hair and pinned it into a neat roll at the back of her head, then donned her spectacles, and by the time Daisy and Tess bundled in, she'd made a pot of tea and only thought about Harry No-Name a dozen or so times.

"So, what happened at Willingham's?" Tess demanded eagerly. "Tell me everything."

"Yes, Eleanor," Daisy said, in a teasing singsong voice.

"Do tell." She sent Ellie a laughing, knowing glance and Ellie felt her cheeks heat.

"We found the prayer book hidden in a safe in Willingham's private study," Ellie said.

Tess clapped her hands in approval. "Excellent work. Bravo!"

Daisy raised her brows with a smirk. "Was that before, or after, your coconspirator ravished you up against the wall, *Signora Pellegrini*?"

Tess turned wide eyes on Ellie. "A ravishing? Double bravo! Did you kiss him? Or did he kiss you?"

Ellie squirmed in her seat. "I'm not exactly sure."

"It looked mutual," Daisy said, with obvious relish, "from where I was standing. And if it was all just for show, then it was *extremely* convincing."

"We needed a reason to be sneaking about in the back corridor," Ellie said.

"Of course," Tess said soothingly. "But was it nice?"

"Very."

"*So* nice, she didn't come back to stay at my house last night!" Daisy crowed.

Tess raised her brows at Ellie. "Harry brought you back here?"

"Of course he didn't," Daisy laughed. "Look at her face! She's blushing like a berry. And you should have seen the way he was looking at her. Like he wanted to take her to bed and keep her there for a month. I bet they went to his house."

Ellie took a calming sip of tea. "We did go back to Cobham House, yes."

"Ha!"

"We put Bullock's Book of Hours in a safe place in his library, and then he showed me how to cheat at cards. It was most instructive."

Daisy waggled her eyebrows. "And what *else* did he instruct you in, dear Eleanor?"

"You sound like William Garrow, cross-examining a witness."

"Answer the question!" Daisy grinned, slamming the flat of her hand against the desktop as if she were a judge demanding order in an unruly court.

Ellie knew her cheeks were scarlet, but she tried to keep the foolish smile off her face. "Well, if you must know, he ruined me quite comprehensively."

Tess gave a delighted squeal.

"I knew it!" Daisy laughed. "How was it? Please tell me he was careful. The first time can be awkward and quite painful."

"It was . . ." Ellie searched for the right word, and settled on, ". . . wonderful. Absolutely wonderful."

Tess smiled. "I'm so glad he made it enjoyable for you. There aren't many men who would bother being gentle with a virgin, and it's a rare man indeed who sees to his partner's pleasure as well as his own."

"I trust you took the necessary precautions?" Daisy asked. "It's one thing to keep a tryst secret, but quite another to have to cover up an unplanned pregnancy. Remember all the work we had to do to hide poor Jane Ashford, when she found out she was expecting her lover's child?"

"True," Ellie said. "And don't worry, we were careful."

"Well, it seems we all had a successful night," Daisy said cheerfully. "Because I found this at Willingham's." She tossed a folded letter onto the desk. "It was in the pile of outgoing mail. I expect the servants were all so busy preparing for the party that nobody could be spared to deliver it."

"Who is it for? There's no name or address on the front."

"It's not clear." Daisy unfolded the paper. "But it says, '*I must postpone the exchange. We cannot meet on Wednesday. I will be at the drinking well at dawn on Thursday, with the item requested. Have the sum we agreed ready.*'"

Tess frowned. "Do you think he's talking about the prayer book?"

"I do," Daisy said. "He'll be handing it over to whoever's been entrusted to deliver it to Bonaparte. And because this letter was never sent, that person doesn't know the plan has changed. They'll presumably still go to the 'drinking well' on *Wednesday.*"

"That's tomorrow," Tess said.

Ellie wrinkled her nose. "I know our mission was to retrieve the book and return it to Mr. Bullock, but don't you think we should try and discover who else is involved?"

"We could go and intercept them," Daisy agreed. "And get the money that would have been paid to Willingham too."

"How do you propose we do that?"

"We could give them a *different* book?"

Ellie shook her head. "The one we recovered is very recognizable. It's got golden covers and is covered in gems. I'm sure they'll know what it's supposed to look like, and I doubt we'll be able to find something similar enough to fool them at such short notice."

"What if we take the real book, then," Tess said, "and hand it over, then get it back at gunpoint as soon as they've paid us?"

"That could work," Daisy mused. "I like the idea of highway robbery. But one has to assume that whoever is making the exchange will be suspicious of being double-crossed. They might even be planning to do exactly the same thing to Willingham, to avoid paying him. There's no honor among thieves."

"The only way to win that situation is to be the side with the most weapons." Tess sighed. "The three of us could go, and we could ask Harry to be the one to meet with the envoy. Four should be enough."

"Won't they be expecting to meet Willingham?"

"Perhaps," Tess conceded. "If they don't know what he looks like, they'll assume Harry is Willingham. If they *do* know Willingham, Harry can tell them he's Willingham's envoy."

"Where do you suppose this 'drinking well' is, though?" Ellie frowned. "There's no point in making these plans if we don't know where the meeting is to take place."

"Willingham's a lazy man," Tess said. "And dawn is a very early time to be meeting someone. I bet it's somewhere close to his house, so he won't have to bother with a carriage, or travel a great distance."

"It could be the drinking well in Hyde Park," Daisy said. "The one up in the woods at the northwest corner. There's a little clearing nearby that men use for duels."

"How do you know that?" Tess marveled.

"Because Devlin met Lord Crowley there a few months ago at dawn to fight over which one of them would propose to Lydia Braithwaite. They fought with their fists, instead of with pistols, and Devlin lost, obviously, because Crowley married Lydia last week at St. George's."

"That's an excellent guess," Ellie said. "Willingham regularly walks in Hyde Park, so he'd definitely want to meet somewhere familiar. Let's assume that's the place."

"Will you tell Harry and get him to come? I'm sure he'll do anything you ask," Daisy teased.

"I'm sure he'll do anything that sounds remotely dangerous and exciting," Ellie countered wryly, "whether I ask him or not. But yes, I'll tell him to meet us at the north gate with the book just before dawn tomorrow."

"Do you think he'll lend me his sword stick?" Daisy wondered.

"He might. Although we might do better to be armed with pistols, instead of blades."

"Agreed."

Chapter Twenty-Six

Ellie couldn't tell if her teeth were chattering with cold or with nerves as she, Tess, and Daisy waited at the northern entrance to Hyde Park.

She'd sent a note to Harry, but still let out a sigh of relief when she saw him ambling down the street toward them, the silver top of his cane glinting in the pale moonlight.

It was still dark, although a faint sliver of lighter gray sky over to the east showed that dawn wasn't far away.

Harry swept the three of them an elegant bow. "Morning. Ready for another adventure?"

"Ready to see justice done," Ellie said.

The sight of him had her stomach in knots, but she forced herself to think of the mission ahead, and not how much she wanted to wrap her arms around his middle and be enfolded in a comforting hug.

"Harry, you wait a few minutes, then make your way to the well. The three of us will be hiding in the trees, and as soon as you have the payment for the book, we'll make our move."

"You've remembered rule number three?" he asked.

"Of course. We're all armed. And hopefully you'll just be meeting a single person, so they'll be outnumbered." She glanced at his sword cane. "Do you have a pistol?"

"No. But don't worry, I trust the three of you to protect me. Now off you go. And good luck."

Ellie smiled. "I thought you didn't believe in luck?"

He patted his breast pocket, where the outline of the little book interrupted the perfect line of his jacket. "I have it right here."

They left him at the gate, and took a wide route through the trees, circling the back of the glade where the meeting was to take place.

The drinking well wasn't so much a well as a small spring that rose from the ground that had been edged with wooden planks to form a pool that trickled away toward the Serpentine. The water was said to be sweet-tasting and beneficial to health, and in the summer months an old lady sat at a table beneath the trees, offering glasses to drink from and ready-filled bottles for people to take home.

There was no sign of an attendant now, nor anyone else, and Ellie was glad of her spectacles to negotiate the shadows as they moved silently between the trees. All three of them had dressed in their darkest clothing.

Tess positioned herself behind a large oak, Daisy hid by a stump in a huge bramble patch, and Ellie made her way to the opposite side of the clearing and concealed herself in a thick stand of beech trees.

The silvery light grew brighter as they waited, and Harry appeared between the trees, walking at an unhurried pace. He stopped at the little spring and checked his pocket watch, then leaned against a tree to wait.

A dark figure wearing a long cloak appeared on the narrow path, and Ellie bit back a curse when two more hooded forms followed. She squinted, trying to see if she recognized the person in front, then choked back a gasp as the figure removed their cloak to reveal a dress instead of breeches, and decidedly *feminine* curves.

The woman came to an abrupt stop when she saw Harry, and her two accomplices—both men—drew blades from within their clothing.

Harry straightened, but didn't appear concerned. His composure was impressive.

The woman was beautiful, with high, angular cheekbones and full, almost pouting lips that curved in a slow smile as she regarded Harry.

"*Enrico? Dio, può essere? Tesoro mio, cosa ci fai qui?*"

She gave an incredulous laugh as she stepped closer and peered at Harry's face.

Harry's own features relaxed into an easy smile.

"*Buongiorno, Sofia. Che deliziosa sorpresa.*" He switched to English, presumably for Ellie's benefit. "And I could ask *you* the same question. The last time I last saw you was at Pauline Bonaparte's birthday party. You were about to steal her letters—and her lover, if I remember correctly."

Ellie's eyes widened. Harry knew this woman! She was another thief!

"I succeeded too," Sofia chuckled. "It was a shame you didn't stay long enough to help me celebrate."

She waved her hand, and her two accomplices lowered their weapons. Her dark eyes roved hungrily over Harry's body, and Ellie felt a sharp stab of jealous outrage. This gorgeous Italian was clearly one of his criminal acquaintances. Had they been lovers, as well as associates? The woman's familiar tones certainly suggested they'd been close.

"But you are not the man I came here to meet," Sofia

purred, taking another step closer to Harry, but still maintaining a sensible distance from his sword stick.

Harry shrugged. "I know. You were expecting Willingham, but as you can see, he's not here. I have the book you came for, though."

"He entrusted you with it?"

Harry raised his brows, and she let out a delighted laugh. "You stole it from him! How delicious."

"I'm afraid so. Old habits die hard."

"Let me see it. But first, drop your cane."

Harry released his hold on the silver-topped sword stick and let it fall to the grass, then reached into his waistcoat.

"Slowly," Sofia cautioned. "Paolo and Luca are very good at throwing those knives. I haven't forgotten what a tricky player you are, my love."

The two thugs raised their weapons again, silently warning him not to draw his own blade from his coat, and Harry smiled at their suspicion. He slid his fingers into the front of his jacket, pulled the little book from the inside breast pocket, and flipped open the cloth wrapping so that the golden covers glinted in the dawn light.

"There," he said easily. "I haven't cheated you. Now, if you don't mind, I'd like to see the money."

Sofia tilted her head to one side with a wicked little pout. "Money? Why do I need to pay you when I can just take it from you?"

She withdrew a wicked little pistol from her skirts, which she cocked with a click and leveled at his chest.

Harry actually *smiled* at the threat, as if he'd fully expected her to double-cross him. Perhaps, Ellie thought, he was remembering rule number seven: *If it looks too good to be true, it probably is.* This Sofia was clearly a very slippery character.

"Always so greedy," he chided. "But I'm afraid I'm going to have to disappoint you. I've brought some friends of my own, you see."

He slid the book safely back inside his jacket, then turned to the spot where Ellie was hiding—he must have known precisely where she'd stationed herself.

Ellie obligingly stepped out from behind the trees and pointed her pistol at the irritating woman's heart.

"Good morning," she said crisply.

Sofia gestured at her two accomplices, urging them to do something, but Tess and Daisy also appeared from their hiding places, each brandishing a pistol, and Sofia cursed softly in Italian, clearly realizing she'd been outmaneuvered.

Harry gave a charming shrug. "It seems we're at an *impasse*."

Sofia's lip curled, but she didn't lower her aim from Harry's chest. "What do you suggest?"

"You should leave."

"Without the book? I can't do that. The man who's paying me to deliver it will be most unhappy." She slid Ellie a sideways, speculative glance, clearly weighing the odds of being hit from that distance, then turned back to Harry.

"I have to have that book."

Whatever Harry had been about to say, it was interrupted by a dark-clad figure exploding from the undergrowth to Sofia's left.

"Hoi!" he bellowed. "Over here!"

Sofia swung toward the noise reflexively, and her pistol went off as her finger tightened on the trigger.

Ellie recognized Ambrose at the same moment as Harry clutched his chest with a shocked, incredulous shout.

"You shot me!"

He staggered backward and fell hard against the tree, then crumpled to the ground as his legs gave out, and Ellie didn't stop to think. She fired her own pistol at Sofia, just as Ambrose tackled the woman to the ground.

Chapter Twenty-Seven

Ellie swore in impotent fury as her skirts got caught in the undergrowth.

She had to get to Harry.

Ambrose and Sofia were rolling over and over in the wet grass, the Italian screaming invectives as she hit at Hugo's head and body with her pistol, but Ellie rushed past them and fell to her knees beside Harry.

Dread and terror coursed through her as she saw his pale face. He seemed to be choking, gasping for breath.

Dear God, where had he been hit? She had to stop the bleeding.

"Harry! God, don't die!" she croaked.

He was clutching at his chest, and she pushed his hands aside and slid her palms over the front of his waistcoat, desperately searching for a wound, fully expecting to encounter the sticky wetness of blood. His dark-colored waistcoat made it almost impossible to see.

He was trying to say something, his chest heaving in great labored gusts.

"Oh, God," she panted. "Lie still. I can't find where you've been hit."

Her heart was beating impossibly fast. God, this had all been her idea. Why hadn't they just returned the book to Bullock and collected the payment? Her stupid need to uncover the whole story had led to this disaster. Harry was dying! And she hadn't even told him how much she cared for him.

"Harry, I—"

"Shh." His hand closed over hers, stilling its frantic movement and shutting off her impetuous declaration. "Ellie," he rasped. "Stop. It's all right." He reached up and caught the back of her neck with his other hand, forcing her to look into his eyes instead of down at his chest.

"I'm all right," he said calmly. "I've not been hit. I'm just winded, I swear."

His steady gaze held hers, but her head refused to believe it. Maybe he'd lost so much blood he couldn't even feel the injury anymore? Oh, God.

"She shot you! I saw you fall." Her voice was a high, reedy squeak.

He pushed himself up a little straighter, and the rational part of her brain finally began to notice that his breathing was easier. The color had returned to his face. "I'm fine, truly."

He slid his hand into the front of his jacket and pulled out the tiny Book of Hours. Ellie sank back on her heels with a gasp. The central gold panel was cratered in, the ball from the pistol lodged in the thick leather binding that lay beneath the golden cover.

Harry's incredulous gaze met her own, and his face broke into a smile. "I don't believe it! Look at that."

Relief flooded through her like a tidal wave, and she put her hand to her throat. Now that the immediate danger was over, she felt sick and horribly shaky.

"You must be the luckiest man in London!" she wheezed.

"Or this is the luckiest book," he countered with a grin. "Bloody Hell, that was a close call."

His eyes flicked to her lips, and suddenly Ellie didn't care that they had witnesses. She leaned in and pressed a brief, hard kiss to his mouth. He started to respond, but a noise behind them made her reluctantly pull back and look round.

Hugo had clearly managed to disarm a furious Sofia. She lay face down in the grass, her hands held behind her back as Hugo straddled her. Her two thugs were being held at pistol point by Tess and Daisy.

Harry groaned as he slowly got to his feet. "My chest feels like an elephant's used me as a chair."

"You're probably going to have a terrible bruise," Ellie murmured. "Are you sure you haven't broken any ribs?"

"I'm sure. But I might as well use my cane."

She retrieved it from the grass, and he leaned on it for support as they hobbled over to Sofia.

Hugo tugged her to her feet, but kept hold of her wrists with one hand while he patted her down with the other.

Sofia spat an incomprehensible stream of Italian at him, which was almost certainly uncomplimentary, as he thrust a hand into her cloak and pulled out an envelope bulging with paper bills.

"The money you were supposed to give to Willingham?" Hugo panted. "I think we'll have that."

Sofia turned furious eyes on Harry.

"I didn't mean to shoot you," she growled, tossing her head toward Hugo. "This fool distracted me."

Ellie curled her lip. "You could have killed him."

"It was an accident!" Sofia protested. "And *you* shot *me*!"

Ellie blinked. Everything had happened in such a blur, she could barely remember firing her weapon. "I thought I missed."

Sofia shook her head and glared at Hugo. "You got my arm. If this fool will release me, I can see how bad it is."

At Harry's nod, Hugo released Sofia's wrists, and she pushed down the neck of her dress to reveal a deep gash on her shoulder that was oozing blood.

Ellie swallowed a sudden flash of nausea and guilt. Her pistol had inflicted that wound. She'd never shot another person before, but she'd acted instinctively, in Harry's defense. She'd do the same again.

She pulled a clean handkerchief from her pocket and gestured to Sofia.

"It's only a scrape. You won't need stitches, but you do need to stop the bleeding."

Sofia submitted to the assistance with a sniff, and Ellie tied the cotton cloth around the wound. She didn't bother to be particularly gentle—it was hard to forgive the near-miss, whether it was accidental or not.

"Now," Harry said, "as exciting as this little reunion has been, I think you and your friends should leave now, Sofia."

Sofia scowled, but clearly accepted when she was beaten. "Bonaparte's brother will be extremely displeased if I don't bring him that book."

"Perhaps you can think of a way to double-cross him the same way you were going to double-cross Willingham?" Ellie suggested sweetly.

Harry smiled at her sarcasm, but addressed Sofia. "You can't win every hand. Go back to Italy. Nothing good ever comes from meddling in politics, especially when it involves the Bonapartes."

Sofia gave a petulant toss of her head. "You may be

right. And from what I have seen of England, it is a horrible place and the people are not at all hospitable." She glared at Ellie, who glared right back. "I can't wait to see the sun again, and eat food that is not *disgustoso*."

She turned with a dramatic twirl of her skirts and sent her two accomplices a scornful look. "What good were you two, eh? Two scarecrows would have done a better job."

Both men looked sheepish. Luca, or possibly Paolo, pointed at Daisy's pistol.

"She would have shot us if we'd tried to help you. I can tell by the look in her eye. *Quella donna è spaventosa*."

"He says you're terrifying," Harry translated to Daisy with a chuckle.

Daisy looked delighted. "I am indeed. Now, go on, start walking. I want to go home and have some breakfast."

Luca, or Paolo, sent her a charming grin and said something in rapid Italian.

"What did he say?" Daisy demanded suspiciously.

"He said he'd like to give you his blade, because he admires any woman who is able to get the better of him," Harry said. "I think you've made a conquest, Miss Hamilton."

Daisy's cheeks turned pink as Paolo or Luca, whichever one it was, bent and placed his knife on the ground like an offering. He stepped back and sent her a jaunty salute.

Daisy gave him a regal nod. "Thank you. I will treasure it always."

With a disgusted snort, Sofia turned on her heel and started tramping back along the path, irritably dusting the leaves from her skirts as she did so. Luca and Paolo fell into place behind her. Only when all three of them were out of sight did Tess and Daisy finally lower their weapons.

Ellie heaved a loud sigh of relief and bent over, hands on her knees. "My goodness, what a morning! I'm so sorry I convinced you all to do this."

Harry shook his head. "It was worth it. How much money is there in that envelope, Hugo?"

Ambrose thumbed through it quickly. "I'd say at least three hundred pounds. Maybe more."

"Worth being shot at." Harry grinned, but Ellie sent him a scowl for being so flippant. No amount of money would have been worth his life.

Daisy glanced between Harry and Hugo. "I'm assuming you two know one another?"

The two men shared an amused look. "We're old friends," Harry confirmed.

Hugo let out a wheeze. "Who are you calling old, you cheeky devil?" He rubbed his side with a pained grunt. "Damn me, but I'm getting too old for rolling around on the grass with ladies of dubious virtue. I think I've cracked a few ribs."

Ellie crossed to him and offered her arm. "Come on, you need to sit down." She glanced at Harry. "You both do."

"Cobham House," Harry agreed. "Hugo, you can stay with me."

The older man's lips twitched, as if he found the offer amusing. "Much obliged."

Ellie turned to her two friends. "I'll go with them. I'll see you back at King and Company."

"Very good." Tess smiled.

Daisy bent to retrieve the knife her unexpected admirer had left her. She turned it over in her hands with a pleased expression.

"On balance, it has been an excellent morning, don't you think? Another case closed for King and Company."

Chapter Twenty-Eight

"You don't think Sofia will try to get revenge, do you?" Ellie asked as she and Harry ushered Hugo into the library of Cobham House. He sank into a chair with a pained grunt.

Harry shook his head. "No. She's been in the game long enough to know not to waste time on a losing streak."

"But do you think she meant to kill you? She aimed right for your heart. If not for that book—"

"I doubt it. When I knew her in Italy, she was just a petty thief, not the sort to commit murder. But who knows? People can change, and not for the better. I'm just glad the three of you were there to save me."

Harry rang the bellpull, and when a servant appeared, he requested tea and toast for the three of them, and laudanum for Hugo.

The older man took a few drops of the painkiller in his tea, and it seemed to take almost immediate effect; he closed his eyes and started to doze, while Ellie sat with Harry on a deep velvet sofa on the opposite side of the room.

"I know it's none of my business," she whispered,

careful not to disturb Hugo, "but was Sofia once a lover of yours? That might explain why she felt so bitter toward you. If you left her, I mean."

As hard as it was to sympathize with the other woman, it was all too easy to imagine how hurt and rejected *she* would feel when Harry moved on to another lover in the future—as he inevitably would.

Harry met her gaze. "She and I had a brief affair. Many years ago, now. I don't think she still holds a torch for me, but she does love drama, and excitement. And perhaps seeing me with someone as lovely as you at my back was hard for her to take."

Ellie shook her head, even as she blushed. "I admit, I was jealous, thinking of you with her. She's very beautiful. And as a fellow thief, you must have plenty in common."

Harry glanced over at a sleeping Hugo, then reached up to brush her cheek.

"Believe me, she doesn't hold a candle to you. She's scheming and opportunistic, and while I know you can be delightfully sneaky yourself, you don't have the ugly, mercenary streak that she does."

"I can't believe I actually *shot* her, though. I'm never normally so violent!"

"I'm glad you defended me with such ferocity." His face took on a wicked look. "In fact, it makes me think of all the other things you can do with such passion."

She sent him a chiding frown. "You're in no state to be exerting yourself."

"I could be at death's door, and I'd still muster up the energy to make love with you. I bet my chest is bruised. Won't you kiss it better for me?"

"You are a very bad man."

"True. But I'm yours. That has to count for something?"

Her heart gave a foolish gallop at his words, but she told herself not to put too much store in them. He was only being glib. Such things came easily to him. He didn't mean it.

"Perhaps. Do you know, I've been practicing a few Italian phrases?"

"Such as?"

"*Vorrei che Harry mi baciasse.*"

His brows rose. "*I wish Harry would kiss me.* That's an excellent one. Allow me to grant your wish."

He leaned in, and Ellie met him halfway, opening her lips beneath his in sheer relief that he was there, alive. She'd been so close to losing him, and her heart gave a painful squeeze at the thought of a world without him in it.

She ran her hands over his chest, needing the reassurance that he truly wasn't hurt, and her fingertip caught in the hole left by the near-fatal bullet. Her heart missed a beat, and she kissed him fiercely, desperately, pouring all her relief and gladness into it. Realization washed over her like a rogue wave.

Dear God, she loved him!

Ellie gasped against his mouth at the shocking revelation. She—sensible, law-abiding, risk-averse Eleanor Law—had fallen irrevocably in love with a nameless, shameless scoundrel!

Oh, this was a disaster.

Their case had been solved. The Book of Hours would be returned to Bullock—albeit with a little damage to the front cover. What if Harry decided to move on to pastures new? What if today's near-miss convinced him that life was more important than solving crimes? What if he decided to take the easy route and simply enjoy his riches without risking his neck?

She'd almost told him she loved him, but now she was perversely glad she hadn't, because she had no idea whether he felt anything remotely similar for her. He was infuriatingly difficult to read. He'd obviously found her attractive enough to make love to her, so he presumably desired her physically, but would he lose interest now that she'd given herself to him?

Ellie gave a hopeless little moan and kissed him again, savoring the precious moment as if it were the last. The embrace turned a little wild as he responded, his tongue delving deeper as he pressed her back against the cushions of the sofa.

"Let's go upstairs," he whispered, "and I'll show you how glad I am to be alive."

"Yes."

He stood, and had just pulled her to her feet when Hugo jolted awake with a snort, and the two of them swung guiltily toward him.

"Oof. Must've dozed off." Hugo's voice was slow and a little slurred, presumably the effects of the laudanum. He ran his hand over his face, then winced in pain as he clearly tweaked his injury. "Harry, m'boy, I think I'll go and have a little lie down upstairs."

Harry exhaled at the interruption, but he released Ellie's hand, and went to help his friend. "Come on then, up with you. I'll see about getting a doctor to check you over."

"You're the very best of nephews," Hugo murmured.

Ellie blinked, certain she'd misheard. "The best what?"

Hugo looked immediately guilty, as if he realized he'd said something he shouldn't.

"Did you say he's your nephew?" Ellie repeated.

Hugo let out a wheezing chuckle as he pushed himself to his feet. He looked like a naughty puppy. "Well, that's done it. The cat's out of the bag. Yes, Harry here is my nephew."

Ellie studied his face, then glanced at Harry, and she couldn't believe she hadn't made the connection before. Of *course* the two of them were related. They had the same cheeky dimples, the same cocky, charming manner. They even shared the same gestures.

"So your name is Harry Ambrose?" she said to Harry.

"Not exactly." For the first time since she'd met him, Harry actually looked uncomfortable, and Hugo laughed.

"No. His *full* name is—"

"Stop! I haven't told her!" Harry blustered, but it was too late.

"—Henry James Charles Brooke," Hugo said happily. "And he's the twelfth Earl of Cobham. Isn't that right, my boy?"

Chapter Twenty-Nine

Ellie glanced at Harry, sure he was about to burst out laughing and chide Hugo for the joke, but instead he sent his uncle a filthy glare.

"I wasn't ready to tell her!"

"It's true?" she gasped. "Wait . . . Is this *your* house? Are you the 'lost earl'?"

Harry ran his hands through his hair. "I am."

She backed away from him as disbelief melted into fury at his deception.

"You lied to me, you scoundrel! When we first met, I asked you what your name was and you said you didn't know it."

"No," he said quickly, holding up his hands in a placating gesture. "What I said was, 'I wish I could tell you,' which is *technically* the truth. You interpreted that to mean that I didn't know my own name, but it also meant that I *couldn't* tell you at that moment. I didn't know you. I couldn't trust you with the truth."

"Ohhh! You are so good at twisting words! You lied by omission, if nothing else. You still deceived me."

"I know, and I'm sorry, but now you *do* know, and I'm

glad. I didn't like misleading you. I almost told you the truth a hundred times."

His expression was open, pleading, and despite Ellie telling herself not to fall for his practiced charms, she couldn't help but believe him.

She pointed at Hugo. "Explain to me how this came about, please."

Hugo leaned back against the arm of the chair he'd just vacated.

"With pleasure. Harry's father, James, was my older brother. He and Harry's mother, Mary, both died of influenza while Harry was away at boarding school. Harry was just fifteen. As his next of kin, I was named as his guardian, but only a few days after their funeral, I got into that ridiculous duel with Barclay. Knowing I had to flee the country, I decided to take Harry with me, and broaden his education."

"You educated him in the gentlemanly art of thieving," Ellie said succinctly. "How was that a good example to set?"

Hugo shrugged. "The world's full of scoundrels. Better to know how to spot them than be cheated and taken advantage of at every turn. I taught him to be independent and resilient, and I'm proud of the way he's turned out."

"In my defense," Harry said, "the vast majority of our money has been acquired by completely legal means— earned, or fairly won on the gaming tables without cheating."

"Didn't your parents leave you any money?" Ellie asked.

Hugo crossed his arms. "Ah, well, there's the rub. It wasn't until we'd been out of the country for a few years that I realized I might have made things a little difficult. I'd appointed men I trusted to run the estate in our absence, but as time went on, it was becoming harder and harder to prove Harry's identity.

"Barclay refused to die, curse him, and Harry's appearance changed. The man he became in Italy was almost unrecognizable from the fifteen-year-old schoolboy who'd left England, and the people who might have been able to vouch for him, like his old tutor, and his nursemaid, began to die off."

Hugo shrugged. "As soon as I heard that Barclay was at death's door, I decided to come back to England and have Harry reclaim his rightful place in society. It's about time he started living as the Earl of Cobham."

Harry sent her a pleading look. "But to do that, I need to prove who I am—which is precisely the kind of challenging case King and Company is famous for solving."

Ellie shook her head, her mind in a whirl. "So that's why you came to us. You wanted to see how competent we were! Oh, I *knew* you were a charlatan. All that rot about wanting a reason to get out of bed in the morning. Ugh!"

"No!" Harry said, then he smiled wryly. "Well, maybe that's a little bit true. I wanted to see your investigative skills in action, and you've impressed me no end. Please say you'll help me?"

Ellie didn't know what to think. "Are you going to pay us?"

"Of course. I wouldn't dream of cheating you."

"Ha!"

He sent her another pleading look, the kind that melted her heart and made it almost impossible to refuse him anything, curse him.

"Please say yes. I've been playing a role, using a fake name, for half my life. I want to stop pretending to be someone else and start being me, Harry Brooke."

Ellie crossed her arms around her middle. "How do I know you're not just some charlatan who's come here *pretending* to be the lost earl? How do I know you didn't kill the real earl, and plan to cheat your way into his title and his fortune?"

"I don't blame you for being skeptical. It's a ridiculous story, the kind one only hears about in fairy tales. Like 'Puss in Boots.' But if you take the case, I know you'll unearth enough evidence to prove I'm telling the truth. If you don't, and still think I'm a liar, I'll leave London and you'll never need to see me ever again."

Ellie's heart did an odd little jump at his fervent ultimatum. He sounded so convincing, but natural caution made her wary.

Ten minutes ago, she'd been about to make love with Henri Bonheur. Now, she didn't know what to feel about Harry Brooke.

"I'll discuss your proposal with my partners," she said stiffly. "If you'll excuse me, I'd like to go back to Lincoln's Inn Fields."

Harry seemed to accept that she'd reached the limits of her endurance. With a nod, he went to arrange for the horses to be hitched to the carriage, and in no time at all she was seated on the padded bench looking down at his worried face.

"Please don't take too long to come to a decision," he said softly. "You know you're the best investigators in London. Better than Bow Street by a mile. Nobody else will do a job as good as you."

She compressed her lips at his flattery, even as her heart beat at his proximity.

Ugh. Had he only been flirting with her to make her more likely to help him? Had his lovemaking been a cynical ploy to gain her allegiance? She hated the fact that she was questioning him, but she refused to avoid the possibility, even if it was painful.

She'd dealt with too many cases where the truth was blindingly obvious to an outsider, but invisible to those closest to the problem. Emotions clouded good judgment, and she needed some distance from Harry to get her thoughts in order.

"Here, take these with you," he said abruptly.

He reached into his coat and handed her the Book of Hours, and the envelope of banknotes they'd confiscated from Sofia.

The morning's events already seemed a lifetime ago.

"I trust you to return that to Bullock." He smiled. "And as to the reward, it's only fair that you three have it. You saved my life, after all."

He kissed her hand, then rapped the side of the coach with his knuckles—the panel that bore the painted crest of his family—*if* his tale was true.

"Goodbye, Ellie. Don't make me wait too long."

Chapter Thirty

"The lost earl of Cobham?" Daisy said. "It sounds like the title of a bad Drury Lane melodrama."

"I know," Ellie sighed. "Should we believe him, or not?"

"The only way to find out if he's telling the truth is to take the case and start investigating," Tess said reasonably.

Ellie glared at the basil plant in the corner. She'd watered it yesterday, since its leaves had started to droop, and now it looked remarkably jaunty. Like its previous owner.

"I'm sure there have been other examples of people returning from the dead," Daisy said. "Do you know any particular legal cases, Ellie?"

"My father dealt with one a few years ago, but I don't remember the details. People often think that once someone's been missing for a few years it's easy for their family to have them declared dead, but it's not necessarily true. The courts look at each individual case and assess how likely it is that the person is dead. If the missing person was known to have been on a ship that sank, for example, or was last seen wounded, during a terrible battle, then the likelihood that they're deceased is high.

"But if someone just disappeared while traveling abroad, there's a chance that they might still be alive. In some cases, courts have required an absence of more than a decade before they finally grant permission for the estate to be distributed to other parties."

"Harry's been gone for almost that long," Tess said. "But his family never had him declared dead."

Ellie nodded. "Petitions usually happen when there's property involved, or when a wife wants to marry someone else. If she's officially declared a widow, then she can't commit adultery or bigamy, even if the 'dead' husband turns up alive later on."

"That makes sense," Daisy said. "Although think how conflicted the poor woman would feel! What a situation to find yourself in." She shuddered.

"The courts aren't usually in a hurry to declare someone dead," Ellie continued. "Especially if that person is heir to an estate and a title. If it was a young, unmarried man, with no legitimate sons, then there would be a chance of him marrying and having a son while he was absent. They'd need to be sure there were no legitimate living heirs."

Tess snorted. "That's why it took so long to name Justin the new Duke of Wansford. Two years to find him and name him the heir!"

"But surely it shouldn't be too difficult to prove Harry is—or isn't—the earl?" Daisy said. "There must be documentation, like a record of his birth in the parish register."

"I'm sure there is, but all that proves is that the eleventh earl and his wife had a male child named Henry. We still have to prove that Harry is that same child who left the country, aged fifteen."

Daisy tilted her head. "Even parish records can lie. After all, my birth certificate lists the Duke of Dalkeith as my father, when everyone knows my *real* sire was the Italian fencing master my mother ran off with."

Daisy's tone was matter-of-fact, and even though Ellie knew she wasn't bothered by her unusual parentage, she still sent her a commiserating look. The duke might acknowledge Daisy as his legitimate daughter, but he was a cold and distant man who had little time for any of his children, including her three elder half brothers.

"I'm surprised Harry didn't just forge some documents," Tess said with a smile. "He must have the criminal connections to do such a thing. Perhaps the fact that he *doesn't* have any proof is actually a mark in his favor?"

Ellie sniffed. "I'm sure he has plenty of fake passports and travel papers, considering how many different aliases he has. Henri Bonheur. Enrico Castellini. The list goes on. But even if he does have a real passport for Henry Brooke, that doesn't prove he's the same man either. There's no description of the person on the paper, just their name. A judge would argue that he could have stolen it from the real recipient."

"There must be someone who can vouch for him, though. What about an old schoolfriend? Or a teacher from school?"

"Or a family portrait?" Daisy suggested.

"A portrait might show a family likeness, but it would have been painted before he turned fifteen, and there's rarely enough detail in them to make a strong enough case," Tess said. "It could show a younger brother, or an illegitimate child. Unless Harry has some obviously distinguishing mark, like a visible scar, or a birthmark?"

Ellie tapped her cheek. "I don't know if you've noticed, but he does have the most extraordinary eyes. One looks blue, while the other looks green-brown. I doubt a painter would have captured that useful detail, though."

"I hadn't noticed," Tess admitted. "I've been too busy admiring his tailoring."

"We haven't *all* been gazing into his eyes like a lovesick puppy, like you have, Ellie," Daisy teased.

"I don't look at him like that!"

Daisy made a comical face. "Oh no? Perhaps it's me that needs to wear spectacles, then. Because I'm sure you go all misty-eyed whenever you look at him."

"Is it really that obvious?" Ellie was appalled.

"That you're in love with him?" Tess grinned. "I'm afraid so. To us, at least. But we've known you for years, so we know you the best of anyone."

Ellie dropped her forehead to her desk and groaned. "It's a disaster. How did this happen? Last week I disapproved of everything about him, but yesterday I thought my heart would stop beating if he was dead."

"At least you fell in love with him before you knew there was a chance that he's an earl." Daisy shrugged. "Nobody could accuse you of being after his title."

"I haven't told him." Ellie raised her head. "And don't you dare say anything about it to him either. He isn't in love with me, and even if he was, what good could come of it? If we prove he's just a charlatan trying to sneak into the role of earl, then he's going to leave London and never come back.

"And if we *do* prove he's the earl, he'll be the toast of the town. The prodigal son, miraculously restored to his rightful place. The single women will be all over him like wasps on a honey sandwich. He'll have his pick of brides. If he chooses to marry, he can do much better than me, who has neither a fortune nor a title. Whatever happens, there's no future for the two of us."

Tess sighed. "He certainly plays his cards close to his chest, but perhaps that's just habit. He's so used to concealing his true intentions it's probably become second nature."

"He definitely desires you," Daisy added. "He never takes his eyes from you whenever you're together. And he likes you too. He laughs at your jokes, and appreciates your talents."

"Yes, but that doesn't necessarily mean he *loves* me, does it?"

"Perhaps he's been too distracted by his quest to prove his name to give the matter real consideration. Men, in general, aren't terribly good at saying what they feel. They just assume you *know*, or they use strange, often incomprehensible gestures to show their regard."

"The way cats show their love by bringing you dead mice." Daisy grinned.

"What a lovely image." Ellie grimaced. "God, why can't our hearts be as sensible as our brains?"

Daisy laughed. "It keeps things interesting, I suppose. Just think of all the drama we'd have missed out on if people didn't do stupid things for love. There'd be no opera, no Shakespeare. No Lancelot and Guinevere, no Antony and Cleopatra. All those poets like Byron and Shelley would have had to get proper jobs, instead of mooning about, composing sonnets to someone's eyelashes."

"It would certainly cut the number of cases at the Old Bailey." Ellie smiled, rallying. "Half of those are crimes of passion. Or committed because of love."

Tess chuckled. "And the gossip sheets would have nothing to write about, except fashions and the weather."

Daisy tossed her dagger into the air, then snatched it back with impressive dexterity. She'd taken to throwing it across the room at a playing card she'd affixed to the door, and Ellie winced every time the blade skewered the poor queen of hearts. It was hard not to remember the night she'd learned to cheat with Harry.

"Well, I think you're worrying over nothing," Daisy said. "As strange as it seems to say I trust a man as unashamedly conniving as Harry, I *do* trust that he's telling the truth about his family."

Ellie sighed. "We'll see."

"Write to him and tell him we'll take the case."

"We should charge him double," Ellie muttered. "For emotional aggravation."

"Actually, I was going to suggest that he pay us with his time and skills," Tess said.

"What do you mean?"

"Do you remember last year, when Edmond Rundell asked us to listen out for information about a jewel that had been stolen from his workshop?"

"An aquamarine." Ellie nodded.

"Well, one of the girls who works at The Golden Ball—that new gaming hell in St. James's—told me a player by the name of Christopher Blake put up a large blue gemstone as collateral in a card game last week."

Daisy raised her brows. "You think it's the one taken from Rundell, Bridge and Rundell?"

Tess gave an elegant shrug. "There can't be many stones of that size knocking around London. It's been several years since the theft. The culprit probably thinks enough time has passed for the jewel to resurface without arousing suspicion."

"Did this Blake lose the jewel?"

"No. He won a purebred Arabian stallion from Lord Kidner, and kept hold of the gem. Kitty said he's an excellent player, even in his cups."

"Harry could win the jewel from Blake," Ellie said firmly.

"My thoughts exactly. If his skill at cards is as good as you say, then he has the best chance of anyone of beating him. And if Blake's 'luck' is down to the fact that he cheats, then Harry should be able to recognize it—and counter it with a few tricks of his own."

Daisy nodded. "If the jewel is the one taken from Rundell, then we'll get a reward for its safe return. And if it *isn't*, we can sell it to Rundell, or another jeweler, for a tidy profit."

"Agreed." Ellie smiled. "I'll tell Harry those are our terms for taking his case."

Chapter Thirty-One

Ellie glanced sideways at Harry. She'd told him to meet her at Harriet Winthrop's party, and the sight of him, looking so effortlessly elegant in formal eveningwear, made her stomach flip. "So you agree?"

His lips curved as he glanced down at her. "To 'acquiring' the gem? Of course. It's a small price to pay for reclaiming my identity."

Ellie couldn't argue with that. She'd never really considered what it must be like to not have the security of a name, but she imagined it might be quite disconcerting.

"And besides," he continued silkily, "I couldn't possibly refuse such a mutually beneficial arrangement."

The tone of his words suggested he wasn't merely talking about work, and Ellie tried not to blush. Working with him would be a lot easier if he wasn't so attractive. And if she didn't know exactly what lay beneath those beautiful clothes of his.

Her face heated at the memory of his skin sliding against hers, the look on his face when he'd joined his body with hers. Even now, more unsure of his identity than she'd ever been, she wanted him.

His insistence that he was the Lost Earl seemed so genuine that it was becoming increasingly difficult to believe him a charlatan, but rule number seven could still be applied to Harry himself.

If it looks too good to be true, it probably is. She would be foolish to get her hopes up.

But it was hard to be formal when they'd been so intimate. A new, reckless part of her wanted to drag him into the nearest storage room or broom closet and kiss him senseless, exactly as they'd done at Willingham's. She wanted to beg him to make good on his promise to make love to her up against the wall, but that would only complicate matters. They had a job to do.

"You look very lovely tonight."

She accepted the compliment with a smile. She was wearing a dress she'd borrowed from Tess, a lovely lavender-blue. It was another of Madame Lefèvre's creations, and although it was nowhere near as revealing as the emerald-green silk she'd worn to Willingham's, it was still different enough from the dresses she usually wore to have made her the subject of numerous admiring male glances.

Gentlemen who'd never paid her any attention before were suddenly looking her way, and instead of ducking into a corner to hide, she found herself lifting her chin and smiling back at them.

Was her increased confidence because she was no longer a virgin? Had the experience imbued her with some kind of magical feminine power?

Certainly, she looked at every man now with new eyes, trying to imagine what they'd look like beneath their clothes, or wondering what making love to them would be like.

Unfortunately, most of those musings led to a repulsed

shudder. None of them could compete with the memory of Harry.

Curse him.

"I see your cousin is here," Harry said softly, breaking into her thoughts. He sent a charming smile toward a pair of elderly matrons, who'd passed by on at least two previous occasions. Ellie recognized them as Prudence and Constance Davies, great-aunts of her old schoolfriend Carys Davies, now Carys Montgomery. The two were inveterate gossips. Heaven only knew what rumors they would be cooking up, seeing her talking so intensely with Harry.

"Edward? Yes."

"He seems like a nice chap."

"He *is* a nice chap. In fact, he's everything I admire in a gentleman. He's selfless, kind, honorable—"

"—law abiding, morally upstanding." Harry rolled his eyes and pretended to yawn. "I'm surprised you haven't married him."

"My parents would certainly approve of the match. He's exactly the kind of man they'd like me to wed."

"He couldn't take his eyes off you, when the two of you were talking earlier."

"You were spying on me?"

"Of course not. I was acquiring wisdom by observing. And was therefore an unwilling witness to his clumsy attempts at flirtation."

Ellie made a face. "Edward wasn't flirting with me. He doesn't think of me in that way. We're friends, that's all."

Harry's brows rose toward his hairline. "Take it from someone who knows, he definitely finds you attractive. I think he's finally realized just how rare you are. You're not just beautiful, you're as intelligent as he is, and you were right under his nose this whole time. He's thinking he's been a fool to take you for granted for all these years."

Ellie gaped at him. "That's a lot to deduce just from watching us talk."

He shrugged. "You would have made just as good a barrister as he is, if you'd been born a man. Don't you envy his career? Don't you resent the fact that you've been prohibited from doing something you would love?"

She bit her lip. He'd done it again. Pierced her straight through the heart with a disarmingly accurate comment. How did he do it? Could he read minds as well as predict playing cards?

"I have been frustrated, sometimes," she said slowly. Truthfully. "Edward started his career as an apprentice to one of my great heroes, William Garrow, the legendary defense counsel. He's attorney general for England and Wales now—and a good friend of my father's. I admire him immensely. He was the first to insist that a person was innocent until proven guilty, and that accusers and their evidence should be thoroughly tested in court."

Harry's eyes were sympathetic. "Bravo."

"I resigned myself to the fact that being a woman bars me from becoming a lawyer many years ago. But I'm glad to have forged a career that achieves very similar goals—namely, helping those in need, and the pursuit of justice for all."

Harry nodded, and she had the impression that he understood her, *knew* her, in a way no one except perhaps Tess and Daisy had ever managed. For all her closeness with Edward, he'd never once asked her a probing question like that. He'd probably never even considered things from her perspective. Harry, on the other hand, seemed able to see things from every angle.

He plucked two glasses of wine from the tray of a passing waiter and handed one to her. Ellie took a fortifying sip.

"So, when do we go to The Golden Ball and relieve this Mr. Blake of his jewel?" he asked lazily.

"We?"

"Yes. I need Carlotta again."

"Why?"

"A man who goes to a gaming club on his own immediately singles himself out as being serious about winning. It puts the other players on guard. A man with a beautiful woman on his arm, however, is there for some fun. He's easily distracted, only giving half his attention to the game. He's hardly a threat at all."

"That makes sense," Ellie said. She slid him a sly, sideways glance. "Aren't you afraid Carlotta will distract *you*?"

His eyes darkened, and his gaze fixed on her mouth as if he were thinking of kissing her. Her heart seemed to stutter.

"It's definitely a risk," he growled. "You'd have to promise to be on your best behavior."

The thought that she might actually have the power to distract him was heady, and a mischievous smile curled the corners of her mouth.

"I'll do my best," she murmured.

❧

Harry watched Ellie saunter away and clenched his hand into a fist against the urge to grab the back of her dress and pull her back against him for a kiss.

Cheeky little minx. She never would have teased him like that a week ago, but it was as if their lovemaking had brought out some previously hidden strand of wickedness in her. It was glorious to see, even though it increased her ability to be dangerously distracting.

If he had any sense at all he'd take Daisy or Tess to The Golden Ball with him instead. Someone beautiful, who'd do the job without providing any temptation. But where Ellie was concerned, he seemed to have lost his wits entirely.

He only wanted her.

Making love with her should have reduced his desire. He'd removed the mystery and anticipation. But now that he knew the sweetness he could find in her arms, and the pleasure he received from pleasuring her, he craved her even more.

He took a deep breath.

That dress she was wearing made her look delicious, and the fact that he wasn't the only man in the room who'd noticed made his blood heat even more. He tamped down a hot sweep of possessiveness, even as he glared at a foppish marquis who raised his quizzing glass to his eye and ogled her as she passed him in the doorway.

She was not his. Not yet. He couldn't make any claim on her until he'd proved who he was, and to do that he had to win that jewel.

He would not fail.

Chapter Thirty-Two

The only experience Ellie had of disreputable gaming hells was from their raucous depictions in the satirical prints displayed in shop windows.

Unlike the elite "gentlemen's" gaming clubs like White's and Brooks's, which catered only to the aristocracy, hells like The Golden Ball in Covent Garden were open to all levels of society.

Ellie couldn't quite believe she'd agreed to accompany Harry, and she tried not to stare as they ducked into a crowded taproom filled with tables and wooden booths.

The smell of the place was almost overwhelming. The odors of stale beer, hot beef pies, and strong coffee assaulted her nose, along with the dizzying mix of hot, sweaty bodies and unwashed skin unsuccessfully masked by a hundred different perfumes and pomades. It was an assault on the senses, and yet there was a thrilling vibrancy about the place that made her blood sing with excitement.

Or perhaps it was Harry's presence that had that effect. The bare wooden floorboards were sticky beneath the soles of her shoes, and a cacophony of conversation, shouts, and laughter from the men and women crammed into the room made her head spin.

It was nothing like the elegant ballrooms of Mayfair. Boisterous aristocrats who'd tumbled out of the nearby theaters rubbed shoulders with artists and merchants, shopkeepers and pickpockets. The women seemed to be a mixture of tarts and bawdy tradeswomen.

Ellie was glad that the place was so poorly lit. She'd reprised Carlotta's red curls and gaudy makeup with Daisy's help, and had opted for a dress in deep purple satin that was only slightly less revealing than the one she'd worn to Willingham's. Daisy had borrowed it from the costume room at Drury Lane Theatre, and Ellie could quite believe that it was worn by an actress playing a woman of easy virtue.

Harry, for his part, was dressed just as informally. His custom-fitted coats had been replaced by a jacket that had once been expensive but was now showing subtle signs of wear, and his diamond cravat pin had been swapped for a simple gold bar. He looked exactly as he wished to appear: as a member of the gentry or lower aristocracy keen to fritter the night away.

He seemed completely unaffected by the lively chaos, but Ellie's pulse leapt as he causally draped his arm around her waist and tugged her closer to his side as they pushed through the crowd.

"Beer?" he murmured, then laughed at her expression of disgust. "Maybe not. But I'm not ordering you a bottle of blue ruin. As much as I'd love to see you drunk and disorderly on gin, Miss Law, we need to keep our wits about us tonight."

She elbowed him in the side and chose to discount the time she, Tess, and Daisy had become utterly inebriated on stolen brandy when they were younger. "I've never been drunk and disorderly in my life."

"That's a great pity. I feel sure you're one of those people who become insatiably amorous when they're in their cups."

Ellie snorted. "You think I wouldn't be able to keep my hands off you? That I'd lose all restraint and ravish you in an alleyway?"

His eyes flared with mischief as he glanced down at her. "A man can dream."

Her stomach clenched at the mental image, but she shook her head and looked away.

He ordered a tankard of beer for himself at the bar, then steered them toward the back of the property.

The gaming rooms were only slightly less crowded than the taproom. In one, men sat around a number of wooden tables playing dice and other games of chance. The second room was given over to cards, and men and women crowded round the various games in progress, giving drunken cheers and loud groans of commiseration in reaction to the players' throws.

Ellie gave a start of surprise and put her lips to Harry's ear so she could whisper. "Do you see that portly man over there, the one with the voluptuous brunette on his lap?"

Harry nodded.

"That's Lord Sowerby. He's a judge, and a friend of my father's."

"I'm guessing that charming lady isn't his wife," Harry drawled with a grin.

"Definitely not. And that gentleman playing cards in the straw hat is the Earl of Glamorgan."

At that moment a pretty girl with golden ringlets who was carrying a tray full of pewter tankards stopped at

Ellie's elbow and leaned in. "Are you the lady sent by Mr. King?" she murmured.

Ellie nodded, but kept her face turned toward the card tables. "I am. And you must be Kitty. Tess said you'd be able to point out our friend Mr. Blake."

The barmaid tilted her chin subtly in the direction of a card table set in the far corner. It had drawn the largest crowd, but without her glasses Ellie couldn't see the players at all.

"He's over there, wearing a bottle-green coat and brown boots," Kitty said. "He's been here for an hour or so, and won most hands. He's been drinking, but he's not drunk."

"Has he wagered the jewel you saw the other night?" Harry asked.

Kitty's eyes widened in admiration as she glanced up at Harry, and her cheeks dimpled prettily. "He hasn't, but that's probably only because he hasn't needed to. The stakes haven't been high enough."

"Then it's high time someone gave him a proper game." Harry smiled, and Ellie rolled her eyes at the way Kitty giggled in response.

Honestly, did the man have to flirt with every woman in a skirt?

"Thank you, Kitty," she said. "If your information proves to be right, you'll get the five pounds we agreed."

Kitty nodded and bustled off, and they moved closer to the corner table.

Christopher Blake sat easily in his chair, and played with a speed and assurance that even to Ellie's untrained eye seemed extremely confident. His face was thin and clever-looking, but there was a cynical curl to his lips and an air of impatience about him that made her oddly uncomfortable.

The game was vingt-et-un, and Harry pressed close to her back in the crowd as they watched the next couple of rounds. His fingers still rested on her hip, and her mouth grew dry at the feel of his strong body pressing up against hers every time someone in the crowd jostled them. It was slow, delicious torture, and she thought with a silent laugh that she didn't need to be drunk to feel "insatiably amorous" toward him. He was horribly addictive.

She forced herself to stay still as he stroked aside her curls to expose her neck, then dropped his head so his chin touched her shoulder and his lips brushed her ear.

It's a game. I'm the harlot he's paid to accompany him tonight.

But her body couldn't seem to tell the difference. Her blood pulsed thickly in her veins, and for the first time in her life she envied girls like Kitty, who could take their pleasure with any man they fancied, without fear of social ostracism.

"I've seen enough," Harry murmured.

Ellie turned her head, just a fraction. Her lips were so close to his that his warm breath shivered across them.

"Is he cheating?" she breathed. "Or just very good?"

"Oh, he's cheating, all right. And he's extremely good at it too."

"Is he working with an accomplice?"

Harry's hand slid to her lower back, and she suppressed a shudder of desire.

"No. But he's dealing the best cards to himself, bringing the ones he wants to the top of the pack, then shuffling the deck in such a way that he has the advantage."

"What about when another player shuffles?"

"I suspect he's also marked some of the cards, by nicking the edges with his thumbnail, or something similar, so he knows where certain cards are, even face down."

"Impressive."

"I'm better."

He chuckled as she deliberately nudged her shoulder into him to punish him for his arrogance.

"Pride comes before a fall," she chided softly.

His lips ghosted the shell of her ear. "It's not arrogance if it's true. Now let me get to work and stop distracting me."

A moment later, Blake's last remaining opponent let out a groan and dropped his cards face down on the table in defeat. Blake gave a knowing grin and scooped the pile of coins in the center of the table toward him. He took a deep swig of ale from the tankard at his side, then glanced around with an air of challenge.

"Anyone else want to try their hand? Who knows, I've had the Devil's own luck tonight. It has to end sometime." He smirked, as if not truly believing it.

"I'll play a few rounds with you, sir."

Chapter Thirty-Three

Harry stepped forward and took the seat opposite Blake. Two other men filled the seats on his left and right, and Blake pushed the playing cards toward Harry for him to deal.

Ellie could only watch in wonder as Harry made a complete mess of shuffling the cards. Instead of making them fly effortlessly between his fingers, as she'd seen him do when they'd played at Cobham House, he seemed awkward and fumbling, as if he'd barely handled cards in his life.

He shook his head with an embarrassed apology, and she bit back a smile as Blake gave a sly smirk of anticipation. He clearly thought Harry was going to be an easy mark.

Over the course of the next few hands Harry played solidly, but without noticeable success. The coins in the middle of the table ebbed and flowed among the four players, but the pile grew steadily as they gradually increased the stakes.

When Harry won a hand, he glanced up at her with an expression of surprised delight, as if he hadn't expected the win at all. He kissed the inside of her wrist, sending a shiver up her arm, and drew her to stand at his shoulder.

Ellie almost applauded his acting ability. She had absolutely no doubt that he was biding his time, lulling his opponent into a sense of false security before he pounced.

"What say we double the odds for this next game, eh, gents?" he suggested. "I think Lady Luck is finally smiling on me."

The other three men agreed, and Ellie's nerves increased along with the stakes. When the pot reached two hundred pounds, the man on Harry's left withdrew. When the stake reached five hundred, the man on his right folded, too, leaving only Harry and Blake.

Blake sent Harry a condescending smile. "Do you wish to continue, sir? Or is it too rich for you?"

Harry tugged his cravat. He took another deep gulp of his beer, then looked up to Ellie, as if seeking her opinion. She bent and kissed his cheek, taking her cue.

"I love a man who plays deep," she cooed, biting her lip at the deliberate innuendo. She slid her hand up his shoulder and toyed with the hair at the back of his neck, then gave his ear a teasing nip with her teeth. Her breasts pressed against his shoulder. "Win this round, and I'll make you the happiest man in Covent Garden."

Harry sucked in a breath, as if he was finding it hard to breathe, then gave a laugh that sounded full of bravado.

"Why not?" He pushed all of his previous winnings into the center of the green baize. An impressed murmur rippled around the spectators.

"I'm all in," he said. "A thousand pounds."

Blake's eyes gleamed at the prospect of a windfall. He pushed his own coins forward, then reached into his jacket pocket. "Will you accept this as the second half of my bet?" He placed a sparkling blue stone on the table between them. "It's an aquamarine. I'm told it once belonged to a prince. It's worth at least five hundred pounds."

Ellie gazed at it in interest. The gem was shaped like a sphere that had been cut in half; flat on the bottom and curved on the top. The facets glittered invitingly, although she had no idea if it really was precious, or simply a colored piece of glass.

Harry, however, gave an easy laugh. "I'm no expert in gemstones, but I'll take your word as a gentleman. Let's play."

Blake reached to pick up the deck, but Harry gave a polite cough. "It's my turn to deal, is it not?"

A few others in the crowd muttered their agreement, and Blake's jaw hardened as he slid the cards over to Harry. "My mistake."

Harry dealt the cards and Ellie watched with bated breath to see if she could detect any hint that either he or Blake were cheating. She could not.

Blake gazed at his hand, then called for another card. Harry slid it over to him, and when Blake picked it up his expression revealed neither dissatisfaction nor pleasure.

"I'll stay."

Ellie's heart was pounding in her chest as Harry lifted his own hand for her to see, and she tried to keep her face expressionless as she saw the queen of hearts and the ace of spades; a winning total of twenty-one.

How on earth had he managed it?

He placed the cards face up on the table with a laugh that sounded completely incredulous. "Bloody Hell! Would you look at that!"

Blake blinked and sucked in an audible breath. Then

an angry flush mottled his cheeks as he tossed down his own hand: a king, an eight, and a two. A total of twenty.

"Your hand, sir," he said stiffly.

A roar of delight burst from the crowd. Harry was enthusiastically clapped on the back, but Ellie glanced nervously at Blake. Would he be so angry at the loss that he'd accuse Harry of cheating?

But Blake seemed more amazed than annoyed, as if he'd been so certain of winning, he couldn't quite believe he'd lost. He rose from his chair and then pushed angrily through the crowd, ignoring the commiserating comments thrown his way.

Harry reached forward, picked the jewel from the pile of coins, and held it up toward Ellie. "For the lady!"

Conscious of her role, she caught hold of his cravat, yanked him toward her, and kissed him soundly on the mouth. The crowd cheered as she plucked the jewel from his hand and pushed it down the front of her bodice, into the cleft between her breasts.

"I'll look after that for you, sir!" she said with a saucy grin.

Harry laughed and gave her bottom a playful pinch. He gathered the rest of his winnings and put them in his pockets, then turned a regretful look to the men all clamoring to play him in the hopes of winning back some of his coin.

"Sorry, gents, but the lovely Carlotta's promised me a night I won't forget. I bid you good evening."

A chorus of ribald comments followed them as they left the gaming room, and Ellie tried to calm her racing pulse. She half expected Blake to be lying in wait for them in the street outside, to rob them of their winnings, but Harry must have arranged for Carson to be waiting.

A plain black carriage—not the one with the Cobham crest on the panels—rattled up almost as soon as they stepped out onto Henrietta Street.

Harry turned to her. "Can you come back to Cobham House?"

She shook her head, even as she swallowed a groan of disappointment. "I wish I could, but I have to get back home."

He gave the address to Carson, then climbed in after her, and as soon as the coach started forward, he caught the back of her neck and toppled her into his lap for a kiss.

Ellie gave a helpless groan of delight. She melted against him as his tongue invaded her mouth, her blood fizzing with excitement.

"Brilliant girl," he panted against her lips. "The perfect partner in crime."

He pressed feverish kisses across her jaw and down her throat, then slid his fingers into her bodice. She gasped as he brushed her nipple.

"Now, where did you hide that lovely jewel?"

His breath was hot on her skin. She tilted her head back and arched into his touch, even as she let out a shivery laugh. "Oh, no you don't! It's mine, remember? The price for helping prove who you are."

He nipped the top of her breast with a playful bite before soothing it with his tongue. "Vixen. You drive a hard bargain."

Ellie laughed. She kissed him again, then gave in to temptation and slid her hand down his chest and then lower, to the impressive bulge between his legs. "Not as hard as this," she murmured wickedly.

He let out a hiss between his teeth. "God, Ellie. You'd drive a saint to drink."

She caressed him through his breeches and he kissed her almost savagely in response. His hips bucked as she unbuttoned his falls, and he groaned as she took him in her hand.

"You don't have to—"

She cut off his protest. "I want to. Let me. Please."

He was hard and hot and she delighted in the feel of him, the way his breath hitched as she pumped and squeezed.

His hand came up to cover hers, moving up and down, but the erratic motion of the coach added an extra complication, making it hard to maintain a rhythm. He swore savagely as they went over a particularly deep rut, and Ellie giggled. She loved the thought of him being out of control. Of taking him to the very edge of sanity. It was only fair. He'd done the same to her.

Their joined hands pumped faster. He gripped the leather strap on the wall with his free hand and arched his spine, tilting his head back on the seat and exposing his throat. The sight of him made her own body thrum with desire, but she was determined to give him this gift. She pumped her hand, and with a groan that seemed dragged from his chest he went rigid, pulsing in her hand.

He let out a long, satisfied sigh and sprawled back into the seat. "Bloody Hell. I love the way you celebrate a successful mission."

His wetness was on her fingers, probably on his breeches, too, although it was hard to tell in the dim light. Ellie pulled a handkerchief from her pocket and wiped her hands as he straightened his clothing, then leaned against him as he pulled her to his side.

"Naughty," he chided weakly. His voice was low in the darkness as he pressed a kiss to her forehead.

Ellie chuckled. "You're a terrible influence. You definitely bring out the worst in me."

"Or is it the best?" he murmured. "I wish there was time to return the favor, but we're almost back at Bloomsbury."

"It's all right. Will I see you tomorrow at King and Company?"

"I'll be there at ten o'clock sharp." He sent a laughing look at her bodice, where the aquamarine still nestled against her skin. "I've kept my side of the bargain. It's time for you to keep yours."

Chapter Thirty-Four

"Good morning, *Mr. King*," Tess teased drily as Harry sauntered into the King & Co. offices the next morning, looking as handsome as ever, and bringing a waft of cedar-scented air with him. "Would you like some tea?"

He sent her a charming smile. "That would be lovely, thank you."

Ellie rolled her eyes as Tess poured him a cup and added milk. Had she forgotten he was a scoundrel? And possibly a shameless liar, as well?

He could still be lying about being the lost earl. She felt a little stab of remorse for continuing to doubt him, but her *job* was to doubt things until sufficient evidence had been provided to ascertain the truth.

"Tess and I just returned the Book of Hours to Mr. Bullock," she said, sliding behind her desk.

Harry leaned against the edge of it, and took a sip of tea. "Was he annoyed by the damage?"

"He didn't react half as badly as I thought he might," Ellie conceded. "I'd removed the shot, and pressed the gold back into shape a little from the inside. None of the jewels had been broken, and when I explained how it had been dented, he became almost giddy."

"He actually *laughed*," Tess said. "He said he was never one to let the facts get in the way of a good story, and that he liked the book even better now. He's going to put it back on display exactly as it is, and tell everyone the shot that made the hole was fired at Napoleon himself!"

Harry shook his head. "See how the truth can get distorted? You can't believe everything you hear."

He glanced over at Daisy, who was using a cotton cloth to apply a thin layer of oil to the blade she'd received at Hyde Park, and whistled in admiration.

"That is an impressive weapon. I'm quite jealous."

Daisy grinned. "Isn't it? I've been doing a little research, and this type of blade is more common in Italy than here. They call it a *cinquedea*, which means 'five fingers,' because that's the width of the blade here at the base, next to the guard." She pointed to the fattest part of the lethal-looking blade.

Harry nodded. "I've encountered a couple of those myself, on my travels. It's basically a long dagger. See how the leather scabbard has a loop on it? That's for attaching to your belt, at the back, horizontally. That way, you can easily draw it with your right hand. It's designed for close combat and self-defense."

Daisy looked delighted. "I've persuaded a friend of Devlin's to give me some extra lessons with it. I'm not bad with a rapier, but I need to practice my knife skills."

Harry made a face. "As if you weren't terrifying enough."

Daisy chuckled at the compliment.

Harry turned back to Ellie. "Have you shown them our spoils from last night?"

"Not yet." She slid open the drawer in her desk and held the blue stone up to the light.

It was impossible not to appreciate the beauty of it. The angled facets made it sparkle, and the pale blue color reminded her of the sky in springtime.

"Pretty," Tess murmured. "Let's hope it's real, and the one Rundell's been looking for. I'll invite him to come and inspect it for himself."

Harry took another sip of tea. "So, now that I've paid your fee, how do you mean to prove my identity?"

"We need more information," Ellie said. "We'd like to talk to Hugo, since he's known you the longest. He might be able to tell us something that will help the investigation. How is he feeling?"

"I had Dr. Wilson come and look at him. He really did damage a couple of ribs wrestling with Sofia in the park. He's been told to rest and not do anything strenuous, but he's certainly up to receiving visitors. He's driving me mad, he's so bored."

Ellie started to rise. "In that case—"

"I need to get something, first," Harry said.

He glanced at the basil plant she'd relegated to the corner of the room. "I'm glad to see you've been taking care of my gift. Do you remember I told you it's supposed to bring good luck and ward off poverty?"

"It's brought us Bullock's five hundred pounds." Tess smiled. "And that aquamarine. So maybe there's something to that superstition."

Harry put down his teacup and rounded the desk. "I meant it in a more literal sense."

He picked up the plant pot and placed it directly in front of Ellie. "I apologize in advance for the mess."

He grasped the basil at the bottom of its stalks, and pulled the entire plant out of the pot, raining soil and roots all over her green leather desktop.

"What are you doing, you madman?" Ellie shrieked.

He laid the plant gently down on the surface, careful not to crush the leaves, and reached into the bottom of the pot, rummaging through the remaining soil with his fingers. A moment later, he withdrew a glittering gold object.

Ellie glared at him. "What's that?"

He held it out for her to inspect. It was a man's signet ring, the flat top engraved with a crest she'd seen a dozen times on the door of his carriage. Three lions rampant on a shield with a chevron.

"The Cobham family seal. It belonged to my father."

Ellie almost sent him a commiserating look, but stopped short. She was *almost* certain that he wasn't acting—that he truly was the Earl of Cobham—but the investigator in her still wanted proof. He could still have stolen it from the *real* earl, or had a plain ring inscribed by a jeweler.

"You hid your family ring *here*, in our office?"

He sent her a cheeky grin, amused at her irritation. "The safest places are those where nobody would think to look."

"That was incredibly risky. What if I'd killed the plant? What if I'd thrown it on the compost heap, pot and all?"

His eyes twinkled. "I suppose I would have had to go digging around in the tea leaves and the potato peelings. But I had faith in your ability to keep it alive. You're extremely conscientious."

He slipped the ring into his pocket, then made a terrible

job of trying to sweep the mess back into the pot and replanting the poor, abused basil into the soil.

Ellie pushed his hands away. "Leave it. I'll clean it up later. Let's go and speak to Hugo."

Chapter Thirty-Five

Hugo's face lit up in a roguish grin as Ellie, Tess, and Daisy all entered the drawing room at Cobham House.

"Ladies, welcome! What a lovely sight for these old eyes." He sat up straighter in his chair, clearly delighted to have company.

Ellie suppressed a smile as she watched Tess and Daisy shoot furtive glances around the room, noting the décor and every other detail. They'd both been keen to have a good snoop at the interior of the house, and to be formally introduced to Hugo.

Tess shook his outstretched hand. "So, you're Harry's uncle? I can definitely see a family resemblance."

"I'm better looking," Hugo chuckled. "Improving with age, like a fine wine."

Harry rolled his eyes as Hugo released Tess to kiss the back of Daisy's hand. "Enchanté, mademoiselle."

"Please, have a seat," Harry said. "I'll ring for some tea."

"And cake?" Daisy asked hopefully.

Harry laughed as he tugged on the bellpull to summon

a servant. "And cake, certainly. I understand interrogations can be very hungry work."

"Who's being interrogated?" Hugo demanded with comical faux alarm.

"The ladies of King and Company want you to tell them all about my murky past," Harry said with a dry smile.

"I'll be happy to tell you whatever you wish to know," Hugo said. "Except for what really happened that one time in Venice, when we dressed as gondoliers and borrowed that scepter from Prince Gustav of Sweden—"

Harry gave a strangled growl, and Hugo gave a wicked chuckle. "I'm teasing, of course. Some secrets will follow me to the grave."

Ellie pulled out a notebook and pencil and balanced it on her knee. "We need to prove that he"—she tilted a glance at Harry—"is the legitimate son of the last Earl and Countess of Cobham."

"Which he is," Hugo said stoutly. "And I'd swear it in front of a judge if I thought my word would carry any weight. Unfortunately, I doubt my word would be enough, considering I'm a bit of a black sheep."

"I've been thinking a lot about his eyes," Ellie continued.

Harry's lips quirked teasingly. "Oh really? That is excellent—"

She sent him a quelling frown for his deliberate misinterpretation. "About how unusual they are. As an identifying feature. Tell me, Hugo, did he always have eyes like that?"

"Ever since birth," the older man said. "I saw him as a baby, about a week or so after he was born, and my brother remarked on it. James was worried that the difference in color indicated something sinister—a defect, or a weakness in the eye, perhaps, that meant Harry would be blind."

Hugo wrinkled his brow, and his own eyes lost their focus as he tried to think back to that time. "In fact, he didn't believe the local doctor, old John Williams, and demanded a second opinion from a specialist who dealt only with the eyes. They brought Harry here, to London, to see the man."

Harry took the empty seat next to Ellie on the chaise longue. His knee casually brushed hers, and her pulse fluttered even as she told herself to concentrate on the task in hand.

"The specialist presumably reassured them that, although rare, the condition is harmless," Harry said. "It's called heteroglaucos. I remember my father telling me about it when I was about ten or so. He said I was in exalted company, because apparently Alexander the Great had eyes that were two different colors too." He gave a wistful smile. "Of course, that made ten-year-old me feel quite special and invincible."

A sudden image of Harry as an adorable boy formed in Ellie's mind and her heart gave a little squeeze for the carefree, innocent child he must have been before his parents had been taken from him. To lose both of them in one fell swoop must have been devastating, and she found herself fervently glad that he'd had the loving, if slightly disreputable, presence of Hugo to help him navigate his grief.

She blinked as she realized Harry was still talking.

"A mixture of pigments is needed to make certain eye colors," he said. "Hazel and green eyes need a combination of both blue and brown flecks dispersed within the iris. Sometimes, however—as in my case—one eye has a concentration of pigment that gives it a colored segment, or even produces two completely different color eyes."

He turned to Ellie and stared unblinkingly at her, and she took the opportunity to study the strange feature at close quarters again. Her stomach fluttered as his pupils darkened with desire, almost obscuring the iris. Heat pooled low in her belly.

"So you could be the only person in the world with that particular arrangement of colors?" Tess asked.

Harry nodded, breaking the silent hold he'd had on Ellie's gaze. "Most likely. It's certainly a very specific identifying feature."

Ellie tapped her pencil on her pad. "I think it's rare enough that if we can show that Harry and young Henry Cobham share the same unique eye coloring, that's enough to prove that you are one and the same person."

Tess leaned forward. "Hugo, can you remember the name of the doctor your brother consulted?"

Hugo squinted up at the ceiling. "I'm not sure I ever heard it. Besides, it was over twenty years ago."

Daisy gave a sigh of frustration. "That's a pity. Because if we could find him, he might be willing to give evidence in Harry's defense."

Ellie frowned down at her paper. "Even if he did, it's unlikely his testimony alone would be enough. A competent lawyer would argue that his memory could be faulty and unreliable after all this time."

Hugo gave a start, as if hit by sudden inspiration. "Wait! I might not know the name, but I *do* remember that they took you to see him once a week for several months. The man was so intrigued by your case that he presented his findings to the Royal Society. They published the article. I remember reading it."

Tess raised her brows. "That article, or his notes, would be excellent evidence."

Ellie's excitement grew. This, potentially, was a breakthrough. "Surely the Royal Society will have a copy of the article in their archives?"

"They will, but without knowing the name of the author it's going to be hard to find."

"It ought to have been published a year or so after Harry was born," Ellie said. "Is that right, Hugo?"

The older man nodded. "Yes, he was only a baby."

Ellie turned to Harry. "When were you born?"

"September the twentieth, 1790."

Ellie did some swift mental calculation. He was twenty-six. Four years older than herself. "So that would make the article published in 1791 or '92. That's a good start."

"The Royal Society's headquarters are in Somerset House," Daisy said. "In the opposite wing to the Royal Academy of Arts. I went there last summer for an exhibition."

The tea arrived, along with a delicious-looking lemon cake, and Daisy's expression turned joyous. Tess took on the task of pouring them all a cup.

"I happen to be free to visit Somerset House this afternoon, if you are?" Harry said to Ellie.

She shot him an amused glance. "I thought you wanted King and Company to handle this investigation? You're paying us to do so, in fact."

"Do you object to me tagging along as an interested party?"

Ellie bit back a smile as she caught Tess's amused glance in her direction. "Of course not. You can come if you wish."

Chapter Thirty-Six

The entrance to the Royal Society's rooms in Somerset House were guarded by a bust of Sir Isaac Newton, who glared in friendly rivalry across the shared vestibule at a bust of Michelangelo, placed before the Royal Academy's door. Harry laughed as he pointed out the perpetual standoff between the Arts and the Sciences.

Daisy and Tess had both returned to the office, so Ellie was once again alone with Harry. She'd already put on her spectacles to project a suitably serious, scholarly air, partly to appear more competent, but also to remind herself that she was there to work, and not merely flirt with Harry.

The gruff gentleman at the front desk frostily inquired if they were members, and she lied shamelessly to gain access.

"We are not, but my father, Lord Ellenborough, has tasked me with undertaking some research in your archives which he hopes will prove invaluable in cracking a case."

She didn't dare glance over at Harry, sure that his expression would make her blush guiltily.

The man's coldness evaporated. "It's for the Lord Chief Justice? Oh, well, in that case, of course. May I ask exactly what it is you'd like to see?"

Ellie pushed her spectacles higher on her nose, as if their admittance had never been in doubt, and inspected her notebook. "I believe the paper we're looking for would have been published in your yearly journal, *Philosophical Transactions of the Royal Society*."

"Do you know the name of the member who presented the article?"

"I'm afraid not, but it would have been in either 1791 or '92."

The man nodded, his long side-whiskers twitching. "Ah. This way."

Harry shot her a congratulatory glance as they followed the man into a huge two-level library, its floor-to-ceiling shelves stacked with innumerable leather-bound tomes. A few desks with chairs for private study were dotted about, and Ellie received several raised eyebrows from their inhabitants at her feminine presence in such a male sanctum.

She raised her nose a little higher in the air. The only reason there were currently no female members of the Royal Society had absolutely nothing to do with the inferior ability of the female brain—as one obnoxious dinner companion had once suggested to her—but more to do with the fact that women were denied the same education as their male counterparts.

She considered mentioning it to Harry, but since idle talk seemed to be frowned upon in the library, she held her tongue.

The clerk led them to a section of shelving and pulled out two enormous leather-bound volumes, numbered 81 and 82, with the dates 1791 and 1792 detailed in gold on the spines. He placed them carefully on a nearby table.

"All the papers published by the society are in here. Do you know the subject, if not the author?"

"I think it's an article on the human eye or iris. Under the biological sciences."

The old man shrugged. "The articles aren't indexed, I'm afraid. You'll just have to look through each one and see if it's the one you're after."

Ellie sent him a grateful smile and sat in one of the hard wooden chairs. "Thank you."

The man left them, and Ellie pushed one of the enormous books across the desk toward Harry, who took a seat opposite.

He grimaced at the thickness of the books. "That is a *lot* of papers."

"It's for your own good," Ellie teased. "Get reading."

She opened her book, and spent the next half hour scanning through the most mind-boggling array of articles, with titles such as "Experiments on the analysis of the heavy inflammable air," and "An account of some extraordinary effects of lightning."

She glanced up at Harry. "Have you ever wondered about 'The rate of traveling, as performed by camels, and its applications, as a scale, to the purposes of geography'?"

"Can't say that I have," he whispered back, his eyes flashing with amusement. "Have *you* lain awake at night pondering the 'Astronomical observations on the Planets Venus and Mars, made with a view to determine the heliocentric longitude of their nodes'?"

"Regularly," Ellie murmured, trying to suppress a giggle. How was it that even the dullest task became fun in Harry's company?

They each returned to their books.

Finally, just when she thought she'd go cross-eyed with boredom, she found an article entitled "Observations on the natural variation of pigmentation in the human iris, including an unusual case of heteroglaucos," by Dr. William C. Emberton, F.R.S.

Her heart gave a triumphant leap and she glanced up at Harry.

"I've found it!"

Her loud squeak immediately earned her disapproving glares from several of the other library occupants, and a cacophony of shushes, and she sent them an apologetic wave.

"Sorry!"

She turned the book around on the desk to show Harry. There, on the page in front of him, was a printed illustration showing a pair of eyes, one with a distinct section of the iris segmented. Green and brown watercolor had been added over the black-and-white engraving, and the unique pattern of brown wedge and green flecks was an exact match for Harry's own eyes.

He stroked the paper with his finger and his face held an expression of delighted awe. "That's it! Those are my eyes!"

"Without doubt, but we still have a problem. Look." Ellie pointed to the words below the illustration. "Nowhere in this article does it say that those eyes belong to Henry Brooke, son of the Earl of Cobham. He only talks about 'the patient,' or 'the child in whom I observed this rarity.'"

Harry skimmed the document himself, then looked up with a shrug. "That's not the end of the world. All we have to do is find this Dr. Emberton and get him to confirm that I was the original patient. That should be more than enough to satisfy a judge that I am who I claim to be."

Ellie nodded.

Harry leaned closer, and her heart rate increased as the smell of his body enfolded her.

"So, are we going to steal this article?" he whispered. "The best way to remove a page from a book is to leave a wet piece of thin cotton thread closed inside, on the inner edge. It softens the paper so it tears neatly."

"How on earth do you know that?" Ellie whispered, appalled.

Harry grinned. "Learned it from a fence who used to deal in stolen maps in Milan. But you really need to leave it a day or two, to work properly."

Ellie shook her head.

"I suppose if you cough loudly," he continued, undeterred, "or pretend to sneeze at exactly the same moment as I rip the pages from the book, it should cover the sound."

"We are not stealing or defacing anything. Behave." She scribbled the name Emberton, and the title of the article, in her notebook. "We've got the doctor's name. Now we can go and look him up and find out where he practices."

She glanced up, and the sudden intense way Harry was looking at her sent a bolt of heat straight through her. He leaned even closer.

"Have you ever fantasized about making love in a place like this? Somewhere completely forbidden? Because I have." His gaze fell to her lips and she squirmed in her seat.

She'd be lying if she denied it. The thought of doing

something so naughty made her almost quiver with excitement, and she could clearly imagine the thrill of trying to stay quiet while Harry's hands roved all over her.

"You'd have to be extremely quiet, of course," he whispered, a wicked twinkle in his eyes. "I might even have to put my hand over your mouth to stop you making any noise. I could press you against the shelves and lift your skirts." His pupils flared. "Or perhaps I'd spread you out on one of these library tables and lick your—"

A cough and the scrape of a chair made Ellie flush guiltily. Dear God, the man was a menace! He could reduce her to a puddle of lust right in the middle of a reading room.

She sent him a disapproving glare. "*Not* an appropriate way to celebrate our success."

He gave a playful pout. "A bit of rebellion is good for the soul. I'm determined to make you break a few rules, Miss Law. Even if it kills me."

Chapter Thirty-Seven

Once they were safely back on the Strand, Harry gave a whoop of triumph loud enough to startle the pigeons.

"Success! I didn't think we'd find anything, to be honest."

Ellie smiled, secretly delighted that the lead had paid off. She'd spent hours on similar cases and never had a jot of luck. "Let's head back to the office."

She glanced around for Carson and the carriage, but Harry caught her arm and tucked it into the crook of his own.

"What's the rush? The sun is out, the air is bracing. Let's take a stroll."

She glanced up at him in suspicion. "Why?"

"Why not? You've heard the adage 'All work and no play makes Jack a dull boy.'"

"Are you saying I'm *dull*?"

His teeth flashed in a grin. "Not at all. You're fascinating. But you're also in danger of working too hard. You need to learn to enjoy the moment."

"By wandering about aimlessly?"

"Wandering aimlessly is an art. What's wrong with a little spontaneity?"

"Well, nothing, I suppose, but I prefer to—"

He looked down at her, a teasing glint in his eye. "You prefer to plan. I know. You read the whole guide book before going to a museum, and then you set out to see four or five very specific items on your list."

Ellie drew back a little, stung by his accuracy. "What's wrong with that? Don't tell me you had such success as a thief without *planning* things."

"Of course not. But you also need to leave room for the unexpected. For improvisation."

"Is that what this is? Improvisation?" she said drily.

"Indeed. One must be open to being surprised, or to discovering something new. Because who knows? That unexpected thing might just end up being your favorite piece in the whole museum."

"Hmm," Ellie said. Still, she turned her face up and enjoyed the faint warmth of the sun on her skin.

"The Italians have a saying for it," Harry continued easily. "*Dolce far niente*. It means 'sweet idleness.' But doing nothing is actually very difficult. We often feel like we should fill every minute of the day with something productive, but sometimes just lying on your back and finding shapes in the clouds, or watching the bubbles float past in a river, is as much diversion as one could possibly need."

"You sound like you've mastered it."

"I have indeed."

They strolled past a variety of shops, peering into the windows of each. Ellie admired the coats on display in the furriers, the pianofortes in Mr. Mott's establishment, and the satirical engravings in the print shop of George Peirce.

Two rather inebriated gentlemen stumbled down the steps of Hunt's Cigar Lounge and Billiard Room, but their open admiration of Ellie stopped abruptly when they saw Harry's sword cane, and the subtly threatening way he toyed with the lion's head handle.

Harry spent far too long considering the wares in the window of Edward Cahan, tailor, and Baddeley the boot-maker, but when Carson finally appeared with the carriage Ellie was glad that they'd taken the time to get some fresh air.

Being near Harry was both a pleasure and a bitter-sweet torment. He seemed to enjoy her company, to want to be her friend as well as her lover, but she couldn't help worry that his attention was only temporary.

She was afraid to trust this newfound closeness. Perhaps he only saw her as an amusing fling, a necessary stepping stone in his path to reclaiming his rightful place in the world.

For her part, she couldn't regret giving herself to him, but it would be better for her heart if she didn't make love with him again until she was absolutely certain of his identity.

If it wasn't for the fact that he'd promised to leave London if she proved he wasn't Henry Brooke, she'd almost prefer him to be a liar. The chances of him choosing to continue their liaison if he was an earl were remote. The *ton* was full of prettier, more socially accomplished girls who'd make him the perfect partner. The fact that he desired her physically would hardly be enough of a draw. She had to be realistic.

Tess and Daisy were both at the office when they got back. Tess pulled down their well-worn copy of Boyle's *Town Visiting Directory*, and it was a simple enough matter to find that there was a physician by the name of Emberton with an office on New Bridge Street, near Blackfriars Bridge.

"Is it too late to call on him now?" Tess queried, looking at the clock on the mantelpiece.

Ellie shook her head. "We might as well try." She glanced over at Harry, who was showing Daisy a gruesome-looking move with one of her knives.

"Do you want to come?"

"Wouldn't miss it for the world," he said.

"I'll come too," Daisy added with a smile.

The elegant gray dome of St Paul's Cathedral loomed over the rooftops as the three of them stepped down onto New Bridge Street. A steady stream of carts and carriages rattled across the Thames, and Daisy pointed to a sign shaped like a pair of spectacles swinging above one of the doors. The gilt letters below read EMBERTON & SONS, OPTOMETRIST.

The smartly dressed young man who greeted them was pleasant enough, but when he introduced himself as Dr. Emberton, Ellie's spirits dropped. He appeared no older than twenty-five; he couldn't possibly be the man who'd examined Harry's eyes. He would have been a boy himself.

Still, she needed to eliminate all doubt. "I wonder if you can help us, sir? I don't suppose your father, or even your grandfather, also practiced from this location? We're looking for the Dr. Emberton who published a paper on the human eye for the Royal Society."

"Ah. That would be my father."

"Could we speak with him?"

"Sadly not; he passed away last summer."

Disappointment flooded her. "Oh, I'm sorry," she murmured automatically.

The young man nodded to accept her condolences.

"I don't suppose you still have his notes, do you?" Daisy asked. "Harry here was the subject of that paper."

The doctor gave a visible start. He twirled toward Harry and stared intently at his face. "*You're* the one!" His tone was one of awed wonder. "At last! I can't believe it! Please, come closer so I can see your eyes."

Harry did so, turning to the light that streamed in through the shop windows, as the doctor peered closely at his irises.

"My father spoke of you quite often," Emberton said, his voice rising in excitement. "He was intrigued by your case. I always hoped you'd come back one day so I could see you for myself."

He was staring at Harry with fascinated delight, as if Harry were a strange creature in a circus. Ellie felt oddly protective of him.

"His notes?" she prompted.

The doctor turned from his inspection of Harry and heaved a deep sigh. "Ah. Now there's a little problem there, I'm afraid. In the last few years of his life my father became a little . . . erratic." He made a pained face. "His mind began to wander, and he became convinced that there were secrets and conspiracies around every corner."

"What do you mean?" Harry asked.

Emberton gave a sad little laugh. "Well, he thought our neighbor, old Mrs. Brown, was secretly a witch who could turn into a black cat. And he thought that *you*, sir, had been kidnapped!"

Harry blinked, then let out a bark of incredulous laughter. "Me? Kidnapped? Why?"

"You disappeared," Emberton said, his face serious.

"Father kept trying to find you, to do a follow-up to his paper, to see if your eyes had changed over time, but Harry Brooke, son of the Earl of Cobham, had vanished without a trace!"

He shook his head. "I told him he was being ridiculous, imagining things. But he was right."

"Not entirely," Harry said. "I left England, but I wasn't kidnapped. I went to Italy with my uncle, after my parents died."

An embarrassed flush stained Emberton's cheeks. "I knew there would be a reasonable explanation. Still, Father became convinced that there had been foul play. People began talking about the 'Lost Earl,' and his mind spun all manner of elaborate fantasies. He was sure that if you were still alive, and somehow managed to escape your captors, that you'd return to claim your rightful inheritance."

"That's not too far from the truth," Daisy said. "We're hoping to prove that Harry's the Lost Earl."

"Your father told you that the child he'd studied for the paper was Lord Cobham's son?" Ellie pressed. "Because there was no mention of his name in the published paper."

Emberton nodded. "Yes. It was written in his notes. There was a letter signed by Lord Cobham agreeing for the study to be published, and records of the payments made to my father for his services."

Ellie's heart gave an excited leap. This was exactly the kind of evidence they needed.

"Father was sure his notes would be important in helping you prove who you were," Emberton said to Harry. "He wanted to store them 'somewhere safe,' but he refused to keep them here, or at our house in Chancery Lane. He didn't trust sending them to Cobham Hall, or to your house here in town, either, in case they fell into 'the wrong hands.'"

He shook his head with a laugh that was filled with bleak humor. "I suggested a bank vault, but he pointed out that even if he left instructions for Henry Brooke, Earl of Cobham, to be permitted access to the contents, you wouldn't be able to *prove* you were him to get to them."

"Like Plutarch's riddle about the chicken and the egg," Ellie murmured. "One has to come before the other."

"Exactly!"

"So what did he do?"

"He said they needed to be kept somewhere safe and dry, but in a place that didn't require any particular identification to visit. He considered hiding them somewhere in the British Museum, but in the end, he made me put them in the one place he considered the safest in England."

Emberton's face scrunched up as if he were embarrassed to finish the story.

"And where's that?" Ellie was already dreading the answer.

"The Tower of London."

Ellie gaped at the doctor. "You can't be serious."

Emberton unscrewed his face and looked at her. "I'm so sorry. I honestly never thought anyone would come back and ask for them. I was just humoring him."

"Where *exactly* did you hide them?" Daisy asked. "A storage room? An office?"

"They're in one of the cells that used to house prisoners in years gone by. In the Beauchamp Tower. You used to be able to visit it if you went on a tour. I put them on a ledge, about two feet up inside the chimney breast in the room with the name Arundel scratched into the wall."

Emberton shrugged. "I'm sorry. I just did as Father asked."

Harry gave his shoulder a reassuring pat. "You were a dutiful son. I don't blame you in the slightest. This just makes things that much more interesting."

Ellie rolled her eyes. Harry used words like "interesting" where other people used "difficult" or "dangerous" or "bloody impossible." Still, she admired his optimism. No doubt he was delighted to have been presented with yet another challenge.

"Thank you, Doctor. You've been extremely helpful. We'll let you know if we meet with any success." She crossed to the door and stepped out into the street as Daisy and Harry took their leave.

Chapter Thirty-Eight

Tess was waiting for them when they got back to the office, and her brows rose as they told her about the latest development.

"I don't suppose even *you* know a way of strolling into the Tower of London unchallenged?" she said to Harry.

His lips twitched. "Afraid not. But I'm fairly sure I could come up with one, given time."

"It would be easier to get a tour, though, wouldn't it?" Ellie said.

Daisy wrinkled her nose. "Not necessarily. It used to be easy to get a tour. They'd let in anyone who asked, for a small fee. Devlin went every day for a whole week to study the antique weaponry when he was sixteen. But they increased the security last year after an incident."

"What happened?"

"A woman viewing the crown jewels reached through the bars, grabbed the state crown, and tried to smash it to bits. Now, the warden only conducts a few tours a week, for a maximum of six people at a time. You have to put your name in a drawing and see if you get picked."

"It would be hard to look for those documents with

other witnesses," Tess mused. "If it was just the warden, he could be distracted, but having strangers there would make it trickier."

"Is it possible to get a private tour?" Harry asked.

"Occasionally, if one knows the right people, or has the right leverage."

"Someone of a *criminal* bent might suggest bribery or blackmail," he murmured. "But I know you ladies frown on tactics like that."

"We do indeed." Ellie tapped her pen against her lips.

"The Lord Chamberlain's office is responsible for the upkeep of the crown jewels," Tess said. "Perhaps that's a way in?"

Ellie nodded. "Francis Ingram-Seymour-Conway, the Lord Chamberlain, is a friend of my father's. I'll write and ask him for a tour. I'll say I'm researching a family descendent, the Earl of Arundel. That would provide a reason to see inside the cells and look for the name scratched on the wall."

"Excellent," Daisy said. "And we might as well apply for a regular tour via the lottery as well. If any of us manage to get a place, we can think of an alternative plan."

A knock on the front door interrupted them, and Tess stood. "That will be the man from the jewelers. Mr. Rundell said he'd send someone to see if our gemstone is real."

Ellie pulled the jewel in question from the drawer and placed it in the center of her desk, while Harry slid easily into one of the armchairs by the fire.

Tess returned with a pleasant-looking gentleman of perhaps thirty-five years old named George Fox, who was apparently superintendent of the jewelry workshops at Ludgate Hill.

She introduced Harry as "Henri Bonheur, a friend of Mr. King's."

"This is the stone in question," Ellie said, holding it up.

"It's certainly the right size and shape," Fox said approvingly. "But appearances can be deceptive."

He withdrew a jeweler's magnifying glass from his coat pocket and set it into his eye, then held the stone up to the light, inspecting it with calm thoroughness.

"You're checking to see if it's paste, or colored glass?" Ellie asked.

"I am. Real aquamarines show different colors when viewed from different angles. And they typically don't contain any visible flaws or bubbles. This also feels cool to the touch, which is another test to differentiate glass or paste from a true gem."

"So it's real?" Daisy asked.

Fox gave a smile. "It is indeed."

Ellie's shoulders relaxed and she sent a glance over at Harry. He didn't seem remotely surprised; he'd probably known the stone was genuine the minute he'd seen it, given his intimate acquaintance with precious gems.

Fox patted his pockets again and withdrew a piece of paper. "Mr. Rundell authorized me to give you this bank draft as payment if the stone was real."

Tess glanced at it and sent him a wide smile. "Thank you. I'll be sure to relay Mr. Rundell's appreciation to Mr. King. He'll be delighted to have another happy customer."

Fox placed the aquamarine in a small velvet bag. "Do you know the story behind this particular gem?"

"I'm afraid I don't."

Fox lowered his tone as if to impart a juicy piece of gossip. "Can you keep a secret?"

Tess shared an amused glance with first Ellie then Daisy. "Better than anyone you know, Mr. Fox."

"Most people don't know this, but a large proportion of the jewels used in any royal coronation don't actually belong to the royal family. They're almost all borrowed, hired for a four percent fee, from various jewelers. As soon as the pageantry is finished, they're removed from their settings and returned."

"I had no idea," Daisy murmured.

Fox nodded sagely. "This stone was in King George's coronation crown, some fifty years ago. It was *not* one that had been borrowed, however. It was part of the permanent royal collection. One of Rundell's silversmiths had been tasked with removing the hired gems from the crown after the ceremony, but he took the opportunity to swap this aquamarine with a glass replica that he'd made. The substitution was only noticed months later, during a routine cleaning, by which time the culprit had fled the country.

"Old Mr. Rundell was mortified that a once-trusted employee had sullied their reputation. He and Bridge secretly paid the king two hundred pounds for the stone, and vowed to get it back, no matter how long it took."

Fox gave a wry smile. "And now, finally, it's back in their possession. Mr. Rundell will be ecstatic."

"Will he sell it back to the king?" Ellie asked curiously.

"Oh no. He plans to give it to the crown. As a noble subject, he wants to return the missing jewel for the glory of England."

Harry gave a cynical smile. "That's very patriotic."

"It's not *entirely* altruistic," Fox chuckled. "We receive an excellent income from all the royal commissions the prince regent sends our way. It makes good business sense to stay in his good graces with a benevolent gift every now and then."

Harry snorted. "Of course."

When Fox had gone, Ellie composed a letter to the Lord Chamberlain's Office requesting a private tour of the Tower. "I'm not sure how long it might take to get a reply. It could be days, or even weeks."

Harry rolled his shoulders. "I suppose we'll just have to be patient. I've been without a name for so long, a little bit longer won't make any difference."

The following week dragged by with the speed of honey falling from a spoon. Two new cases came in: a request to investigate the theft of a painting during a country house party in Kent, and a complaint from a woman who suspected that her absent husband had married another woman, therefore committing bigamy.

Ellie would normally have relished the thought of diving into either one of those cases, but concentration eluded her.

Harry seemed to be keeping his distance. He didn't call at King & Co., and she didn't see him at any of the social functions she attended with Daisy and Tess.

He was probably spending his time entertaining Hugo, but she missed him, more than she'd thought possible. She wondered if he thought of her at all.

She spent her time researching the layout and history of the Tower, and trying to think of alternative ways to get inside the walls if her request for a tour was denied. It would have been easier a few years ago, when the Royal Mint had been housed there. They could have disguised themselves as one of the many hundred workers employed there, and slipped through the gates.

Or they could pretend to be delivering ale to one of the inns that provided food and drinks to the garrison of soldiers and yeomen guards stationed within the walls.

Her mind whirled with possibilities.

If their visit proved successful, and the doctor's notes proved that Harry was indeed the rightful Earl of Cobham, she would be happy for him, even if it meant that she'd probably lose him in the subsequent social whirl.

Armed with a title to accompany his good looks, money, and quick wit, he'd be inundated. Every debutante, spinster, matchmaking mamma, and widow would be hoping to catch his eye or become the next countess, and despite the fun they'd had together, she was sure he'd choose someone other than herself.

"What will we do if the documents aren't in the Tower?"

Ellie glanced up at Tess and frowned. She'd been daydreaming, looking out of the window at the tree-lined square, but it was almost as if Tess had been reading her thoughts.

"It's certainly a possibility," she said slowly. "Emberton could have lied about leaving them there. Or someone could have discovered them by accident and disposed of them. I suppose if we come back empty-handed, we'll just have to try every other avenue of investigation before we admit defeat."

A letter bearing the seal of the Lord Chamberlain's office finally arrived the following Tuesday, and Ellie ripped it open with impatient fingers.

She let out a shriek of triumph that caused Daisy to miss her playing card target; her knife embedded itself in the frame of a charming painting of Venice that Tess had hung on the wall.

Tess appeared in the doorway. "You've been granted a tour of the Tower?"

"Yes! With the Keeper of the Jewel House, a gentleman by the name of Edmund Swifte."

"When?" Daisy demanded.

Ellie checked the letter again. "I'm to present myself, and one guest, at the Lion's Gate entrance at nine o'clock on Friday night. I'll write and tell Harry."

"You mean you don't want Tess or me to go with you?" Daisy teased.

"Well, you have to admit that finding the documents is more important to Harry than to either of you. And while you're both excellent partners when it comes to being sneaky and creating diversions, I think we can all agree that Harry is the master."

Tess laughed. "That he is."

Harry's reply was short and sweet.

I'll be ready. H

Chapter Thirty-Nine

Ellie dressed with care for the Tower, in a practical blue dress and a dark navy cloak, and by the time Harry's coach pulled up at the front door she was almost shimmering with nervous energy.

Remembering rule number three, she'd armed herself with a small folding knife—the kind that might come in useful for opening a letter, not for stabbing someone. Daisy had offered her a blade, but Ellie had refused on the grounds that she'd probably slice off her own fingers if she tried to use it.

Her leg started jiggling with nervous excitement as she sat on the seat opposite Harry, and he leaned forward and pressed his hand to her knee, stilling the motion. The warmth of his palm spread through her skirts and the silk of her stockings, and heat spread up her leg at his touch.

She wanted to cross the carriage and sit next to him, to have him put his arm around her and hug her, but she didn't move.

His face alternated between light and darkness as they passed the rows of newly installed gas street lamps.

"I've wanted to prove who I am for years," he said softly. "But since coming back to London, since working with you, that desire's become even more imperative."

Ellie frowned. She was about to ask what he meant, but the carriage rocked to a stop in front of the impressively high walls of the Tower. The crenellated tops disappeared up into the darkness.

Determined to see as much as possible, she slipped her glasses onto her nose.

An imposing stone gate with two rounded turrets and a carved royal crest above the entrance stood before them, the way barred by a set of black ironwork gates. Two yeomen, in their uniforms of scarlet and gold, stood guard, but when Harry approached, a third man dressed in a dark coat and white shirt stepped out of the shadows.

"Eleanor Law to see Edmund Swifte?" Harry called.

The man smiled. "I am he. Welcome, ma'am, and sir."

When the gates were opened, Ellie shook hands with Swifte, then jumped in fright as the low, unmistakable roar of a lion echoed through the night. It sounded incredibly close.

Swifte chucked. "Fear not, Miss Law, you're perfectly safe. That's just Harry, one of the royal tigers who live here in the menagerie. He's a handsome fellow from Bengal, but he does like to make himself known."

She slid an amused glance at Harry. "A handsome beast named Harry, hmm? Is he fierce?"

"Oh, no, he's very tame," Swifte continued with a grin. "At least according to his keepers. But I shouldn't wish to be inside the cage with him myself!"

"I visited the menagerie a little while back," she said. "I particularly remember the bear named Martin. And the ravens, of course."

"Then you know the superstition about the ravens?"

Swifte asked. "If they ever leave the Tower, England will fall to her enemies."

"The keeper told me that their flight feathers are clipped to prevent that ever happening."

Harry raised his brows and sent her an amused look. "Nothing like giving luck, or fate, a helping hand."

Ellie gestured to Harry. "This is my friend, Monsieur Henri Bonheur."

Swifte produced a set of keys on a huge metal ring and handed it to one of the guards, who unlocked the gate and ushered them inside. Ellie hid a shudder as the metal closed behind them with an ominous clang.

Swifte looked at her again. "I'm told your father is Baron Ellenborough, the Lord Chief Justice?"

"He is."

"How wonderful! I'm a lawyer myself, and I studied several of his cases and verdicts when I was in training. His trial of Lord Cochrane, for the Stock Exchange Fraud two years ago, was extremely enlightening."

Ellie smiled. She'd helped her father for hours with that particular case. "It was indeed."

"And you're doing some research into your family tree?"

"Yes, a distant relative, the Earl of Arundel? Family legend has it that he was a prisoner here, and scratched his name or initials into the stone walls of his cell. I'd love to see if it's true."

"Almost all of the cells have some sort of graffiti in them," Swifte said. "There are hundreds of names, but I can't say I've ever studied them particularly closely."

"I think he might have been held in the Beauchamp Tower?"

"You're welcome to look," Swifte said, "but first we must wait for one other guest."

Ellie's spirits dropped at the news that another person would be joining them. She'd assumed she and Harry would have a private tour, with only Swifte to deal with.

Another carriage clattered to a stop outside the gate and she glanced at Harry in surprise as the jeweler, Mr. Fox, approached the gates and was admitted.

"Evening, Mr. Swifte," he called jovially, then gave a smile when he recognized Ellie. "Miss Law! Good evening. What a surprise to find you here. And Mr. Bonheur too." He shook Harry's hand warmly.

"It seems you've already met?" Swifte said. "Mr. Fox is a regular visitor here. He conducts the twice-yearly inspection and cleaning of the jewels."

Fox nodded. "Miss Law works for the private investigator, Charles King. Mr. Rundell used Mr. King's services to find the aquamarine that I'll be replacing on the state crown tonight."

"It's a small world, is it not?" Swifte marveled with a smile. "If you don't mind, Miss Law, we'll escort Mr. Fox to the Martin Tower, which is where the jewels are kept, so that he can start work. Then I can take you to the Beauchamp Tower."

Harry flashed Ellie a delighted sideways smile. "Oh, I have absolutely no objection to seeing the crown jewels, Mr. Swifte. In fact, it's always been a lifetime ambition of mine. I'm quite the collector of precious gems myself."

Ellie stifled a smile, even as she sent him a stern look to remind him that this was *not* a reconnaissance mission for a potential future heist.

They crossed a bridge over the water-filled moat, and she wrinkled her nose as the unpleasant smell of stagnant water and sewage rose to her nostrils. The Thames, just visible in the moonlight to their right through the sluice gate, was never sweet-smelling, even when it was moving swiftly, and the Tower moat was presumably the destination for both human and animal waste.

They reached a second tower, and Swifte unlocked a small door cut into the larger wooden gate. Once they were through, he lifted his lantern to show they were in a narrow, cobbled walk between the outer walls and a second set of inner walls, almost as high.

Ellie pressed closer to Harry. There was little doubt that this place was a prison, as well as a fortress, and her heart beat with both excitement and dread at the mission ahead.

Swifte pointed to their right. Beneath the arch of a half-timbered brick building was a wooden gate, beyond which a set of stone steps led down into the inky-black water of the river, visible through an iron portcullis.

"That's the water gate entrance, also known as Traitor's Gate. Many poor prisoners had their last taste of freedom coming through there."

Ellie shuddered. "Has anyone ever escaped?"

"A few." Swifte smiled. "In fact, it's rumored that the Tower's very first prisoner, one Ranulf Flambard, the Bishop of Durham, was also the very first escapee. He climbed through one of the White Tower's windows using a rope that had been smuggled to him in a gallon of wine."

Ellie chuckled. "Bravo, Bishop."

"The most *ingenious* escape, in my opinion," Swifte continued, clearly warming to the theme, "was by a Stuart loyalist named William Maxwell, the fifth Earl of Nithsdale, back in 1715. The day before his execution his wife, Lady Winnifred, and several of her friends visited him in his cell, and smuggled in layers of women's clothing under their own garments.

"The earl put on the clothes, and heavy makeup, while the ladies distracted the jailers by coming and going, and flirting shamelessly. Nithsdale eventually walked out of the Tower with the other ladies—despite being over six feet tall and having a large bushy beard—while his wife kept up a one-sided conversation in the cell, pretending to be talking with him. When she left, she asked his keepers to grant him a few hours of solitude to pray, which they did, so his escape wasn't noticed for quite some time."

Harry caught Ellie's eye and sent her a private smile. No doubt he was full of admiration for such a ruse. He was probably tucking the idea away as inspiration for future use—if he hadn't already done something similar himself at some point in his blackened past.

"So the earl and his lady managed to leave London?" he asked.

Swifte nodded. "In the Venetian ambassador's carriage. They escaped to the Continent, and lived out their days happily in Rome, or so the story goes."

"That sounds like a fairy tale." Harry smiled. "But I imagine the vast majority of prisoners didn't share such a happy fate."

"Certainly not."

They turned left and passed beneath another archway. "That grassy area is the Tower Green, where special executions took place."

Ellie grimaced. "Special executions?"

"Most traitors were executed in public, outside the walls, on Tower Hill to the north of here. But royals and other high-ranking nobles had the honor of a private execution."

"*What* an honor," Harry drawled, and Ellie sent him a chiding look.

He might joke, but he could so easily have been sentenced to execution himself, if any of his previous crimes had been uncovered. Her heart skipped a beat at the thought. He might not have faced the executioner's axe, but he could certainly have been sentenced to hang on the gallows. Or sent on board a stinking prison hulk, condemned to transportation to the other side of the world for seven years, which in many cases was tantamount to a death sentence.

She could only hope that this solemn reminder of the risks he'd taken were enough to convince him that his decision to stop his illegal activities was the right one.

Swifte continued talking. "Only seven people were actually executed here, including two of Henry the Eighth's wives: Anne Boleyn, his second wife, and Catherine Howard, his fifth. Thomas Cromwell was another victim, and so was poor Lady Jane Grey, known as the Nine-Day Queen."

"I'm glad we don't live in such bloodthirsty times now," Ellie murmured.

Ahead of them, in the center of the courtyard, rose a tall stone building with four square towers, one on each corner, each capped with a domed gray roof.

"That's the White Tower, the oldest part of the Tower, built by William the Conqueror," Swifte said.

"How many guards are there here, Mr. Swifte?" Harry asked.

"There are twenty yeomen guards on duty, both day and night, who do most of the ceremonial duties, but there's also a whole garrison of King's Fusiliers, commanded by the Constable of the Tower, whose role it is to defend the actual fortress and guard the jewels. They all live here in barracks."

"That sounds like excellent protection," Harry murmured, and Ellie sent him a laughing glance. No doubt assessing the level of security in any location was second nature to him.

They stopped in front of a tall, square tower set in the eastern corner of the walls.

"This is the Martin Tower. My family and I have apartments directly above the jewel room."

A uniformed soldier stood guard at the entrance, and he nodded at them as Swifte unlocked yet another door.

"Ready to see the crown jewels?"

Chapter Forty

"My assistant, Mr. Tombley, is already in the jewel room," Swifte said as he led them along a gloomy stone hallway. "Visitors are locked in during their visit, and they're usually only permitted to see the jewels from a distance."

He opened a second heavy oak door and swung it wide, and they finally stepped into the room where the crown jewels were kept.

Ellie looked around in wonder. The room had a high, vaulted ceiling, like a church, but there were no windows at all. A series of lamps had been lit all around the perimeter, and in the center of the room the jewels sat on a large stepped display stand surrounded by high iron railings.

Jewels and gold glittered in the flickering light, and she stared at the numerous crowns, scepters, and other shining regalia laid out on the purple velvet cloth.

Swifte stepped to her side. "Impressive, is it not?"

"Indeed. What a sight!"

Ellie managed not to look at Harry, even though she was sure he was relishing the sight of such splendor and fighting the temptation to steal something.

"Legend has it that King James the First's wife, Anne of Denmark, enjoyed performing Shakespeare's plays at court. She and her ladies would borrow the jewels to use as props, and several were returned with damage."

Swifte's tone was disapproving, but Ellie stifled a giggle. She could imagine herself, Tess, and Daisy doing exactly the same, given the chance.

Tombley stepped forward. "Since then, we've added this rail to keep people at a greater distance from the regalia, and there, you see, the repaired state crown and the Exeter Salt have been put inside glass cases on revolving tables."

"Excellent improvements," Harry murmured.

Swifte turned. "Mr. Fox, let's get you started on replacing that aquamarine."

He unlocked the glazed case in which the state crown lay and placed it reverently on a baize-topped table that had been positioned beneath one of the lamps.

The lower edge of the crown was trimmed in white ermine fur, and the central cap was a deep purple velvet. The part that circled the king's head was gold, as were the four curved arches that came up and over the top and joined together in the center below an orb and a cross.

A huge, irregular bloodred stone glittered on the front band, above a large blue sapphire, and the whole piece was encrusted with a profusion of diamonds and emeralds. It reminded Ellie of the tiny Book of Hours they'd returned to Mr. Bullock.

Swifte turned to her with a smile. "Before we leave Mr. Fox to his work, would you and Mr. Bonheur like to hold the crown in your own hands?"

"Absolutely!" Ellie breathed immediately, and Harry laughed at her childlike enthusiasm.

Swifte picked up the crown and handed it to her, and

she held her breath at the incredible sensation of holding something so precious. It was heavier than she'd expected, and she felt a pang of sympathy for poor mad King George, who'd had to wear the uncomfortable thing for so many hours on the day of his coronation.

"What an incredible piece of history. Thank you for letting me hold it."

She handed the crown to Harry, and watched him with an eagle eye. She couldn't see how on earth he might manage to steal any part of it with so many of them in attendance, but she wouldn't put it past his abilities. She'd witnessed his incredible sleight of hand before.

His dimples flashed as he caught her eye, and she was sure he knew precisely what she was thinking.

Her heart clenched with a strange, almost painful happiness. He was a perfect rogue. Even if there was no future for the two of them after tonight, she was glad they were sharing such an unforgettable experience. How many people could say they'd touched the crown of England?

"Has anyone ever tried to steal the jewels from inside the Tower?" Harry asked, his tone one of perfect innocence.

Swifte placed the crown safely back on the table. "A man named Captain Thomas Blood almost succeeded, back in the late 1600s. He and a group of accomplices tied up my predecessor, the Jewel House Keeper named Talbot Edwards, and stole St. Edward's crown, that golden orb, and the Sovereign's Sceptre." He pointed to the pieces on display. "They almost escaped, but Edward's son returned home unexpectedly and foiled the plot. They were captured just outside the walls."

"Were they executed?" Ellie asked.

"Incredibly, no. Blood was granted an audience with King Charles, and managed to convince him he deserved a second chance. He was not only pardoned, but granted lands in Ireland worth five hundred pounds!"

Harry shook his head with a wry chuckle. "The fellow must have been the most persuasive rogue."

Ellie almost rolled her eyes. The parallels between Harry and this Captain Blood were striking. Being pardoned and then *rewarded* for a theft was something that Harry would undoubtedly manage too.

She took one last look around the treasure chamber, trying to fix the sight onto her memory so she'd be able to tell Daisy and Tess as many details about it as possible. She wanted to remember this night forever.

Swifte jangled his keys. "Mr. Fox, we'll leave you to your work. Mr. Tombley will see you out when you're done."

Harry took one last, wistful glance at the jewels, and sent Ellie a wry smile. "Let's be off, then."

Chapter Forty-One

"Now for your research," Swifte said as they stepped back into the cool night air. "The Beauchamp Tower's not usually included in the tours we give to the general public, since most people prefer the menagerie and the armory, but the cells are very interesting."

Harry caught Ellie's arm and slowed their steps so they wouldn't be overheard. "Do you have a clever plan to make him leave us alone?"

"Of course," she whispered back, trying to ignore the tickle of his warm breath at her ear. "Do *you*?"

"Of course," he echoed, giving the tip of her nose a teasing flick. "But ladies first. I'll follow your lead."

They followed the walls around the back of the looming White Tower, and Swifte raised his lantern as he unlocked a door in the curtain wall. A rusting suit of armor loomed out of the darkness and Ellie jumped in alarm before it came fully into focus. Harry snorted in quiet amusement.

"The cells used for aristocratic prisoners are up here."

A curving staircase led onto a narrow corridor with a

series of closed doors. Swifte pushed one open, and they stepped into a large, bow-fronted room that was clearly part of the rounded turret, with leaded-glass windows, and a fireplace large enough to roast an ox.

"This is the room with the most profuse carving, but there are smaller cells with names and dates too."

It was much larger than Ellie had expected it to be, although it was still cold and unwelcoming. Her heels clicked on the bare floorboards and echoed strangely in the empty space.

The walls were covered in a profusion of scratched names, designs, and initials. She reached out and traced the name Iane, an older spelling of Jane, with her fingertips. Had it been carved by the seventeen-year-old Lady Jane before her untimely execution? The thought was depressing. Women had so often been at the mercy of more powerful men, mere pawns in the ruthless cut and thrust of history.

In the flickering lantern light, she found the name Thomas inscribed above a crudely carved bell with an *A* on the side, a cross, a shield, and even a lion and the date 1564.

"So many names!" she exclaimed. "It could take hours to read them all."

Harry stepped forward and sent her a chiding look. "Where's your usual optimism, Miss Law? I feel sure we'll find what we're looking for if we work together."

He began prowling the room, tilting his head back to read the inscriptions that were higher up, while Ellie started by the window and methodically moved her way from left to right.

Swifte did his best to provide them both with sufficient illumination.

"Perhaps it would be better to come back when it's daylight?" he suggested.

"Wait!" Ellie exclaimed in triumph. "Here it is! Arundel!"

Sure enough, the name had been carved in a slanted, flowing script, along with a longer inscription, next to a small tree.

She shot Swifte her most charming, pleading smile. "Oh, this is wonderful! My father will be so delighted. I don't suppose you have a piece of paper and a pencil, or a charcoal stick, do you, Mr. Swifte? I'd just *love* to take a rubbing of this, as proof."

"I suppose there might be some paper down in the guardroom," Swifte said reluctantly. "But we only have the one lantern. I wouldn't want to leave the two of you up here in the dark. These rooms are said to be haunted, you know."

Harry reached into the pocket of his coat. "As luck would have it, I have a candle with me. I once got locked in a cellar as a child—accidentally, of course—and now I have a dislike of the dark. I always carry one."

Ellie had no idea if there was any truth to that statement, but her heart still squeezed at the thought of him alone and afraid in the darkness. Oh, the man had the ability to tie her up in knots.

He lit the candle from Swifte's lantern and sent the other man a confident smile. "Don't worry about us. Miss Law and I will stay right here until you return. I'm far too wary of encountering one of your infamous ghosts to go wandering about this place at night." He sat himself down on the seat in the window embrasure, and gestured Swifte toward the door.

Poor Swifte clearly thought the request was an

annoyance, but he obviously didn't want to offend them by refusing. "Very well. I'll be back shortly."

Ellie waited until the sound of his boots disappeared down the stairs before she turned to Harry and lifted her brows. The single candle gave off far less light than Swifte's lantern had done, and his face was uplit in its glow, giving his handsome features a wicked cast and making his dimples deeply shadowed.

"Brilliant girl!" He balanced the candle on the stone seat and strode over to her. "Your deviousness leaves me breathless."

"Thank you."

"As does kissing you." He caught her by the hips, and pulled her up hard against him.

Ellie's stomach somersaulted, and her heart almost doubled its pace as their lips met. She pressed herself even closer, kissing him back with fervent urgency, and Harry's tongue swept against hers, tasting her with a fierce demand that made her blood heat and her belly tingle.

He tightened his grip for a brief moment, then thrust her away from him with a low, gasping laugh. "God, woman. You're a terrible distraction!"

She laughed too, elated, practically shaking with nervous energy. "You're right. Let's find those papers."

Harry strode to the enormous fireplace and ducked beneath the lintel. The walls around him were streaked black with soot and age. "It doesn't look as if an actual fire's been lit in here for decades. That's a good sign."

He reached up and began feeling along the inside of the chimney, dislodging a small avalanche of soot that rained down on him. He turned his face away, coughing, while Ellie held her breath and prayed they hadn't been sent on a wild-goose chase.

"Now I see why you wore a coat that was almost black," she said. "It hides the soot beautifully."

Just as she was beginning to give up hope, he stilled and glanced up. "I've found a ledge. It's like a single stone's been removed to make a hiding place." He repositioned his arm, and a cloth-wrapped bundle tied with brown string fell onto the hearth at his feet.

Ellie pounced on it just as she heard the slam of a door below and Swifte's footsteps ascending the stairs.

"Quick! He's coming!" She thrust the packet through the side slit in her skirts and into the pocket beneath. The bundle was so large it made a bulge at her hip, but she pulled her cloak around her to conceal it.

Harry ducked out of the chimney and retook his place in the window, but as he turned in the candlelight Ellie's heart missed a beat. She ran to him and wiped an incriminating black smudge of coal dust from his cheek. He cleaned his dirty palms on her cloak a moment before Swifte reappeared, clutching a large sheet of paper and a handful of sharpened pencils.

Ellie clapped her hands, her happiness unfeigned. She could barely contain her excitement. "Ah, marvelous."

It was a matter of moments to place the paper over the inscribed name and take a rubbing with the pencil, and she stepped back with a triumphant sigh when she was done.

"Thank you, Mr. Swifte. I appreciate your patience." She rolled the paper and tucked it beneath her cloak. "Shall we go?"

She barely glanced at Harry as they retraced their steps through the arched guardhouses. It was only when the final gate clanged shut behind them and they were safely ensconced in the carriage that she allowed herself a deep, relieved exhale.

She pressed her palm flat to her heart as if she could calm its racing. "We did it! Good heavens, what a night."

Harry tilted his head toward the bulge of documents in her skirts. "Let's just hope those papers are what the doctor says they are, and not something completely different. What if they're the last words of a prisoner, a confession, or even love letters?"

"Shall I open them now?"

He shook his head. "Not enough light. Wait until we're back at Cobham House."

She sent him a laughing, teasing look. "It must have been incredibly trying for you, to be so close to all those precious gems and not steal a single one of them. Were you imagining ways to do it?"

His dimples flashed. "Force of habit. Purely *theoretically,* mind you."

"I'd say it was impossible."

"Nothing's impossible. Only extremely unlikely. I bet I could do something with a carrier pigeon. Or a highly trained dog. Or a wooden leg."

Ellie shook her head, loving his inventiveness. He was certainly never boring. "But that's all behind you now, isn't it?"

He pressed his palm over his heart. "From now on, I'm going to be a model citizen."

She let out a disbelieving snort. "Ha!"

For a delightful moment she entertained herself with a lurid fantasy of Harry making good on his promise to make love to her against the wall by sweeping her upstairs as soon as they reached Cobham House to celebrate their success.

And then she remembered that Hugo was undoubtedly still in residence and anxiously waiting for news, and her spirits fell.

The luck they'd had tonight finally seemed to have deserted her.

Chapter Forty-Two

Hugo was indeed waiting for them in the study of Cobham House, elegantly attired in a burgundy velvet banyan robe and matching slippers, and his brows rose in question when they came through the door.

"Well, did you find them?"

"We found *something*," Harry hedged.

He poured all three of them a glass of wine, while Ellie delved into her skirts and set the bundle on the desk. She flicked open her little pocket knife and held it over the string. "May I?"

Harry nodded, and both he and Hugo leaned forward expectantly as she unwrapped the outer layer of soot-blackened parchment to reveal a thick stack of folded documents. Several were sealed with red blobs of wax, which clearly hadn't been disturbed.

Harry turned over the topmost letter, and her heart skipped a beat as she read *For the attention of Henry Brooke, Esquire.*

His hands shook slightly as he began to read the contents. "It's Emberton's signed testimony of his inspection of master Henry Brooke, son of James and Mary Brooke, Earl and Countess of Cobham." He turned to the second page and smiled. "And look! Here's the original drawing of my eyes."

The watercolor illustration, although rather amateurish, clearly recorded the unique patches of blue and brown Ellie was so familiar with. She smiled, pleased on Harry's behalf.

"That's undoubtedly enough to prove that you and young Henry Brooke are one and the same. Congratulations."

Harry beamed. He looked like he wanted to kiss her, but Hugo's presence held him back.

"You still have to apply to the Lord Chancellor for a writ of summons to the House of Lords to be officially recognized as the next Earl of Cobham," she reminded him, trying to keep her mind on business. "But that's just a formality. You'll need to prove your parents were legally married—which can be done by providing a copy of their marriage registration—and that you were born legitimately after that date, which means providing proof of your birth."

"His parents were married at St. George's, Hanover Square," Hugo said. "Their names are in the register. And his birth was recorded in the church near Cobham Hall, in Kent."

Harry's eyes took on a faraway look as he clearly pictured the place in his mind, and Ellie's heart tugged painfully in her chest. *Of course* he owned a country estate, as well as this magnificent town house. He was an earl.

"Cobham Hall's lovely," he said with a smile. "I grew up there, until I went away to school."

A wave of yearning to see the place seized her, but she pushed it away. "Who's been managing the estate, while you were away?"

"His parents' old steward," Hugo supplied. "He sent us annual reports on how the place was faring. When he died, his son took over the role. I can't wait to see it again."

Ellie forced a smile, despite the awful feeling that Harry was already slipping away, far beyond her reach.

She'd fallen in love with Harry: rogue, reformed criminal, of no fixed abode. Henry Brooke, Lord Cobham, was a completely different proposition. He wouldn't need to fill his days "working" for King & Co. or accompanying her on cases. He'd be too busy running his estate, joining debates in the House of Lords, hosting society parties. He'd need to find a suitable wife to play hostess and bear his children.

He wouldn't need *her* to entertain him.

A bittersweet ache twisted her gut. Clearly it was possible to be glad for him and feel sorry for herself at the same time.

She cleared her throat as he fished his golden signet ring from his pocket and slid it onto his finger with a satisfied smile.

"Well, that's another case closed for King and Company."

He sent her a confused look. "What do you mean? We're not done yet."

"You hired us to prove—or disprove—your identity. We've done what you asked."

"What about introducing me into society?"

Ellie removed her spectacles and pinched the bridge of her nose. When they'd left the Tower, she'd been fizzing with excitement, buoyed up with finding the documents, but now she just felt exhausted.

"You don't need an investigative agency for that. As soon as you're granted your letters patent, you just need to get someone well-placed in the *ton* to give their personal seal of approval." She shrugged. "Tess is the Duchess of Wansford. I can ask if she'd be willing to host a party to introduce you as the Earl of Cobham, if you like."

Harry frowned at her formal tone. "I would appreciate that very much, thank you. And tell her I'll cover all the expenses."

"Well, it's late. I'd . . . better be getting home."

He opened his mouth as if intending to say something, then shook his head and changed his mind. "Of course. I'll tell Carson to ready the horses."

When he left the room she said goodbye to Hugo, but he was waiting for her when she stepped out into the hallway. Before she could say anything, he wrapped his arms around her and pulled her into a crushing hug.

"Thank you," he breathed, pressing his nose into her hair. "You've given me back my name, my future. Everything." He pressed a kiss against her forehead and his voice dropped to a husky groan. "I wish you could stay and help me celebrate. I want to show you *exactly* how grateful I am."

Ellie swallowed a sudden lump in her throat even as her body urged her to throw caution to the wind. "I wish I could, too, but I have to go."

She would *not* cry. If this was goodbye, the last time they were alone together, then she would take it like a strong, sophisticated woman. She would not wail and make a fuss. Heartbreak wasn't fatal.

She pulled out of his arms and stepped back as the rattle of the carriage sounded outside. "I'm glad tonight was a success. I'll let you know what Tess says. Good night."

Chapter Forty-Three

Harry's official confirmation as the twelfth Earl of Cobham sent a shock wave through the *ton*. Society was agog with the news that the man who had been amongst them as Henri Bonheur, Comte de Carabas, was, in fact, none other than Henry Brooke, the Lost Earl.

As if that wasn't enough, there was a persistent rumor going around that the same man was also Charles King, the mysterious owner of King & Co. investigative agency.

Despite being the ones who'd *started* that particular rumor, with Harry's permission, Ellie, Tess, and Daisy all strenuously denied it whenever they were asked, which naturally did nothing but fan the flames of speculation.

The man in question, however, was being remarkably elusive. He'd kept a frustratingly low profile for the past two weeks; Ellie hadn't seen him since she'd checked his papers were all in order and addressed them to the Lord Chancellor's office herself.

Tess had jumped at the chance to host a party, much to her husband's dismay, and invitations had been sent out to over a hundred of society's most respected and fashionable members, for attendance at a special ball to introduce the Lost Earl.

Acceptance letters had been piling up on the silver tray in the hallway of Wansford House for days.

"I don't think we've had more than a dozen people say they can't come," Daisy said excitedly, as she and Ellie compiled a final list in Tess's elegant drawing room. "It's going to be an absolute crush."

Tess beamed. "It's going to be the biggest event I've ever hosted. Poor Justin thinks we've all gone mad."

"At least Harry's paying for it all." Daisy grinned. "That should keep your husband happy. The only time he likes to spend money is when it's on you."

Tess glanced at Ellie. "Will your dress be ready in time?"

"Madame Lefèvre has promised to have it delivered by tomorrow morning."

"I can't believe you've finally ordered something so wonderful for yourself." Tess smiled. "I can't wait to see you in it."

Ellie's stomach did a little nervous flip. She'd used some of her share of Bullock's money to buy her very first dress from the fashionable couturier, a beautiful peacock-blue silk gown with velvet ribbon along the neckline and hem.

If the dress made her look and feel beautiful, then she might also be able to feign confidence and effortless ease for the evening as well. She was about to witness Harry's ultimate triumph, and it wouldn't do to appear dispirited. Even if that was how she felt inside.

"Does anyone know what Harry's planning to wear?" Daisy asked idly.

"No idea, but I can't imagine it'll be anything less than magnificent."

Ellie adjusted her spectacles. "Are you sure we've made the right decision, letting everyone think that Harry is Charles King? After all, *we* were the ones who started this enterprise. We've done all of the work. Don't you think it's unfair to let a man just swan in and take all the credit?"

Daisy shook her head. "We've already discussed this. And no, it's perfectly fine. I wouldn't have agreed to it otherwise, and neither would Tess."

Tess gave a fervent nod. "Agreed."

"After all, it's as advantageous for us as it is for him," Daisy continued. "We always let clients assume our employer was a man, so this really isn't that different. If anything, I predict we'll get even more business now, because of his charm and natural charisma. People just can't help believing in him."

"And it's the perfect explanation for everyone who previously met him as Henri Bonheur, or Enrico Castellini," Tess added. "He can just say he assumed those roles to work undercover for a case."

Ellie toyed with her pen. "Well, he'd better not embarrass us, now that he's the very visible figurehead of the company."

"I'm sure he won't. Now that he's been confirmed as the earl, he's unlikely to do anything that will risk his position. He came to us saying he was determined to stay on the right side of the law, and I don't think he's in any danger of going back on that now."

"But do you really think people can change?" Ellie sighed. "They say a leopard never changes his spots."

"They also say a reformed rake makes the best husband, so there's clearly room to maneuver," Daisy quipped with a laugh. "Have a little faith."

"I think it's absolutely possible for people to change,"

Tess said earnestly. "Just look at Justin. When I first met him, he was adamant that he would only marry because it was expected of him. He certainly didn't believe that he could fall in love. But miracles *do* happen, especially when we least expect them to. I have no doubt that he loves me just as deeply as I love him."

"True," Daisy sighed. "So there's still hope for both of us, Ellie, my love."

Ellie declined to comment. She couldn't decide if she was excited about tomorrow's event, or terrified. To watch from the side of the room while Harry was fêted and adored by a bevy of beautiful women would be almost impossible, but she had her pride. If necessary, she would prove she could act just as well as Harry. She would smile, and look happy, and generally behave as though her heart wasn't breaking.

It would be the performance of her life.

Chapter Forty-Four

"I knew he'd cause a sensation!"

Daisy's laughing comment forced a reluctant smile from Ellie. As predicted, Tess's ballroom was filled to bursting with an avid crowd, all desperate to make the acquaintance of the newly minted Earl of Cobham.

Tales of his mysterious ten-year disappearance were rife with so much exaggeration and embellishment that Ellie was convinced he'd started most of them himself.

"Someone told me he's been a spy for Wellington," Daisy murmured. "And that he infiltrated Napoleon's birthday party."

"*I* heard he had something to do with finding the French Crown Jewels." Tess snorted from behind her fan.

Ellie rolled her eyes. "He couldn't have been more than five years old when those were stolen. Wherever do people get these ridiculous ideas?"

"The best one was that he'd been kidnapped by Barbary pirates, negotiated his own ransom, and ended up at the court of the Bey of Algiers as his translator." Daisy shook her head.

"I like the rumor that he helped the banker Rothschild smuggle gold to the army in the Peninsula."

"To be fair, with Harry, any one of those could actually be true." Ellie sighed.

All three of them glanced over to the opposite side of the room, where Harry was holding court at the center of a throng of rapt admirers, and Ellie's heart squeezed painfully in her chest.

She'd expected him to wear something extravagant and flamboyant, like the powder-blue coat he'd worn to Willingham's, but he'd surprised her yet again. His stark black evening jacket was so perfectly cut to accentuate his lean, muscled physique that he made every other man in attendance look scruffy and unkempt in comparison. His buff breeches and frothy cravat were the epitome of understated elegance.

At this distance, he was barely in focus, since she'd forgone her glasses in favor of not looking like a studious bluestocking.

"They couldn't have welcomed Lazarus rising from the dead with any more enthusiasm," Daisy said drily.

"Everyone loves a fairy tale." Ellie shrugged. "He'll be the toast of the town until someone else with a more exciting story comes along. They're all so fickle."

Tess slid her a sideways glance. "I'm so glad you wore that dress, El. You look sensational. Lord Ware's asked me three times for an introduction, and James Coutts begged me for your name the moment you entered the room."

"I've spoken to James Coutts on at least three separate occasions this season. He's called me Sophie every single time. The man's an imbecile."

Daisy chuckled. "It's a rare thing to find a man with money *and* brains."

"I have to say, I adore Harry's uncle Hugo. The man's an incorrigible rogue." Tess smiled and waved at the man in question, who was flirting outrageously with Emma Sydenham, the *ton*'s most eligible widow.

"It's a shame your parents couldn't come, Ellie. It would have been nice to introduce them to Harry."

"It would, but my aunt Eliza fell and sprained her ankle while coming out of church on Sunday, so Mother's traveled down to stay with her for a week." Ellie shrugged. "And you know what my father's like. He'd rather bury himself in depositions and witness statements than endure the agony of attending a ball. I'm sure he was delighted when that last-minute petition for clemency was delivered, needing his urgent attention."

She glanced over at Harry again, and squinted. He seemed to be moving.

"Is Harry coming this way?" she muttered. "I can't see."

"He is," Tess murmured. "And he's looking at you as if you're the key to the jewel chamber at the Tower! I'd say that dress is doing its job."

And then Ellie couldn't breathe, because Harry was there, in front of her.

She hadn't seen him in person for over two weeks, and when she finally managed to suck in her breath, her pulse stuttered at the familiar scent of his cologne.

"Good evening to my three favorite ladies."

Tess and Daisy both swept him extravagant, mocking bows.

"Good evening, Mr. King," they echoed, in perfect unison.

"Sorry, force of habit," Daisy added loudly with a grin, fully aware that they could be overheard by those closest to them. "Although I suppose now the cat's out of the bag."

Ellie barely dipped a curtsey. Her legs were suddenly like jelly.

Harry turned to her and held out his hand. "May I have the honor of this dance, Miss Law?"

Heat rose in her cheeks. "Oh, no, really, I don't—"

"She does!" Daisy said, pushing her forward with a hand on the small of her back.

"She definitely does," Tess echoed with a glittering smile.

Ellie sent each of them a glare that promised retribution.

Harry leaned in. "You can't wear a dress like that and expect to stand at the side of the room like a wallflower. There's not an unmarried man here who hasn't been trying to pluck up the courage to ask you to dance."

Ellie had to smile at his hyperbole. "Am I so fierce, then? Or is it just that you're bolder than most?"

His dimples flashed as he smiled that irresistible smile. "Oh, I am *definitely* bolder than most. Faint heart never won fair lady."

She sighed, and her desire to be held in his arms overrode her reluctance to be the center of attention. "Oh, very well."

The whispers increased as Harry's choice of companion was noted, but he merely turned her in his arms as the first swirling strains of the orchestra filled the air. Ellie tried to relax as his hand settled on the small of her back, and his other hand held hers at precisely the correct angle near her shoulder. She'd never felt so self-conscious in her life.

"Do you remember our first dance, at Willingham's?" he murmured.

"Yes." Her throat was inexplicably dry. There was so much she wanted to say to him, but now that she had the opportunity, her mind was an unhelpful blank. At least this close, she could see the fascinating colors of his eyes. They were wonderfully distracting.

"In the carriage, on the way to the Tower, I told you how important it was for me to prove my real name."

"I remember."

"It's because I realized, several years ago now, that I couldn't ever marry without it."

Ellie's spirits plummeted. Had he considered marrying someone in the past? Or had it just been a general, theoretical observation? A thought that he might want to marry, *eventually*.

She was too afraid to ask. "People sign fake names on the marriage register all the time. My father prosecuted a man only last month who'd married two different women under two different names."

"Those marriages weren't legal, though, were they?"

"Well. No."

He looked down at her. "If I loved a woman enough to want to marry her, then I couldn't trick her into a sham marriage and risk disgracing her. That wouldn't be love at all. Love is caring for the other person so much that you'd do anything to avoid hurting them."

Ellie's heart was hammering in her throat at his closeness. The room was unseasonably warm. She moistened her lips, and his gaze dropped to her mouth before flashing back to hers.

"But now you have your real name, beyond all reasonable doubt. You can marry whoever you like with a clean conscience," she said.

He'd probably already made a short list of candidates from the women he'd met this evening. She could think of half a dozen ladies who'd be perfect as his countess, all of them beautiful and accomplished in their own ways.

His lips twitched. "I don't think I'll ever have a *completely* clean conscience, but at least in that particular instance I would be innocent."

She braced herself to hear the worst. She'd always known that theirs would only be a temporary fling, and while she'd hoped it might last longer than it had done, she would accept defeat stoically, if not willingly.

Still, she couldn't seem to look away.

"I have someone in mind, actually."

She missed a step, but he covered the stumble with his usual effortless grace, swinging her round in an impromptu twirl that made her skirts wrap around his legs like seaweed.

"Oh?" she croaked, grateful for the small mercy that she sounded interested, and not soul-crushed. "Anyone I know?"

"It is, as a matter of fact."

She was starting to feel sick, but she managed to twist her lips into a parody of a smile. "Who?"

"Do you know, Miss Law, for a woman with an incredibly brilliant mind, you are, on occasion, incredibly stupid."

Ellie gasped, momentarily shocked out of her misery by the insult. "What?"

"You've already refused to be my partner in crime, because you're far too sensible, but how do you feel about being my partner in life?"

Ellie blinked, sure she was dreaming and had somehow slipped into an alternative universe without realizing it. She almost looked around to see if the rest of the guests had turned into cats, but Harry's gaze held her hostage.

"You want to marry *me*?"

"Of course I want to marry you." His brows twitched

in the merest hint of masculine confusion. "Who on earth *else* do you think I'd want to marry? I love you. And I'm pretty sure you love me too."

Ellie was sure she must be staring up at him like a simpleton.

"Wait. Say it again. You love me?"

His mouth creased into a smile and his dimples appeared. "Why do you sound so astonished? Yes, I love you. I have no idea precisely when it happened, but I've never been more certain of anything in my life."

He turned them both in another elegant swirl, and in the small part of her brain that wasn't frozen with shock, Ellie was grateful that at least one of them had retained their coordination.

"*Because* I love you," he continued with devastating normalcy, as if they were discussing something as unimportant as the likelihood of rain, "I am not going to get down on one knee in the middle of this enormous crowd of people and propose to you, because I know you'd likely die of mortification to be the focus of such a spectacle. But what I *can* tell you is that as soon as we are alone, I'm going to beg you for your hand."

He smiled down at her. "Do you think you're going to accept?"

Ellie swallowed, hardly daring to trust the glowing ball of happiness that seemed to be lodged beneath her sternum.

"I don't see why not. Because I love you too. Quite desperately."

His fingers tightened on hers for a fraction of a second, and as his shoulder relaxed beneath her palm, she realized with astonishment that he'd actually been tense. The idea was so ridiculous it brought a smile to her face.

"Did you honestly think I'd refuse you?"

"The thought had crossed my mind. Someone like you can do a million times better than me. But I think you loved me before I had a name, so I had a little hope."

She shook her head. "I don't care what you call yourself. I don't care if you're a thief, or an earl, or the son of a chimney sweep."

His eyes bored into hers. "Now I *really* wish we weren't in such a public place, because I want to kiss you very much."

Mischief flashed through her. "You have only yourself to blame. This was an ill-conceived plan."

"Probably the worst I've ever concocted," he agreed ruefully. The heat in his gaze made her hotter than ever, and just the promise of his lips on hers made excitement tingle through her veins.

"But what should I call you? Charles? Harry? Henry?" she teased, suddenly bold.

"Yours," he murmured. "Just call me yours."

The music came to a rapturous end, and Ellie smiled up at him, breathless. He released her right hand reluctantly, but kept his left hand at her waist as he escorted her off the dance floor and back toward Tess and Daisy, who were watching them with undisguised interest.

Ellie was sure they could discern her happiness even from across the room. She felt like she was glowing with it.

"Do you think your father will agree to you marrying me, now I'm the Earl of Cobham?" he murmured. "As opposed to a nameless ne'er-do-well."

She deliberately bumped his hip with hers. "He and Mother always wanted me to find my perfect match, whoever that was. They've never pressured me to marry a man with a title, or to settle for someone I didn't love."

"I've got a good chance, then."

"I'd say so."

Daisy was practically hopping from foot to foot with curiosity. "That seemed a very *intense* conversation you two were having out there."

Ellie sent Harry an amused, questioning look. "Would you call it intense?"

He tilted his head and pretended to consider, and she almost burst out laughing.

"A spirited negotiation," he said solemnly.

"Regarding what?" Daisy pressed, trying—and failing—to keep her voice to a low screech.

"Another joint collaboration," Ellie said, delighting in being deliberately evasive.

"A mutually beneficial arrangement," Harry added.

Tess raised her brows, clearly intrigued but not daring to read too much into their loaded words. "Business? Or Pleasure?"

Harry glanced at Ellie and his eyes darkened as his pupils expanded. "Oh, most definitely pleasure," he drawled.

Daisy let out a tiny, muffled squeak of excitement and clapped her hands over her mouth.

Tess's lips curved into a smile and she turned to address Harry. "In approximately ten minutes my husband is going to ask you to go to his study to discuss a business venture," she said softly.

Harry raised his brows. "He is?"

"Yes, because I'm going to ask him to. *You* are going to accept, but when you get to the study, you're going to open the door that's concealed in the wall in the corner next to the large globe."

"Interesting," Harry smiled, clearly intrigued.

"That door leads to a servants' passage, and a staircase that goes up to the third floor. Wait in the first room on the right."

Harry took her hand, bowed low over it, and kissed it. "Thank you, Your Grace."

Tess sent him a gracious nod watched as he took his cue and walked away without a backward glance.

Daisy turned to Ellie, and raised her voice just enough to carry.

"Ellie, my love, you're looking extremely hot." She fanned her enthusiastically.

Tess pretended to look equally concerned. "Oh dear, yes. Perhaps the dancing was too much? Why don't you go upstairs and cool down for a moment?"

Ellie caught the wicked twinkle in their eyes, and a wave of gratitude for her wonderful, devious friends swelled inside her.

"Indeed, I *do* feel a little overheated. I think I'll take your advice."

Chapter Forty-Five

Ellie's heart was pounding as she waited in one of Tess's spare rooms. It was where she always stayed when she was at Wansford House, and a few of her things lay scattered about on the dressing table and chairs.

Too excited to sit on the bed, she paced nervously between the window and the cheval mirror, and just when she thought she'd splinter apart from anticipation, Harry opened the door and stepped inside.

The distant hum of the ball far below faded away completely as she rushed into his arms. Her mouth opened under his, and he pressed her roughly against the wall, his big body the perfect combination of urgency and restraint.

Ellie bit back a gasp of delirious happiness. She kissed him back, twining her arms around his neck as her tongue tangled with his. The taste of him, so wonderfully intoxicating, made her lightheaded.

"Mine," he growled against her lips. "God, Ellie, I want you so much."

"Wait!" She pushed lightly on his shoulders. "You said

as soon as we were alone, you were going to beg for my hand."

His playful growl of frustration warmed her heart, but he fell back from her and raked his hand through hair she'd already disordered with her fingers.

"Such a stickler," he groaned. "But fine. I did say that." With jerky motions he tugged his gold signet ring from his finger, sank to his knee on the floor, and gazed up at her. "Eleanor Law—"

"Jane," she said with a smile.

"What?"

"My middle name's Jane. Do it properly."

He let out a sound of playful fury. "Right. Eleanor *Jane* Law, you infuriating little baggage"—he held out the ring—"will you do me the very great honor of becoming my wife?"

"Henry James Charles Brooke," she said with mock solemnity, repeating the names she'd seen listed on numerous documents in the past few weeks. "Yes."

She held out her hand, which was only shaking a tiny amount, and he slid the ring onto her fourth finger. She didn't get time to admire it, or to marvel at the miracle of a man like Harry wanting a girl like her. The moment it was on there, he surged to his feet and pinned her back against the wall.

"Bloody fantastic," he growled. "And now we've got the formalities out of the way, I'm going to pleasure you up against this wall until you can't think straight. Agreed?"

"Agreed."

The kiss went from soft to carnal in less than three beats of her heart. Ellie clung to him, seeking with her tongue as a burning urgency rose within her. She grabbed the lapels of his jacket and pushed the garment off his shoulders and he shrugged out of it, paying no heed to the expensive fabric. He flung it away and reached down to pull her skirts up her legs, gathering the fabric in huge swathes.

His hand slid up, over her silk stockings' garters, then encountered the bare flesh of her thigh, and he groaned against her mouth as he palmed her bare bottom.

"Quel vestito mi ha fatto impazzire tutta la notte."

"Meaning . . . ?"

"This dress has been driving me mad all night."

"It was meant to," she admitted with a laughing gasp.

"Vixen! I always knew there was a devious streak hidden behind that studious veneer."

He kissed his way down the side of her neck and pressed little nibbling bites to the top curves of her breasts, which were shown to devastating effect by her bodice. Ellie threaded her fingers through his hair and held him tight, loving his passion, his fervency.

A moment later he'd unbuttoned his falls, and she wrapped her leg around his thigh, letting him settle between her own. His seeking fingers found her core, and he made a deep sound of approval at finding her already wet. She was more than ready for him.

"Ellie. Love."

He kissed her again and she tilted her hips, going up on tiptoe so their bodies could fit together. He slid inside, and the strange angle made her suck in a breath. It wasn't particularly comfortable, but when he started to withdraw, she clutched at his shoulders, determined to allow him his pleasure even if she took none herself.

She pressed her back more firmly against the wall, and he took more of her weight, lifting her off the floor and wrapping her legs around his hips, and suddenly their bodies aligned perfectly.

Ellie closed her eyes. Every rock of his hips produced a wicked, delicious friction that made her body clench around him. The same building tension she'd felt before began to grow, as he pressed and withdrew in a maddening rhythm.

His hand cupped the back of her head, tilting it back until she gazed into his extraordinary eyes.

"I love you," he breathed harshly, as if it were somehow a punishment and not a blessing, and she laughed with sheer joy.

"I love you too."

She held her breath, reaching for that ultimate prize, and then it happened. Her head tipped back, her eyes fluttered closed, and pleasure claimed her, hot and deep and sweet. She gave herself up to it with complete abandon, letting it fill her, loving the physical connection of their bodies and the merging of their souls.

Harry kissed her again, his lips hard against hers, and with one last thrust he withdrew from her body. As soon as her feet touched the ground again she reached between them, determined to help him. He was fisting his cock, and she placed her hand over his.

He slammed his free hand against the wall next to her head and buried his face in her neck, and a moment later found his own release. His guttural groan reverberated through her and she reveled in the way his big body shuddered and flexed.

For a moment they simply stood together, panting, utterly spent. And then he lifted his head and stroked his fingers over her jaw. He pressed soft kisses to her cheek, her nose, the corner of her eye, and she smiled in exhausted contentment.

He gazed deep into her eyes, and those beloved dimples creased his cheeks.

"What are you smiling about?" she demanded.

"Just remembering rule number eight."

She wrinkled her nose and tried to think, but her brain was still a nebulous mess thanks to his marvelous debauchery. He'd made good on his promise to stop her thinking straight.

"Remind me which one that is again."

"*What you take, you sell. What you're given, you keep.*"

She raised her brows, demanding a silent explanation, and his smile widened.

"I'm going to keep *you,* Eleanor Law. You've given yourself to me. Freely. And I'm never going to let you go." He pressed another kiss to her lips. "Do you remember that tale I told you, the one about the thief who stole the bluestocking's heart? I didn't tell you the whole story."

"Fancy that, you omitting certain pertinent facts," she said drily, and he mock-scowled at her sarcasm.

"After the thief stole her heart," he chided, "she stole *his* right back, in the ultimate revenge. They kept each other's hearts forever, and never returned them."

"Sounds like they deserved each other," she said.

"Sounds like they met their perfect match."

He straightened, and they spent a moment rearranging their clothing. Ellie crossed to the bed and sat on the edge, while he bent and rescued his poor coat from the floor and shook his head in mock despair at the creases. "At least we'll keep the tailors of Cork Street and Bond Street in business."

He glanced at her. "Are you happy for me to speak to your father tomorrow?"

She nodded, her heart almost overflowing. "Yes. And then I suppose an announcement in *The Times*? Unless you'd like to marry by special license, we'll have to wait for three weeks until the banns are read."

He groaned. "It will feel like a lifetime, but I'm sure we'll be able to find some time to be together like this in private. I happen to be *extremely good* at planning clandestine activities. Especially when I have such excellent motivation."

She chuckled. "Finally, a way to use your skills that I can approve of."

He caught her hand and kissed it, as he'd done the very first night they'd met. "I live only to please you, my love."

Epilogue

"Excellent cake," Daisy mumbled through a mouthful of icing. "I love weddings."

Tess sent her a fond smile and turned to Ellie. "Especially when it's for someone we adore. Congratulations, Lady Cobham."

Ellie put her hands to her warm cheeks. "That sounds so strange. I've been 'Miss Law' for so long."

"It took me months not to turn around and look behind me whenever someone called me Your Grace. Don't you remember?" Tess chuckled. "You'll get used to it."

"Those emeralds look wonderful on you." Daisy sighed. "And you know that dress is my absolute favorite."

"It's Harry's favorite too," Ellie admitted, growing even pinker.

Hugo joined them, looking very dashing in a bottle-green coat and the shiniest boots Ellie had ever seen. He'd clearly been paying the tailors of Bond Street a visit.

"I've heard from a common acquaintance that dear

Sofia is back to her old tricks in Venice," he murmured. "She won't be bothering us again here in England any time soon."

"That's excellent news," Ellie said. "I won't be tempted to shoot her, for flirting with my husband."

"I wonder what became of Paolo and Luca? I still have my lovely knife." Daisy patted her thigh.

Tess's mouth dropped open. "You're wearing it *now*? Here?!"

Daisy shrugged. "Rule number three: Always carry a weapon. That's sensible advice. Who knows what could happen at a wedding? Emotions are high. Things could easily get out of hand."

"Will you be carrying it at your own wedding?" Tess teased.

Daisy made a disgusted face. "If such an unlikely event should ever occur, then yes, I'll be armed. Why wouldn't I be in a position to defend the people I love?"

Ellie chuckled. "A heartwarming, if slightly blood-thirsty, sentiment."

"It definitely might come in useful to stop Devlin hogging all the cake." Daisy sent a dark scowl at her brother, who was loitering with hungry intent by the wedding breakfast buffet.

"As you once said about Harry, I'm so glad you're on *our* side, Daisy."

Daisy grinned, just as there was a commotion out in the hall. A flustered-looking footman stepped into the doorway, and announced in awed tones, "Her Majesty, Queen Charlotte!"

After a moment of stunned surprise, everyone in the room dipped in either a deep bow or a formal curtsey.

Ellie straightened as the queen made a beeline toward her, trailing two handmaidens in her wake.

Tess recovered her voice first. "Your Majesty, what a wonderful surprise! We are honored."

The elderly monarch bowed her head graciously. Her gray hair was powdered and curled, as befitted an elderly dowager with grown children, and the pearls she wore shimmered under the light from the chandeliers.

Ellie had last seen the queen a few months ago, when she'd called upon King & Co. to help retrieve a series of sensitive and embarrassing love letters written by Princess Charlotte, her granddaughter. It seemed that their success had marked all three of them for Her Majesty's special affection and gratitude.

The queen took Ellie's hand and patted it maternally. "Miss Law, you are now Lady Cobham, and I for one am most delighted." She leaned in a little closer and her eyes twinkled with a mischievous gleam. "I've heard a great number of tales about your new husband, which have been vastly entertaining, and I must say, I'm so pleased that you've found a man worthy of your considerable talents."

"Thank you, ma'am." Ellie smiled.

The queen gestured to one of her companions, who stepped forward and handed her a small tissue-wrapped rectangle.

"I've brought you a little wedding gift, to wish you a happy union."

"Should I open it now?"

"By all means."

Ellie untied the ribbon and her face broke into a delighted smile as she realized what it was.

"It's a Book of Hours," the queen said softly. "Her Grace"—she nodded to Tess—"told me about your recent case concerning a similar book. I found it most diverting. And since that book was thought to be lucky, I thought perhaps something similar might bring you the same."

Ellie turned the little book over in her hands, stunned at the generosity of the gift. It was clearly as old and as valuable as the one she and Harry had returned to Bullock. The beaten gold front and back covers were inset with two large circular red hardstone roundels, each exquisitely carved with biblical scenes. Smaller gems studded the borders, like tiny, multicolored berries.

"I don't know what to say, Your Majesty," she breathed. "Thank you."

"After what you did for my dear Charlotte, it was the least I could do. Ah, Lord Cobham!" The queen smiled as Harry came to join them. "My felicitations. Your choice of bride shows you are a man of exquisite taste."

Harry bowed low and sent her his most charming smile. "Thank you, ma'am. I shall endeavor to keep her as happy as she's made me today."

He caught Ellie's eye, and her heart swelled with love. She'd already felt like the luckiest woman in England, but perhaps with the book they'd be the luckiest couple in the world.

The queen took her leave, and when the commotion had died down, Ellie glanced over at Daisy.

"Do you know, I'm beginning to think that hermit who told our fortunes at Vauxhall Gardens might not have been a complete charlatan after all. He accurately predicted happy endings for both Tess and myself."

Daisy looked immediately wary. "He said I'd meet my match on a dark highway. What on earth does that mean?"

Ellie shrugged. "I've no idea, but if you're doing any traveling, I'd certainly be on your guard." She sent Harry a laughing look. "After all, there's no telling when you might fall for a scoundrel of your own."